12/10

DATE DUE

MAY 1 8 2011			
JUN 0 4 2011			
JUN 3 0 2011			
AUG 0 1 2011			
SEP 2 6 2011			
ILL 11/12			
ILL 3/13	WITHDRAWN		
JUN 0 9 2014			

Demco, Inc. 38-293

Twenty Boy Summer

by Sarah Ockler

LITTLE, BROWN AND COMPANY

New York   Boston

Little, Brown and Company

Hachette Book Group
237 Park Avenue, New York, NY 10017
Visit our website at www.lb-teens.com

Little, Brown and Company is a division of Hachette Book Group, Inc.
The Little, Brown name and logo are trademarks of Hachette Book Group, Inc.

First Paperback Edition: May 2010
First published in hardcover in June 2009 by Little, Brown and Company

The characters and events portrayed in this book are fictitious. Any similarity to real persons, living or dead, is coincidental and not intended by the author.

"Ask for Me" lyrics written by R. Alex Morabito.

Library of Congress Cataloging-in-Publication Data

Ockler, Sarah.
20 boy summer / by Sarah Ockler.—1st ed.
p. cm.
Summary: While on vacation in California, sixteen-year-old best friends Anna and Frankie conspire to find a boy for Anna's first kiss, but Anna harbors a painful secret that threatens their lighthearted plan and their friendship.
ISBN 978-0-316-05159-0 (hc) / ISBN 978-0-316-05158-3 (pb)
[1. Best friends—Fiction. 2. Friendship—Fiction. 3. Grief—Fiction.
4. Secrets—Fiction. 5. Vacations—Fiction. 6. California—Fiction.]
I. Title. II. Title: Twenty boy summer.
PZ7.O168Aam 2009
[Fic]—dc22
                                    2008014196

10 9 8 7 6 5 4 3 2

Book design by Saho Fujii

RRD-C

Printed in the United States of America

For Alex,
my best monster and number-one favorite person
in the whole wide world.

Twenty Boy Summer

one

*F*rankie Perino and I were lucky that day. Lucky to be alive —
that's what everyone said. I got a fractured wrist and a banged-up
knee, and my best friend Frankie got a fat little scar above her left
eye, breaking her eyebrow into two reflective halves. Up one side,
down the other. Happy, sad. Shock, awe. Before, after.

Before, all of us were lucky.

After, only me and Frankie.

That's what everyone said.

two

It was just over a year ago.

Twelve months, nine days, and six hours ago, actually.

But thirteen months ago, everything was . . . *perfect*.

I closed my eyes, leaned over my candles, and prayed to the cake fairy or the God of Birthdays or whoever was in charge that Matt Perino — Frankie's brother and my best-friend-that's-a-boy — would finally kiss me. It was the same secret wish I'd made every year since Frankie and I were ten and Matt was twelve and I accidentally fell in love with him.

Frankie, Matt, and their parents — Uncle Red and Aunt Jayne, even though we're not related — celebrated my fifteenth birthday in our backyard with Mom and Dad, just like always. When all the singing and clapping and candle blowing stopped, I opened my eyes. Matt was right next to me, *beside* me, sharing the same air. Mischievous. The back of my neck went hot and prickly when I smelled his apple shampoo — the kind from the green bottle he stole from Frankie's bathroom because he liked how it made his hair look — and for one charged-up second I thought my birthday wish might finally come true, right there in front of everyone. I didn't even have time to *think* about how embarrassing that might be when Matt's hand, full of birthday cake, arched from behind his back on a not-so-slow-motion trajectory right into my face.

While cake in the face was clearly progress from the previous year's Super Bowl coach–style shook-up soda over the head, something in the wish translation was still getting lost as it blew across my candles into the sky. I made a mental note to clarify my demands next year in bullet points with irrefutable examples from Hollywood classics and screamed, shoving both hands into the mangled confection on the picnic table.

I scooped out two giant corners overloaded with frosting flowers.

Then, I charged.

I lunged.

I ran.

I chased Matt around the yard in laps until he dropped to the ground and wrestled the extra pieces from me, rubbing them into my face like a mud mask. We went at it for ten minutes, laughing and rolling around in the grass, Frankie and our parents cheering and howling and throwing more cake into the ring, candles and all. When we finally came up for air, there wasn't much cake left, and the two of us were coated head to toe in blue rainbow-chip frosting.

We stood up slowly, laughing with our mouths wide open as we halfheartedly called a truce. Dad snapped a picture — Matt's arm around my shoulders, bits of cake and colored chips and grass clinging to our clothes and hair, everything warm and pink in the glow of the setting sun, the whole summer stretched out before us. It didn't even matter that Matt was going to college in the fall. He'd be at Cornell studying American literature, just over an hour away, and he'd already started talking about my and Frankie's weekend visits.

When the novelty of the birthday cake wrestling match finally faded, Matt and I went inside to clean up. Beyond the sliding deck door, shielded in the cool dark of the house from everyone out back, we stood in front of the kitchen sink not saying anything. I stared at him in a sideways kind of way that I hoped didn't expose the secret thoughts in my head — thoughts that, despite my best efforts to contain them, went further than I'd ever let them go before.

His messy black hair and bright blue eyes cast a spell on me, muffling the chatter outside as if we'd been dunked under water. I held out a sticky hand and threatened him with another gob of frosting in an attempt to break the silence, afraid he'd hear my heart pounding under my T-shirt. *Thump-thump. Thump-thump. Thump-thump-thump-thump.*

Matt scooped some frosting from my outstretched hand and moved to close the space that separated us, changing absolutely everything that ever was or wasn't between us with a single raised eyebrow.

"Anna," he said, dragging his frosted fingers through my hair. "Don't you know what it means when a boy pulls your hair at your birthday party?"

No. Just then, I didn't know what anything meant. I couldn't remember how we'd arrived in the kitchen, why we were covered in cake, why my best-friend-that's-a-boy was looking at me so differently, or even what my name was. I bit my lower lip to prevent my mouth from saying something lame without my brain's permission, like "Oh, Matt, all my wishes have come true!" I felt the stupidity rising in my throat and bit down harder, staring at his collarbone and the small piece of blue sea glass he wore on a leather cord around his neck, rising and falling.

Rising.

Falling.

Seconds? Hours? I didn't know. He'd made the necklace the year before from a triangular piece of glass he'd found during their family vacation to Zanzibar Bay, right behind the California beach house they rented for three weeks every summer. According to Matt, red glass was the rarest, followed by purple, then dark blue. To date he'd found only one red piece, which he'd made into a bracelet for Frankie a few months earlier. She never took it off.

I loved all the colors — dark greens, baby blues, aquas, and whites. Frankie and Matt brought them back for me in mason jars every summer. They lived silently on my bookshelf, like frozen pieces of the ocean I had never seen.

"Come here," he whispered, his hand still stuck in my wild curls, blond hair winding around his fingers.

"I still can't believe you made that," I said, not for the first time. "It's so — cool."

Matt looked down at the glass, his hair falling in front of his eyes.

"Maybe I'll give it to you," he said. "If you're lucky."

I smiled, my gaze fixed on the blue triangle. I was afraid to look at him, because if I let my eyes lock on his, he might try to — and then everything would be — and I might just —

"Happy birthday," he whispered, his breath landing warm and suddenly close to my lips, making my insides flip. And just as quickly as he'd surprised me with the cake, he kissed me, one frosting-covered hand moving from my hair to the back of my neck, the other solid and warm in the small of my back, pressing us together, my chest against his ribs, my hip bones just below his, the tops of our bare summer legs hot and touching. I stopped breathing. My eyes were closed and his mouth tasted like marzipan flowers and clove cigarettes, and in ten seconds the whole of my life was wrapped up in that one kiss, that one wish, that one secret that would forever divide my life into two parts.

Up, down. Happy, sad. Shock, awe. Before, after.

In that single moment, Matt, formerly known as friend, became something else entirely.

I kissed him back. I forgot time. I forgot my feet. I forgot the people outside, waiting for us to rejoin the party. I forgot what happens when friends cross into this space. And if my lungs didn't fill and my heart didn't beat and my blood didn't pump without my intervention, I would have forgotten about them, too.

I could have stayed like that all night, standing in front of the sink, Matt's black apple hair brushing my cheeks, heart thumping, lucky and forgetful. . . .

"What's taking so long?" Frankie asked, running up the deck stairs outside. "Come on, Anna. Presents."

I pulled away from Matt just before she pressed her face against the screen to peek inside.

"Yeah, birthday girl," Matt mocked. "What's taking so long?"

"Be right out, Frank." I gave him my Don't You Dare face. "I just need to change."

"Can I come?" Matt whispered against my neck, causing a shiver. Or an earthquake.

I suddenly remembered all the baths we'd taken together as little kids, before we got old enough for it to be dangerous. The memories seemed different now. More vulnerable. Raw. My face went hot, and I had to look away.

"So?" Matt pinched my arm as Frankie headed back to the picnic table.

"So you're lucky Frankie didn't see that," I said, not sure I meant it. "And you have to go change your *own* shirt. In your *own* room. I mean, over —"

"Mmm-hmm." Matt grabbed my hand and pulled me in tight for another kiss, his other hand on my cheek, quick and intense. He pressed his body against mine in the same configuration of hip bones, stomachs, and ribs as the first time. I pressed back, wanting to wrap myself around him, anchor myself to him. It was all that kept me from floating away like a tiny, iridescent bubble.

"Do you think she saw us?" I asked when we finally stopped.

"Nah." He laughed, still holding my hand. "Don't worry. It's our secret."

Alone in my bedroom, I shoved my frosting shirt into a plastic bag to deal with later. I rinsed my face and hair with cool water, but my legs wouldn't stop shaking and I couldn't catch my breath.

The brain that was conspicuously absent for the kitchen sink rendezvous was suddenly hyperaware, modeling scenarios and impossible questions that were about twelve-and-a-half minutes too late:

What now?

Will this kill our friendship?

What about our parents?

Does he like me, or was he just messing around?

Will it happen again?

How do we tell Frankie?

Why did he say it's our secret?

Made-up answers raced through my mind, and I had to close my eyes and count to fifty to calm down. Fifteen minutes after everything changed was too soon to start obsessing about the what-ifs of the future.

Back outside, warm and giddy in front of Dad's bonfire, I spent the rest of the night not touching Matt, not laughing too hard at his jokes, not looking at him, afraid that someone would read the thoughts written on my face. After the fire had faded to a soft glow and I'd opened all the gifts, it was time for the Perinos to head back to their house next door. I said my goodbyes and thank-yous to Frankie, Uncle Red, and Aunt Jayne and looked at my feet when it was Matt's turn.

"Thanks for the cake," I said. "And the journal." He knew how much I loved my diaries — as much as he loved his books. It was the best present ever. Well, second best.

"Happy birthday, Anna," he said, picking me up and spinning me around in a giant hug, telling me with a wink that he'd see me tomorrow, just like he'd done on a thousand other nights. "Write something for me tonight."

To everyone else he was regular Matt, the big brother part of the inseparable Anna-Frankie-Matt triangle, the boy who used to bury our Barbies in the backyard and read us adventure stories when we couldn't sleep. But to me, he'd become something else as soon as he pulled my hair at the kitchen sink. Something *other*. Something that would never be the way it was before.

You awake? Matt's text message lit up the phone on my night table later that night.

Ya.

Of course I was awake. In the hours since the party, my heart hadn't slowed its furious beat. Sleep was out of the question.

Meet me out back, k?

K. 5 min.

I pulled on a sweatshirt, brushed my teeth, and put my hair in a loose ponytail. I started to dig for my eyeliner but decided it would look a little strange (and obvious) if I showed up behind the back deck at one in the morning in full makeup. Instead, I opted for hair down with a little mango-flavored lip gloss — casual but cute.

It wasn't sneaking out, exactly. I mean, it was my own backyard, and if I saw any of the upstairs lights go on, I could duck back into the kitchen and pretend I was snagging the last piece of cake salvaged from the birthday battle.

Matt was waiting by the stairs when I tiptoed out the back door. My bare feet hadn't even touched the dewy grass when he pulled me against the side of the house.

"I can't stop thinking about you," he said, kissing me again, this time with a purpose and intensity I'd never seen from him in the long history of our friendship. I kissed him back, wrapping my arms around his neck as his mouth pressed against mine. I must have been shaking, because after a minute he stopped and asked if I was cold.

"Just — surprised," I said. "And happy. And scared." It was barely a whisper, but I hoped it communicated everything I was thinking. Scared of getting what I wished for. Scared of hurting Frankie. Scared of losing my two best friends. Scared of undoing everything the three of us had known and loved since we were kids.

"Me, too," he whispered, breathing hard. "Anna, did you ever —"

Before he could finish, a square of light fell on the grass from Mom and Dad's bathroom window upstairs.

"I have to go," I said. "Tomorrow?"

He grabbed my arm and pulled me close to him, a whisper brushing against my cheek. "Tomorrow."

Then he kissed my neck, his lips alighting on the skin below my ear like a spark from the bonfire that burned long after I crept back to my bed.

He called the next day.

"Hi."

"Hi." I was still dazed from the late-night backyard encounter and kiss-induced insomnia.

"Frankie and I are going for ice cream. Come over?"

Frankie.

"Sure," I said. "But Matt, should we — I mean, did you say anything to her?"

"Not — *exactly*."

Does that mean he doesn't think it's a big deal? That we can just go for ice cream like any other day, like it didn't happen? Like it won't happen again?

"I want to, Anna," he said, reading my mind. "It's just — she's my little sister. And you're our best friend. And now you're my — I mean — we need to look out for her, you know?"

And now I'm your what?

"I know," I said.

"Don't worry, Anna. I'll tell her, okay? Just let me think about the best way to do it."

"Okay."

"Promise me? *Promise* you won't say anything?"

"Don't worry." I laughed. "It's our secret, right?"

I spent an hour getting ready, obsessing over hair and clothes and things that never used to matter so much. I couldn't calm the butterflies in my stomach about seeing Matt again, about feeling his lips on me, about telling Frankie, about the rest of the summer, about the rest of always.

When I first got to their house, I climbed in the backseat of Matt's car and avoided eye contact with him, worried either that he'd already told Frankie, or that he hadn't. We rode the whole way not looking at each other, Frankie chattering in the front seat about their upcoming California trip, seemingly oblivious to the fact that the whole world had changed the night before. It wasn't until we got inside Custard's Last Stand and Frankie forgot her purse in the car that we finally locked eyes.

"Hey, you," Matt said gently, smiling at me. I opened my mouth to say something important, something witty and charming, but in the new dawn of our relationship, where everything suddenly mattered, I was tongue-tied.

"Hey," I said lamely.

Matt jangled his keys and kicked at the floor with his foot.

"What are you thinking about?" he asked, tracing a line across my forehead.

Before I could invent something better than "Last night at the party and behind the house and I wish you would just shut up and kiss me again," Frankie was back with her purse, pressing us to make the difficult decision between the banana split and the fudge brownie sundae.

Sparing Frankie any further agony over the ice-cream selections, Matt ordered one of each, along with a caramel sundae for me, and we shared everything, fifty-fifty-fifty, just like always.

As Frankie shoved a spoonful of brownie into her brother's mouth, laughing her soft Frankie laugh, a flash of guilt squeezed my stomach. Until the night before, there were no secrets between the three of us but the ones I kept for myself — my silent, formerly unrequited feelings for Matt. I could hardly look at him without my insides tying up. *Please,* please let's tell her.

"Listen," Matt said. We were out back under the stars again, sneaking out after everyone else had gone to sleep. "You know she needs to hear it from me. I think the best time for me to tell her is when we're in California. It's only a few weeks away, and then I'll have some time alone with her to tell her about everything. It'll give her a chance to let it sink in."

The thought of keeping something so important, so intense, so unbelievable from my best friend for even one more day almost killed me. Never before in our shared history did I hide so much as a passing crush — she knew everything. She'd been there for every tragedy, every celebration, every embarassing moment. She'd been with me when I got my neon green braces in fourth grade. With me in seventh grade when I walked out of the school bathroom past the entire lunch line with my skirt tucked into my tights. With me when Jimmy Cross and I kissed during the eighth grade assembly and got hauled off to the principal's office. Birthdays, dreams, fears, laughs, obsessions — everything. Inside her head, Frankie had the map to my entire life, and I to hers. I hated that my feelings for Matt were uncharted and unmapped like a secret buried treasure.

But he was Frankie's brother. I trusted him. And when he took my face in his hands and breathed my name across my lips, I knew that I would keep my promise forever.

Days passed quickly into weeks, Matt and I perpetuating our "just friends" charade as best we could in front of Frankie and our families. So many times during family dinners or casual visits in our adjoining backyards, I wanted to end the charade, to throw my arms around him in front of everyone and just make it known. I censored every look I gave him, every word, every touch, certain that I'd mess up and someone would find out.

But no one did.

To our parents and Frankie, we were the same best friends as always, innocent and inseparable. Whenever we could steal a few minutes alone, that's when we became the "other," the charged-up thing that kept me up at night, afraid of falling so fast, afraid of losing, afraid it wouldn't last once Frankie found out. We stole too-short kisses in the front hallway, shared knowing and devious looks across the dinner table when we weren't being watched. We snuck out every night behind the house to watch for shooting stars and whisper about life, about our favorite books, about the meaning of songs and old memories and what would happen after Frankie knew. It wasn't the topics themselves that changed — we'd talked about all of those things before. But now, there was a new intensity. An urgency to know as much as we could, to fit as much as possible into our final nights before Matt revealed the secret.

On their last day before the trip, after they'd finished packing, the three of us went back to Custard's for an ice-cream send-off. I ordered the mint chocolate-chip brownie sundae, Frankie got a dipped cone, and Matt got a strawberry shake. Matt and Frankie were buoyant, floating on the anticipation of their upcoming trip, carrying me along in the current of their excitement. I couldn't wait for them to get to Zanzibar, to their summer house, down to the beach where Matt would tell Frankie about us and she'd smile and laugh and hug him and everything would be perfect again.

"It will be fine, Anna. You'll see," he whispered to me when Frankie went up to the counter for more napkins. "I know we're dragging it out, but she's my little sister — I can't help it. We just have to look out for her."

I smiled, envisioning our final kiss before tomorrow's departure, later tonight at our usual meeting place behind the house.

We split our ice creams three ways again, saving just enough for the ride back home. In the car, Matt turned up the volume on his favorite Grateful Dead CD. Frankie and I sang the melody while he filled in the harmony, his face tight and serious as he concentrated on the words. He drove with one hand on the wheel, the other tapping the dashboard, then his thigh, then back to the dashboard — a wild imaginary drum solo. I stopped singing long enough to shove in another spoonful of my mint chocolate-chip sundae, a pothole causing me to miss, the ice cream toppling down my shirt to my lap. I was in the front seat, right next to him, and I didn't care. In just three weeks, my best friends would be back home, helping Matt get ready for college, enjoying the sunsets of summer, and looking forward to the rest of our days — the rest of our forever.

The chorus started again through the speakers and I sang louder, *"Ca-sey Jones you bett-er . . . watch your speed . . ."* Frankie laughing from the backseat, Matt smiling at me sideways, fingers secretly brushing my knee, the noon sun laid out and happy on the dusty road ahead.

Together. Happy. Whole.

The three of hearts.

The possibilities endless.

And then . . . my sundae flying out of my hands into the dashboard.

Veering.

Screaming.

Slamming.

Broken glass.

A wheel spinning.

Casey Jones skipping, over and over. *"Watch your — watch your — watch your speeeeeed."*

Someone squeezing my hand, hushing, asking for my parents' names and phone number. *Helen and Carl Reiley. But don't tell them,* I think.

An ambulance. Paramedics. Stretchers.

"I've got him," someone shouts. "Get the girls out!"

"Can you hear me? Can you move your legs?"

"Jesus, you girls are lucky to be alive."

In the hospital lobby, I curled myself against Dad's chest, letting him stroke my hair and hum Beatles songs like he did when I was little to chase away the monsters. My head hurt, my knee was bandaged up, and my wrist was immobilized and wrapped in white tape. Frankie, sitting across from me with her knees pulled to her chest, had a fat lip and eight stitches sticking out like angry black spider legs through her left eyebrow. She was still — all but her fingers rubbing the red glass of her Matt-bracelet. I closed my eyes under the fluorescent lights and tried to make another birthday wish, a onetime do-over, a rebate, a trade-in on the kitchen sink kiss that started everything, offered up for just one last miracle.

I thought about Matt's clove-and-marzipan-frosting mouth and his favorite books stacked up on every flat surface of his bedroom as the doctor told us what happened. Matt wasn't a careless driver; he just had a hole between the chambers of his heart, a tiny imperfection that had lain dormant for seventeen years until that moment on the way home from Custard's when it decided to make itself known. They used a more medically appropriate term when they explained it to Red, handing him a plastic bag full of Matt's things. Watch. Wallet. The Syracuse Orangemen T-shirt he'd worn that day. But I knew what it meant. I knew as soon as Red started shouting, as soon as Aunt Jayne collapsed in Mom's arms, as soon as the hospital chaplain arrived with his downturned mouth and compassionately trained eyes.

Matt — Red and Jayne's Matt, Frankie's Matt, *my* Matt — died of a broken heart.

And everything else that ever mattered in my entire existence just . . . *stopped*. I was underwater again, seeing things in a slow-motion fuzz without sound or context, without feeling, without care. The world could have ended and I wouldn't have noticed.

In a way, it *did* end.

They must have let Red and Jayne and Frankie say goodbye to him, but I don't remember.

Mom and Dad must have called relatives and friends and funeral directors, but I don't remember.

There were probably nurses and apologies and organ donor papers and Styrofoam cups of cold coffee, but I don't remember any of it. Not in a way that makes sense.

I don't even remember how I got home. One minute I was underwater in the hard plastic hospital chair, and then I was back in my own bed with the door closed against my parents' muffled conversations downstairs and the endlessly ringing phone.

I must have fallen asleep, because I dreamed about him. In the dream, he gave me his blue glass necklace and Frankie's red bracelet.

"We need to look out for her, you know?" he said. "I have to be the one to tell her. It's the only way."

I know.

And when he smiled at me, I promised. I promised him I would protect her.

I promised him our secret would stay locked up for all eternity. And it will.

three

Stretched out on my stomach across Frankie's new purple comforter in a T-shirt and yoga pants, I read *Rolling Stone*'s Helicopter Pilot interview three times.

"Brandywine." Frankie caps her lipstick and admires her pout before the aptly named vanity mirror. "It might be too dark for you," she says, handing me the tube, "but try it if you want."

I don't need to try it. It *will* be too dark. My skin's so white it's almost blue, save for nineteen freckles that I hate, completely immune to peel-off pore strips and exfoliating citrus scrubs.

"Frank, *please.*" I flip back to the beginning of the interview. We're supposed to be making our packing lists and mapping out all of the exciting things we'll do in California next month, but I've spent the last hour watching Frankie primp, preen, and fluff. "I refuse to get glammed up for this."

"Who's getting glammed up?" Frankie asks. "I'm just — oh, shut up, Anna!"

Frankie gets glammed up for everything — trip planning, movie night, grocery shopping, the rare event of taking out the trash. The earth could get knocked out of orbit by a bend in the space-time continuum, and as North America careens toward Europe at half the speed of light, with houses and pink plastic lawn flamingos and people's dogs whizzing by — *aroooooooof!* — Frankie would be like, "Hold on, Anna. Do I have anything in my teeth?"

Frankie's always been the cute one, even when our moms dressed us in the same pastel sundresses or elastic-waist diaper jeans. But she used to be shy and sweet and a little awkward about it, even.

Last year, when the shock of Matt's death wore off and she stopped calling for him outside his bedroom, Frankie withdrew into a cocoon like a baby caterpillar, lonely and uncertain. She wouldn't talk to anyone — her parents, my parents, not even to me. Not in a way that mattered. Sometimes I wondered if I was going to lose both of my best friends from the same broken heart. But by the time school started again last fall, she emerged, metamorphosis complete, a brand-new butterfly who stopped crying, loved boys, wore sparkly makeup, and smoked Marlboro Lights in secret out her bedroom window.

Now, wherever we go, Frankie enters the room like a dazzling black hole and, in accordance with my Fifth Theorem on Quantum Physics and Beautiful Girls, sucks up all the attention around her.

"Anna, do you want it or not?" she asks.

"Or not. It's too dark for me."

"Suit yourself, Casper." She presses her lips together, blotting them with a tissue and dusting a layer of translucent powder on top.

The Frankie remix. Perfectly applied glitter eye shadow, French manicures, trendy brown-black hair with red highlights flipping out around her chin and *shimmering.* "Anna" and "shimmer" don't belong in the same sentence. My hair is curly, all over the place, and looks an awful lot like wild hay if I don't apply enough gel. Other than the basics of moisturizing and proper hygiene, the last time I spent more than twenty minutes getting in touch with my inner diva was for the time I spent with Matt. Now, my makeup sits in the bottom bathroom drawer under an ever-thickening layer of sparkly pink dust.

"You used to love this stuff," she says, rummaging for a lighter shade. "Here, try this one — Moonlight Madness. It's got ground-up crystals or something."

I shrug and focus on the pictures of Helicopter Pilot's self-appointed mascot, the Air Guitarist, until she gets distracted mixing eye shadow shades on the back of her hand with a Q-tip. I can't fault her for trying. She doesn't know about Matt, the ghost that floats in and out of my heart, haunting and unresolved.

Don't worry. It's our secret.

"Do you like this color?" She bats her eyes at me and laughs. Something about her smile reminds me of him, and I have to look away to block the flood of memory. It's officially more than a year now. I know I should let go, but it never really leaves me. Every morning, I wake up and forget just for a second that it happened.

But once my eyes open, it buries me like a landslide of sharp, sad rocks.

Once my eyes open, I'm heavy, like there's too much gravity pressing on my heart.

I never talk to Frankie about it. Matt's her brother for real, not her best-friend-that's-a-boy in the big-brother way. I never say *anything* about him.

I just swallow hard.

Nod and smile.

One foot in front of the other.

I'm fine, thanks for not asking.

"That color's great on you, Frank," I say.

"Have you seen my big powder brush?" she asks. "I can't find anything since Mom turned my room into the Hotel Sahara."

"Check those treasure box things on your desk." I nod toward a set of gold-colored boxes lined up smallest to largest.

Frankie locates the brush in the middle box. "I have to put a lock on the door or I'll never find anything again."

For the past six months, Aunt Jayne's been on some kind of decorating kick. Every time I walk into Frankie's house, something is different — new throw pillows or moved furniture, more plants or fewer, splashes of color or minimalist neutrals, a whirlwind of throws, shams, swags, and swatches. Last week, she transformed Frankie's 1920s flapper bedroom into a Moroccan oasis, draped in deep purples and reds and wooden beads for curtains.

"It's like a new adventure every day," Frankie said last month when her dragonfly bathroom became sexy cowgirl central almost overnight, complete with real rope lasso towel holders. I guess it's good that Aunt Jayne is excited about something again — running out to the fabric shop or the home-and-garden store whenever inspiration strikes, which is basically whenever one of those leave-town-and-let-total-strangers-redecorate-your-house-in-forty-eight-hours shows comes on. In the past month alone, she's filled half the garage with boxes of magazines, pillow covers, paint swatches, antiques, switch plates, and faux fur. There's only one room she doesn't touch — the one at the end of the hall. The one with the perpetually closed door that might as well not exist anymore.

"Frankie, are you done yet?" I know all there is to know about Helicopter Pilot, including the fact that the rock-star drummer Scotty-O had a liver transplant when he was four, and I'm tired of watching Frankie's head bob around in a hair-teasing frenzy. "I read this article so many times I feel like I'm *in* HP."

"Yeah," she says, "except that they're the best band in the universe, and you can't even sing 'Happy Birthday' in tune."

"Maybe not. But *I* passed my English final, which is more than I can say for *some* people in this room."

"Hey! Sixty-seven is still passing. And for your information, *smarty,* I just signed up for the word-a-day e-mails to expand my vocabulary."

"Oh, really?" I ask.

"Today's word is *judicial.* As in, just because Anna's an übernerd doesn't mean she has to be so *judicial* against people who aren't."

"Judgmental. You mean *judgmental.* And I'm not."

"Judge — *shit.*" She grabs a spiral notebook and pen from her desk and scribbles in it. "Judg-ment-al. *Judgmental.* You," she says, clicking her pen closed and dropping the notebook back on the desk, "love being right, don't you?"

I toss the magazine on the floor. "It's painful, but someone's got to be the smart one in this operation."

Frankie shrugs, taking her powder brush on a final trip across her nose. "I guess I'll have to rely on my looks. There — I'm done." She rises from the vanity chair and smiles, hands frozen on her hips like she's waiting for some kind of stage direction. *My butter-fly.* Just like her brother. When she smiles, her blue eyes light up and put a voodoo magic love spell on everyone around.

"Perfect," I say, twisting my hair up with a pencil. "Now, can we *please* start planning this trip, preferably sometime before it ends?"

Frankie tosses me a purple gel pen and lined paper from her desk. As I work on our packing lists, she paces the room shouting out potential items, sweeping back and forth with her video camera. One of her aunts gave it to her after Matt died to "take her mind off things," and she hasn't put it down since. I think she's afraid of missing something important — or not being able to remember it later, when it matters.

In less than an hour, we cover clothing (casual day, dressy day, casual evening, dressy evening, sleepwear, and nonwater beach attire), swimwear (for which we still need to shop), toiletries and makeup (for Frankie), games, music, and books (for me). We also pick the official name for our upcoming adventure — the Absolute Best Summer Ever (A.B.S.E.) — because that's exactly what it *will* be, according to my newly appointed tour guide.

"You okay, Anna? You don't seem too excited all of a sudden." Frankie sits down in front of me and tilts her head, frowning. Matt used to do that same thing with his head whenever he was worried about one of us and needed a closer look at the situation.

"No, I'm good," I say. "I guess it doesn't seem real yet. You know how weird Dad was about the whole thing. I don't want to get too excited till we're actually *on* the plane."

Dad already thinks I spend too much time over here. "Red and Jayne need to get more involved with Frankie's grief," he's said on more than one occasion, lately following up with something like, "especially since this will be their first trip without Matt." But what does Dad know? His idea of grief support is bringing over a six-pack for Uncle Red and not saying Matt's name.

Frankie shakes her head and flips off the camera. "Don't worry. He already said you can go. You just need to do some — oh, what's that thing called — envisionation, I think."

"Envisionation?" I ask.

"You know, where you think about the thing you want and just picture yourself getting it?"

"*Visualization,* Frankie, and it's not gonna work."

"Visualization. Yeah, that. Just try it, okay?" She closes her eyes and presses her fingers to her temples, switching into monotone. "Anna is arriving in California. She and Frankie are magical and beautiful, like mermaids in the water. They are walking on the beach and lots of boys are waving and drooling because they're *so* irresistible."

She opens her eyes. "Can you see it?"

"Not really," I say. "But I *am* getting very sleepy."

"Be serious, Anna. You aren't trying hard enough. Close your eyes."

I do as she asks and try to picture the scene she's painted. She talks about lying in the sun, the smell of coconuts, writing postcards to my parents, and soon I'm thinking about the postcards Matt used to send me with pictures of sea lions wearing sunglasses or severely overweight women in neon thongs. I saved every one, tucked safely into a box under my bed.

If he'd kissed me a year earlier, would I have gotten love letters, instead?

"See?" Frankie taps my leg, pulling me back to the present.

"We *will* see." I shake off a fading image of Matt's scribbled blue *XO*s.

"Anna, this is going to be so great!" Frankie tacks our packing list to the bulletin board on the wall above her desk and procures a cigarette from the stash in her top drawer. She only smokes in her room, out the window. Never in public. Never at school. Never outside. She denies it whenever I bring it up, but sometimes I think she doesn't even like it; she just wants her parents to catch her and do — I don't know. *Something.*

Last month, when Uncle Red and Aunt Jayne first suggested the return trip to their favorite summer spot with me in tow, Frankie freaked out. She went completely silent for a long time, and none of us knew what would come next. It was like at school or family things right after the accident when people would mention Matt. Her mind would shut off and go away. Or she'd get so angry she'd shake. Other times, early on, she'd just run away and weep. Weeping is different from crying. It takes your whole body to weep, and when it's over, you feel like you don't have any bones left to hold you up.

She didn't weep the night they talked about the trip, though. She just got mad and stormed off to her room, leaving Red and Jayne to fumble through their usual apologies to me. I could see it was hard for them, but I wasn't sure what they expected. As the California announcement took an awkward dive out of Red's mouth and flopped onto the table waiting for a response, all I could think was, *A year later is still way too soon.*

But the next morning, Frankie started to warm up to the idea, and by week's end, it was as though she was in on the Zanzibar Bay plan all along, doodling pictures of palm trees and sunshiny good times in her head.

Frankie kneels in front of the window, pushing aside the wooden beads and leaning against the sill to light the cigarette. Matt's red glass bracelet slides down her wrist, sparkling through the sunlit haze of smoke. The bottoms of her feet are gray with the barefoot dust of summer, and as she turns to blow each puff of smoke at the sky, I can't shake the feeling that it really *is* too soon.

"Frankie, do you think California is happening too fast? I mean, too soon?" My voice is low. I'm not exactly sure it came out right.

"Not really," she says, dropping the half-smoked butt into an old Diet Coke and rejoining me on the floor. "We still have one, two . . . four weeks before the A.B.S.E. officially begins. That means that our hair should grow about half an inch." She holds her hand below her chin, indicating the anticipated length. "Also, we're going on Ultra Quick-Skinny."

"Those fake milk shakes?" I ask. Swallowing my own tongue sounds more appealing than a shake for breakfast, lunch, and dinner. "You're kidding."

"Anna, we *have* to. We can lose, like, ten pounds by then. Think beaches. Think bikinis." She lifts her shirt and pinches the nonexistent fat on her stomach. "And," she says, slapping her belly twice, "don't forget about the A.A."

A.A. — Anna's Albatross. From the Latin *Anna,* meaning me, and *Albatross,* meaning "something that hinders or handicaps; e.g., 'it was an albatross around her neck.'" It's the code name we gave my virginity when Frankie lost hers to the German exchange student after the Spring Send-off dance two months ago and became the expert on such things.

"But Francesca," I say in my breathy romance novel voice, "I want it to be . . . *special!*" Which is at least fifty percent true. Well, maybe sixty. Okay, sixty-eight, but no more. The truth is, I always imagined it would be with Matt. I was in love with him before I even knew what to call it, and when we finally got together last summer, it was a done deal in my mind. I saw the whole of my future in that first kiss, all the way up to the part where I would help him pack on his last night before school, and one thing would lead to another, and he would passionately kiss me goodbye, falling onto his bed, and then we would finally . . .

But when he died, that dream died, too. Guys? Getting close? *That* close? It hurts too much to think about. If I kiss someone else, the spell will be broken, and my memories of Matt and everything I wrapped up in them will be erased. *No, thank you.*

"Special? Yeah, right!" Frankie throws a pillow embroidered with gold elephants at me. "I told you, it's really not that good the first time. It's more like a rehearsal for the real thing — an undress rehearsal. I picked Johan because he was leaving a week later and I knew I'd never have to see him again."

Picked Johan. If I look up *picked* in the dictionary, I won't see any reference to Frankie and Johan. I'll have to flip ahead to *S* for *stalked.* All year, Frankie intimidated Johan's girlfriend, Maria, with dirty looks in gym class, left daily notes in his locker, and made out with his friends in the parking lot so that it would get back to him. Johan was the only guy unwilling to end his current relationship for a shot at Frankie, and that perplexed and frustrated her. So when Maria dumped him a week before the Spring Send-off, Frankie pretended she didn't know about it until the night of the dance, when she approached him with her I'm Totally Here for

You face. Half an hour later, they were out on the dark soccer field doing their own little dance, leaving me to fend for myself in a gym full of gyrating, happy teenagers.

It's been two months. Johan is back in Germany and hasn't returned any of Frankie's e-mails.

That doesn't stop her from plotting the downfall of my innocence on our upcoming trip. In *her* mind, we'll be ignoring a direct missive from the God of Summer Vacations if I don't ditch the big V once and for all somewhere along the Pacific coast.

"How could I forget the Albatross?" I ask. "You bring it up every five minutes."

"Just trying to keep it fresh." She rises from the floor and holds out her hand. "Anyway, your virginity is the least of our pretrip problems. Come on — your house."

four

Upstairs in my room, Frankie pans my closet with her video camera, doing her best movie-announcer-guy voice:

"In a *world* where summer dreams really *do* come *true,* Anna and Frankie plan the vacation of their *lives.* There will be *beaches.* There will be *bathing suits.* And there will be *boys.* But something *lurks* just below the surface, threatening to *ruin* the A.B.S.E. if these clever, beautiful gal-pals don't turn their attention to its *immediate* resolution: *Anna's wardrobe is a total nightmare!*"

Owing to Frankie's tireless quest for the smallest ratio of fabric to flesh legally allowed, her summer attire — and even most of her winter set — is always beach ready, featuring cute halters, short skirts, and strappy black sandals.

Owing to my *mother's* tireless quest for the ultimate deal, combined with her standard-issue fashion immunity, *my* wardrobe — taken as a collection — should be tried, convicted, and hung. Devoid of *anything* cute, short, or strappy, my closet houses an anthology of half-price, off-season sale items typically excavated from the basements of overcrowded department stores where I elbowed my way past mobs of middle-aged women bargain-hunting in the loose underwear bins.

"What do you suggest?" I ask, fingering the shirts that hang in front of us.

"I don't even know where to start." She turns the camera on herself and makes an exaggerated shrug in front of the lens. "Just take it all out and throw it on the bed."

I'm not in the mood to dismantle my entire closet, but I do as she asks. It makes her smile, just a little bit, so I don't fight her. Sometimes when she looks happy like this, I watch her from the corner of my eye and wonder if my best friend is still in there somewhere, the one who used to stage elaborate weddings for our dolls and deal me an extra thousand dollars in Monopoly so we could conspire against Matt. In the postdeath murk of our relationship, I don't know if I'll ever see that Frankie again. We're such different people now; if I met her on the street today, just like this, we would never be friends. But once in a while, her smile comes back — however fleeting — and I see her, really *see* her, and know I'll do anything to keep her here a little longer, to keep her from slipping back into the coma of silence that nearly overtook her last year.

Even if it means talking about clothes and boys and milk-shake diets instead of things that matter.

"Anna Reiley's wardrobe malfunction, take one." Frankie films while I toss heaps of unwearable clothing on the bed by the armful. I have a few passable favorites, supplemented by frequent raids on Frankie's closet, but I force most of the embarrassing ensembles into hiding, where they wait in vain for the day when they, like their more stylish brethren, might be called into fashion service.

"God, Anna. What are *these*?" Frankie sets down the camera to grab a pair of old jeans with her finger and her thumb as though pants can transfer a contagious virus.

"They're my old favorite jeans from middle school. They have good memories."

"Anna, ankle zippers are never good memories. And what the hell is *this* thing? It's completely ruined."

My mouth goes dry as Frankie pulls a white tank top from the plastic bag I've kept it in for the past year, stuffed behind all the shoes on the closet floor. It has splotches of purple, crusty and fading from its original birthday blue. At first I didn't want to wash it because it reminded me of that night and everything it was supposed to turn into. After he died, I didn't want to wash it, get rid of it, or do *anything* to it.

Ever.

"Garbage pile," Frankie says, ready to cast it aside.

"Don't!" I dive toward her and snatch the shirt out of her hands with more force than I intend. It's the only surviving witness to the night Matt and I changed over from friends to whatever it was we became, and it's nearly impossible for me not to cry.

"What's *with* you, Anna? It's just a white tank. You can get a new one for like five bucks."

Don't worry. It's our secret.

"Sorry." I'm surprised and glad she doesn't recognize it. I run my thumb back and forth over a crusty bit on the shoulder strap as a five-second version of the cake fight flashes behind my eyes like a movie stuck on quick search. *Don't cry over spilt frosting, Anna.* "I just — I like this one."

"What for?" she asks.

Just tell her.

"It's from the — it's just the —" I bite my lower lip.

Tell her.

"Anna? What's wrong?"

Oh, it's nothing, really. Just that it's from the first time your brother kissed me and made me promise not to tell you. And I was in love with him forever, and he was supposed to tell you about it in California, and we were all going to live happily ever after. I still write him letters in the journal he gave me, which he doesn't answer, since he's dead and all. But other than that? Honestly, it's nothing.

"Anna?" She watches me with her sideways face again.

"Huh? Oh, sorry. Nothing. I'm fine. I — I'll get rid of it later. Anyway, look at these." I swallow the lump in my throat, shove the tank behind some shoe boxes in the closet, and pull out a pair of tiny Snoopy flip-flops. "Remember when we had matching flip-flops in third grade?"

"Anna, we had matching *everything* back then. This," she sweeps her hand over the clothes, "is a fashion — a fashion *Heidelberg,* as you would say. I don't know when we got so far off track."

I know. I remember the exact moment Red started dropping us off at the mall with his credit card, telling Frankie to get whatever she needed and that he'd be back for us in a few hours. "Nothing like a little family trauma to kick-start a decent wardrobe," she'd say, pretending not to cry while trying on piles of expensive clothes from all of our favorite stores.

"It's *Hinden*burg, Frank. And if you're feeling nostalgic for matching outfits, you're welcome to join me and Mom on our next trip to Shay's House of Bargains."

"There must be *something* savageable in here."

"*Salvageable.* And there isn't."

"Yeah, that's what I said. Salvageable. As in, able to be salvaged. Besides, all we really need are bikinis, jean shorts, and sandals. And maybe a dress or two for going out at night. Come to think of it, maybe we should get a —"

"*Bikinis?* In *public?!*"

My world is crashing down around me! Frankie — long and lean, olive skin, fat in just the right places and nowhere else — will be *stunning* on the beach. But me? I picture my blue-white skin and untoned, freckled arms hanging unattractively out of a two-piece. No one wants to see *that* unprepared. I look Frankie up and down and chew on my thumbnail. Perhaps a beach vacation with my *stunning* best friend isn't such a great idea. "I don't think so, Frank."

"Anna, no one will notice us if we're wandering around in old-lady clothes. They'll think we're pregnant or something."

"Rather than wanting to *get* us pregnant?"

"Exactly."

"I don't know, Frankie. I don't think —"

"Anna, you're gorgeous, and you know it. You just have to stop being so shy about it and start working it. Dab on a little lipstick, walk straight, throw your shoulders back, suck your stomach in, stick your boobs out — and work it!"

In my mental movie of "working it," I do okay with the lipstick but concentrate so hard on straightening, throwing, sucking, and stick-outing that I don't notice a surfboard or driftwood or a small child underfoot and I trip, sailing over said unseen obstacle and face-planting in the hot sand.

"Not gonna work," I say.

Frankie climbs onto the bed and grabs my shoulders. "It *is* gonna work. Believe me. You're perfect!"

"You really think so?"

KABOOM!

Frankie and I both let out a squeal at the unexpected thunder. To me, the sudden change in weather is a clear sign that the universe does *not* want me to wear a bikini. As the sky darkens and the downpour starts, I catch Frankie gazing out the big bay window behind us, watching needles of rain come straight at the glass. She stares at it for a long time, tracing a streak of water down the window, distant. She does that sometimes — like her mind splits and one side stays here with me while the other is off living an entirely different life in the distance with people I can't see or hear.

"He loved the storms at night, remember?" she whispers, more to her reflection in the window than to me. I nod and rest my head on her shoulder. It's the most she's said about him in a long time.

five

The next morning, entirely against my will, Frankie asks Aunt Jayne to drop us off at the mall and leads the charge to her favorite store — Bling. Everything inside — including the staff — is either see-through, rubber, glittered, or some combination thereof.

Leaning against the floor-to-ceiling speaker system behind the counter, a blonde only a few years older than us flips through the pages of this month's *Celeb Style* and bobs her head, dangling silver hearts dancing above her shoulders to the techno bass behind her.

Never deterred by a woman in a black rubber halter-top, Frankie taps on the counter. "Hi," she shouts over the music. "Did you get the new swimsuits in yet?"

Rubbergirl, whose ripped denim shorts look like underwear with pockets, raises an eyebrow at Frankie and jerks her head toward the far corner of the store.

"Thanks," Frankie says.

"Whatever." Rubbergirl turns the page and releases a long, my-life-is-so-hard sigh.

Thankfully Mom isn't here to witness the exchange, or we'd be waiting around for Bling management so Mom could share a long and painful commentary on how Rubbergirl's lack of customer focus reflects poorly on the entire clothing industry.

"She's new," Frankie assures me, dragging me to the corner where the girl had so obligingly directed us.

After handing me her camera with explicit instructions to keep filming, Frankie takes a deep breath and gets to work. She weaves her way through racks of swimsuits, foraging like a mother antelope for her starving babies, passing over colors or styles that are "soooo last year" or "too blah blah blah for the beach." When she finds something with potential, she tugs on the fabric to simulate a hard day in the surf and holds it to the light to ensure it has the right amount of see-throughability.

After fifteen minutes of hunting and gathering, Frankie emerges from the racks with two armloads of try-ons. A broken fingernail and a slight breathlessness are her only battle scars.

"You take this half, and then we'll switch." She passes me a pile of shiny, sparkling spandex as we move into the fitting room and hole up in adjoining stalls.

"I think we should stick with black," I say to Frankie as I crack open the dressing room door to show her a particularly hideous orange thing stretched across my backside — the third atrocious suit I've tried on. "It's supposed to be slimming."

"Everyone wears black," Frankie says. "And we don't need slimming. We need something fun. Something — ew! Not *that* fun!"

She shoves me back into the stall before any passing shoppers can associate her with the orange monstrosity in fitting room A.

"Keep trying, Anna. You'll find the one."

Five more try-ons, five more rejects. *Okay, maybe last year's yellow one-piece with the daisy neckline has potential.*

"Frank, this is hopeless. Can't I just wear my —"

"No," she says, stepping out of her stall. "You are not allowed to mention that yellow suit again. I think I found one I like. Come see."

I crack open my door. Frankie is a vision in a sheer white wrap below the artificial glow of the fitting room.

She opens the wrap to reveal a baby blue halter-style suit that ties at the neck and hips and covers just enough of Frankie to keep everyone wondering. It was made for her; evidenced by the mothers and daughters gathering around her like lost sheep seeking her guidance through the tangled pastures of Bling's swimsuit collection.

"Oh my God, that's it!" I emerge from my stall and hug her as though she's trying on wedding gowns. "You look amazing!"

"Does it make me look too fat?" She tugs at the bottom and turns back and forth to look at her butt and stomach in the three-way mirror. "What about my huge ribs? I have man-ribs."

One of the mothers laughs.

"Honey," the woman says, "if I had that body, I'd go to the beach naked."

Frankie smiles. The other moms agree. A little girl stares. Celeb Style, *here she comes.*

"Frank, it's awesome. You *have* to get that suit."

"You think? Are you sure?"

"Yes," the lost sheep and I say.

"Okay, as long as you're being honest."

"Oh my God, if you don't get that suit I'm not going to California."

"Okay, okay! I'll get it. In the meantime, here." She reaches into her dressing room and pulls out a hanger full of olive green something. "I think I found one for you, too. I know you're a little more conservative about these things."

Locked in my stall, I strip down again and prepare for another painful but predictable rejection. *If this one doesn't work out, I'm going to Alaska instead. No swimsuit required.*

I pull and stretch and tie the various parts into position without looking in the mirror. As I stare at the chipped Cotton Candy nail polish on my toes, I imagine walking down the beach in my childish yellow suit with Frankie, Queen of Summer, in soft baby blue. I'll be the sidekick. The second string. The second helping. The second choice.

My head hurts.

"Well?" Frankie knocks on the door. "Do you have it on?"

I unlatch the door and push it open, still afraid to look in the mirror.

"Wow. *Wow.* Anna, oh my God. Wow!"

"Bad?" I whisper.

"Um, come here." Before I can say another word, Frankie grabs my wrist and pulls me into the main fitting room in front of the three-way mirror. Thankfully, the sheep have disbanded.

"Look." She nudges me closer. I stare at my reflection. The girl in the mirror stares back. I don't recognize her.

"Anna, you're getting this suit."

"It's eighty dollars."

"Anna, you're getting this suit."

"But I —"

"Anna, you're getting this suit. That's it."

I twist and turn and contort all of my appendages in search of some fatal flaw that will force me to abandon the suit, but I can't find one. Not in the lightly padded halter top that ties at the neck like Frankie's. Not in the boy-shorts bottom that makes my stomach look flat and slides over my hips like a second skin.

"See, I told you you're gorgeous," Frankie says.

"Whatever." I'm still getting used to the idea of showing anyone my belly button on purpose.

"Oh my God," Frankie squeals. "Anna, I just thought of the best idea *ever*."

"Great. I'll ask Mom to set aside some bail money."

"No, listen." She puts her arm around me and lowers her voice. "It's about the Albatross." Her broken eyebrow seems to be dancing as she wiggles it suggestively.

"Oh, right. Your little pet project." I am simultaneously intrigued and afraid — a combination I've grown used to over the past year with Frankie.

"It's perfect. We're in California for twenty-three days, right?" She does some quick calculations on her fingers, looking up at the ceiling to concentrate. "If we allow three days for arrival, exploration, and strategy, that leaves us eighteen, nineteen, *twenty*. Twenty days, give or take."

"Twenty days for *what*?"

"Twenty boys."

I think she's joking, but her eyes are set. I must stop this madness before she has us buying the family pack of condoms at the pharmacy.

"Frankie, I'm not sleeping with twenty guys, and neither are you!"

She laughs. "Come on, Anna. I just meant that if we could *meet* a boy a day, and maybe do a little test-drive, certainly you could ditch the A.A. at some point, right? We can even make it a contest. Whoever gets the most prospects — wins."

While the yellow-daisy-swimsuit Anna would never have agreed to such a scandalous contest, the crazy girl in the mirror wearing the olive bikini can't crush Frankie's sincere smile. It's ear to ear, almost all the way to her bright blue eyes, and before I can even *think* about what a bad idea it is, our mission is in motion.

"Twenty days," I say, overjoyed at her lasting enthusiasm. "Twenty boys. I'm in."

Frankie wiggles her eyebrow and takes one more look at our bikini reflections, nodding her approval.

I smile and nod back, challenge accepted.

Cue the movie announcer guy.

Somewhere along the California seashore, a strange wind blows over the ocean, and twenty oblivious boys simultaneously look up from their surfboards.

six

As the days turn into the final hours before the trip, whenever I think about Frankie's twenty-boy contest, I can't ignore the prickly feeling in my stomach that accompanies Matt's face, fading and disappointed.

I never saw you in a bikini, I imagine him saying.

You didn't live long enough, I think.

But twenty, Anna? Does it have to be twenty? What about five? Or three? Or one?

What do you care? You're dead, remember?

I shake my head and pack the last few items on my list. Unless Dad has a last-minute change of heart, we leave tomorrow morning.

"Dead boys don't talk, Anna," I say out loud. "Remember?"

"What?" Mom does her signature knock-while-already-opening move on my bedroom door. "Did you say something, hon?"

"Um, no, just reviewing my packing list." I see Dad behind her and hope they haven't been standing there long. Then I see the serious look on their faces and swallow hard, hoping they're just here to remind me about sunscreen and lifeguards and generally being an all-around well-behaved girl for Uncle Red and Aunt Jayne.

"Can we talk for a minute?" Dad asks, making himself comfortable on my desk chair.

"Um, okay." I remove and refold a few things from my bag to create the illusion that I'm busy.

"So, Frankie's smoking again," he says.

I can't tell if it's a question or a statement, so I play dumb. "What do you mean?"

"I came home between open houses today and saw her," he says. Dad's in real estate, so his schedule can be unpredictable. Frankie should know — her window faces our house. It's been a few months since the last time he busted her, when he grilled me about *my* nonexistent smoking habits and made me promise I'd get her to quit.

"She just — she found — it's just that — I don't know, Dad." I give up. The only excuse I can think of is the truth — she's broken. Until someone can figure out how to fix her, what else *can* she do?

Dad sighs. "Anna, do you think maybe the trip is something the Perinos need to do together, as a *family*?"

"They *are* going as a family," I remind him. His line of questioning makes me nervous. When the Perinos first invited me, it took some convincing to secure Dad's permission. Before Matt died, Dad already struggled with such "living on the edge" activities as me going outside with wet hair in the winter, taking off my sneakers without untying them, and going to bed without flossing. It only got worse after the car accident, and I really thought Dad would say no to a summer vacation across the country — especially with his comments about me spending too much time with Frankie. But after presenting a convincing argument, citing my honor roll final grades, and committing to additional housework without being asked, I won him over. After that, whenever someone mentioned California, I changed the subject. Like I told Frankie — he can still revoke permission until we're on the plane.

"I know they're going as a family," Dad says. "I meant — without the neighbor kid getting underfoot."

He says "the neighbor kid" like I'm some barnacle that even industrial-strength chemicals can't remove from the hull of their family tragedy.

"Dad, she kind of needs me there, you know?" I force myself to keep my voice steady, thinking about Frankie's "positive envisionation." *I am on the beach. There are drooling boys and postcards and something about beautiful mermaids. . . .*

"I understand that, Anna. It's just that . . . do you ever think that part of the reason Frankie isn't moving on is — is that you aren't *letting* her?"

I look to Mom for support, but her eyes are on me expectantly, as if at any minute I'll see their irrefutable logic and unpack my bags. I know Mom and Dad care about Frankie, but they weren't the ones hiding upstairs with her in the weeks after Matt's death while well-meaning relatives and friends stopped by, bearing an endless supply of cards and food in disposable foil pans and saying all the wrong things. "He's in a better place now." "God must have a plan for him." "At least he didn't suffer." "You're still young, Jayne. Maybe you can have another child." "You'd stop thinking about him if you took down his pictures." They didn't hold Frankie as she sobbed for hours at a time without talking. They didn't make sure she ate even when she wasn't hungry. They didn't do her homework when she couldn't concentrate, or explain to our teachers why she was late for every class.

"How do you know Frankie isn't moving on?" I ask.

"Anna," Dad says gently, "all I'm saying is that as long as you're around, Red and Jayne don't really have to worry about Frankie — you're doing it for them. And two thousand miles away on a trip that will be extremely difficult for them — that complicates things. We just want to make sure you're ready to deal with this."

Deal with this? Not only does he reduce my best friend's emotional state to something akin to an annoying rash, he also plants a new seed in my already overcrowded brain.

Could I be the reason Frankie isn't moving on?

Since Matt's death, the earth has made more than one full trip around the sun — plenty of time to be Over It, according to the official books and therapists and school counselors that tried to talk to me about my "caretaker" role in Frankie's life.

But Frankie isn't over it.

I'm not over it.

And I don't want to talk about it, because one day his name will brush against my lips in her presence, and through an involuntary blushing of the cheeks, a misting of the eyes, a breath drawn too tightly, or a single tear, the secret I'm supposed to keep locked up forever will be revealed.

"Sweetheart," Mom says. She looks at me softly with her You Can Talk to Me face, which is only slightly more tolerable than its close cousin, the I Was Young Once, Too, face. Unlike the IWYOT face, which usually means that she knows I'm up to something and I'd better not lie about it, the YCTTM face is equal parts guilt and empathy with a dash of "are we still friends?" and "your father isn't a bad guy" stirred in.

"Dad and I are just concerned about Frankie. We know she's under a lot of pressure, and you've been managing some really tough emotions that maybe Red and Jayne should be more involved with."

I think about Aunt Jayne's constant whirlwind of interior decorating and shopping sprees with Uncle Red's credit cards.

"Well, they *aren't* involved."

"We know, Anna," Dad says. "That's why Mom and I are concerned. California will be especially hard on them, and who knows how that will affect Frankie. You may have to be the strong one out there, okay?"

I stifle a laugh, remembering something Matt said to me in his final days. Frankie was babysitting down the street, and Matt and I were hanging out in his room sorting his books and music into "staying home" and "going to college" piles.

"I know I'm not going far," he said, shuffling through the staying-home CDs. "But I'm worried about Frankie. I don't want her to feel like we don't want her around, or like she's alone. I think it's going to be hard on her once she knows about us. You'll have to be the strong one, Anna."

"Excuse me?" I pretended to be put off by his inference that us girls would just fall apart in his overprotective absence. "It's not like you're going off to war. I think we can handle it."

"I didn't mean it like *that*," he said, coming closer to me on the edge of the bed and taking my face into his hands.

I looked up at him with mock hurt. Then I tackled him, pinning him to the bed with another kiss.

"Who's the strong one now?" I asked him.

"Okay, you win. You win." He laughed. I stayed on top of him, resting my head on his chest while he played with my hair until Frankie got home.

"Anna?" Dad asks. "You okay?"

I nod, blinking away the memory. "I *am* the strong one, Dad."

"I know, Anna. But —"

"Hard parts aside," Mom interrupts, "I do think the trip will be good for you, too. It might help you — I don't know — *visit* with Matt again. Does that make sense?" She looks at me with such compassion that for one second I forget she's my mother and think she might actually *know,* like I wear my feelings in big words across my face and all she has to do is brush aside my hair to read them.

"Yes," I say, hoping they don't see my cheeks go hot.

"All right." Dad rises from the desk chair. "Finish up and get to bed. You've got an early morning tomorrow."

Finally.

Pretrip fears allayed once again, I hug them both good night and recheck my bags against my list. Everything seems to be in order. There's just one problem.

I can't get him out of my mind.

I turn off the overhead light and flip on my reading light. Curled in my bed, I watch a fresh downpour stream along the window and make everything outside soft and blurry. I think about the ocean again and look across my room at the mason jars full of colored glass from Frankie and Matt.

Matt could have died any of a hundred ways, but whenever I look at the glass, I walk through the history of our friendship searching for things I could have done differently or said sooner to break the chain of events leading up to that day in the car, the day his heart stopped working. *Hi, Matt, I'm in love with you. Let's not go for ice cream today. Let's just find a place to hide.*

Back when we were still "just friends," I used to write about him in my old diary, which I carried around everywhere. I'd write about hanging out with him and Frankie on the weekend, or him stopping by my locker between classes at school, or the books he gave me to read so we could talk about them later. Only sometimes did I admit my real feelings for him on paper — I was always afraid that someone would find my diary and show him all of my secrets.

I wrote my first real letter to him in the journal he gave me — though I still didn't want him to actually *read* it. It was after we kissed outside my house, when I was alone in my room with every cell in my body buzzing, still feeling him on my lips. I printed off the picture Dad had taken after the cake fight, taped it inside the journal's purple cover under his "Happy Birthday" inscription, and wrote.

The next few weeks were a blur of happiness, secret midnight meet-ups, talking about the rest of the summer, how he'd write every day from California, how Frankie and I would drive with their parents to take him to Cornell. Every second that I was awake, I wanted to be with him. To see and know him in the entirely new light of our unfolding relationship — whatever it was meant to become — in a way different from all our years as childhood best friends.

I didn't have time to think about what was happening, let alone write letters that he'd never read.

A few months after he died, I started writing to him again — just once in a while. Not in a communing-with-the-dead kind of way, but it did help me feel close to him, especially after a hard night with Frankie or on nights when I couldn't stop thinking about him.

Like tonight, on the eve of our departure — the too-soon family vacation that's only missing one thing.

Dear Matt,

In less than a day, I'll be standing on the same sand you stood on so many times before. Well, not the same sand, with the tides and winds and erosion and all of that, but the same symbolic sand. I'm so excited and scared that I can't sleep — even though I have to wake up in five hours!

You know, I saved every one of your postcards. They're here in a box under my bed — all the little stories you sent, like little pieces of California. Like the beach glass you guys always brought me. Sometimes I dump it out on my desk and press my ear to the pieces, trying to hear the ocean. Trying to hear you.

But you don't say anything.

Remember how you'd come back from your vacation on the beach and tell me what it really felt like? What the ocean sounded like at dawn when the beach was deserted? What your hair and skin tasted like after swimming in saltwater all day? How the sand could burn your feet as you walked on it, but if you stuck your toes in, it was cold and wet underneath? How you spent three hours sitting on Ocean Beach just to watch the sun sink into the water a million miles away? If I closed my eyes as you were talking, it was like I was there, like your stories were my stories. In many ways, I feel as if I have memories of you there, too. Do you think that's crazy?

Matt, please don't think badly about Frankie's contest. It's just a silly game. It's so Frankie, you know?

No, I guess you wouldn't. You'd kill her if you did!

She just misses you. We all do. I'll look out for her, though. I promise.

Please watch over us tomorrow, and for the next few weeks while we're away. You'll be in my thoughts the whole time, like always.

I'm going to find some red sea glass for you.

I miss you more than you could ever know.

Love,
Anna

I trace my fingers over his name on the letter and close my eyes, imagining that when we get to California, he's there waiting for us, smiling with his apple hair and blue beach glass necklace.

seven

"See you in a few weeks." Mom hugs me goodbye in the Perinos' driveway. "Call us every few days and don't forget to send postcards."

"I will. And I won't."

"Remember what I said about sunblock and always swimming where the lifeguard can see and hear you," Dad says. "The ocean can be dangerous, especially during vacation season when the beaches are crowded."

"Dad, we covered this already. Besides, you hate vacations," I tease. "How do you know what the beaches are like?"

"We don't hate vacations," he says. "In fact, Mom and I were just talking about planning our *own* family vacation for next summer."

In my sixteen-year history as an Official Member of This Family, we've never taken a real vacation. In a perfect storm of stupid ailments, Dad's afraid of flying, Mom can't stomach long car rides, and both of them have issues with nonchlorinated water. Sure, we've covered the local circuit — Amish country, the zoo, Oak

Ridge State Park — anything listed in the New York State guide-book and less than two hours' drive. But no exciting, life-altering experiences to write about in those school essays in the fall. No exotic destination from which I could send postcards.

Dear Frankie and Matt,
Here we are at . . . the zoo!
We didn't even have to stand in "lion."
The monkeys miss you.
Love, your world-traveling neighbor, Anna

"Sure, Dad," I say, smiling. "Sounds fun." I give him and Mom one more round of hugs before settling in next to Frankie in the backseat. After a few more words to Red and Jayne about taking care of the Perinos' plants, house, and mail while we're away, Mom and Dad finally let us leave.

I watch out the back window as my parents wave from the yard and get smaller and smaller as we zoom up the street. In less than half a day, I'll be getting off a plane two thousand miles farther than either of them will ever go. I consider their strange antitraveling afflictions for just a minute before realizing that I've never been on an airplane and could very well be cursed with the same fear of flying that keeps Dad's feet planted on the ground.

"Don't even worry," Frankie says when I confess my concerns. She's in full makeup, perfect hair, cute drawstring traveling pants, and a plain pink T-shirt. "It's safer than driving."

I look at her eyebrow and feel a twinge of pain in my wrist — the phantoms of old injuries. She doesn't notice.

The sun is just peeking above the horizon as Red pulls onto the highway. He alternates between scanning the morning talk radio for news and weather and trying to engage Jayne in conversation. She's been kind of far away all morning — nodding and smiling, polite but preoccupied. I follow Frankie's lead and continue our conversation as though we're any other normal family taking any other normal vacation.

Frankie tells me about the itinerary: how long the flight to San Francisco takes, what we do when we land, the drive to Zanzibar, where we eat lunch, what time we should get to the house.

It's barely six in the morning and I already feel like we've been traveling all day.

At the airport, we check in, drop off our luggage, and follow the signs to the security checkpoint.

"I can't believe I'm sixteen years old and I've never been past security at the airport," I say as I take off my shoes and set them on the conveyor belt next to Frankie's. "I'm so sheltered."

"First time through the X-ray machine, first time on a plane, first time in California . . . I'm sensing a theme here, Anna. You know, *first times?*" Frankie wiggles her eyebrows and steps through the machine. If Red and Jayne weren't already through the checkpoint waiting for us on the other side, I'd grab my shoe from the conveyor belt and maim her with it right here.

The security screener takes a few extra minutes to scan Frankie with the handheld wand before waving me through.

"Too bad," I say, grabbing my shoes and bag off the belt. "I think I packed the wrong bathing suit. You know, the *yellow* one. With the *flowers.*"

"You *better* not be serious." She looks aghast.

"I guess we'll find out when we get to the beach."

"Find out what?" Red asks as we reunite.

"Nothing," Frankie says. "Where's Mom?"

"Restroom." Red nods toward the blue-and-white sign down the hall.

"Again?" Frankie asks. It's Jayne's fourth trip to the bathroom since we checked in. "Is she okay?"

"She's fine, girls. Just a few nerves before the trip, that's all." Uncle Red sticks his hands in his pockets and looks back toward the bathrooms. "Just a few nerves."

Frankie slings her backpack over one shoulder. "Can me and Anna go ahead to the food court? It's right up there."

"Sure, hon. We'll catch up in a minute."

Frankie and I find a Jack's Java and order frozen green tea smoothies and nonfat blueberry muffins, the least we can do to maintain our combined two-and-a-half-pound loss on the all-but-abandoned Ultra Quick-Skinny diet.

"I can't believe the airport has a dry cleaners and a Jack's Java," I say, slurping my smoothie. Though I've traveled to the airport with Mom and Dad to pick up and drop off relatives, I've never been this far inside. Above the sound of the overhead announcements and final boarding calls to exotic destinations, parents scold their kids, people shout into cell phones, and friends reminisce about their vacations before boarding the planes that will carry them home. It's like a secret underground world — a constant flux of arrivals and departures, reunions and breakups, hellos and good-byes, befores and afters.

"They have everything here — even a spa," Frankie tells me. "You could totally live in the airport."

"Didn't they make a movie about that?"

"If they didn't, they should. Come to think of it, *we* should." Frankie digs her camera out of her bag and gets into her interviewer voice.

"A.B.S.E., day one. Departure. Anna Reiley, first-time visitor to the airport, sips her smoothie while awaiting her flight to California. The air is charged with excitement as Reiley snarfs down the last few crumbs of her nonfat muffin. Tell us, Miss Reiley, how does it feel to finally see the inner workings of the airport?"

"Well, Francesca, I am admittedly full of trepidation, never having been in the airport before, as you know. Yet I'd be remiss if I didn't tell the viewers how excited I am to travel with the renowned Francesca Perino and her adoring parents. I just can't thank them enough. And thank *you*, Francesca. And I'd like to thank my own parents for agreeing to send me to the airport, and the Academy for believing that I'd make it to the airport when no one else did. Thank you. Thank you all. Please, no more questions."

"No, thank *you*, Miss Reiley." Frankie turns the camera on herself. "This is Frankie P, live from the airport, signing off."

"You're a freak."

"I'd be all full of trepilation and reminisce if I didn't agree."

"Trep*idation* and *remiss*."

"Yeah, them, too."

Red and Jayne collect us in front of Jack's, order two large house blends to go, and lead us down to the gate. After a few sips of the strong coffee, Jayne seems a little better. She even laughs when Frankie and I show her our mock interview.

We still have an hour before boarding, so Frankie and I pass the time by writing stories in the back of my journal about the other waiting-area passengers. We get through Duane Durstein — pervy, wife-cheating insurance salesman; Gloria Masterson of the Boston Mastersons (old money), who long ago snubbed her family when they refused to accept her love of show poodles; and Mickey, a six-year-old with gigantic floppy ears who refuses to listen to his frazzled mother. Actually, that part isn't made up — the boy's mother calls him Mickey, too. Before we can move on to the woman in the crocheted American flag sweater, the counter attendant calls our row.

"That's us," says Red. "You girls ready?"

I smile. I am *so* ready.

Before I know it, I'm buckled tight next to Frankie in row fourteen, window seat, listening attentively to crewmember instructions and following along with the passenger safety information card conveniently located in my seatback pocket. Everything is new to me — bathrooms at thirty thousand feet, free snacks, male flight attendants. I'm an utter child with wide eyes and matching dopey grin, just released from the jungle by the wolves that raised me.

I reach into my bag for my journal so I can write about everything I see on the plane and realize with a sudden panic that my bag isn't as crowded as it should be.

"Oh, *no!*" My pulse starts pounding in my veins.

"Anna, what's wrong?" Frankie asks. "Nervous?"

"I left my journal on the counter when I handed them my ticket!"

"Are you sure?" Frankie pokes around my bag to confirm.

"Yes! I remember setting it down to pull the ticket out of my purse!" I'm practically in tears.

"Don't worry, we're still at the gate." Frankie presses the call button. "They can probably get it for you."

"Frankie, I *can't* lose it!" Passengers in neighboring rows look on with mild interest as I start to hyperventilate. *I'm crawling out of my skin! How can everyone be so calm about this?*

"Everything okay?" A perky flight attendant in a navy blue suit — Darcy, according to her name tag — appears at the end of our row.

"Did anyone turn in a purple notebook?" Frankie asks. "She left it on the counter when we boarded."

"Let me check on that for you," Darcy says, smile firmly in place.

"It's okay, Anna. Breathe." Frankie pats my hand.

After what feels like three days, perky Darcy returns to our row, notebook in hand.

"Is this it?" she asks. "One of the passengers gave it to Meg up front."

"Yes!" I reach over Frankie and the nameless passenger in the aisle seat, practically snatching the journal from Darcy's manicured hands. "Thank you so much," I say, flipping through the pages to make sure nothing has been torn, eaten, spilled upon, or otherwise damaged during our brief but painful separation.

"Better now?" Frankie asks.

"Yes. You have no idea."

"I do. I'd freak out like that if I lost my movies." She smiles and plugs herself into her iPod for the Helicopter Pilot double-live we downloaded last night.

I turn to the window, keeping the journal on my lap. There's no way I'm letting it out of my sight now.

Midway through the flight, I peel my face from the window-pane and realize I haven't felt any of the fear-of-flight symptoms Dad warned me about — nausea, clammy hands and feet, racing heart, white knuckles, generally making an ass of oneself (other than when I lost my journal, which was a freak accident and thankfully over quickly). I watch the whole country go by — rivers, lakes, mountains that look like ripples in the ground, and the yellow-and-green patchwork quilts of Middle America.

"Look, Anna, there's the Golden Gate Bridge." Frankie leans over my lap to point out a huge orange bridge stretching on forever. Beyond that is the Pacific Ocean, dotted with strips of foamy white-caps and the soft, colored triangles of sailboats.

I love the flying and the sights so much that if we had to turn around and go home right now, it would still feel like a complete vacation.

It's almost one when we finally get off the plane, though it's only ten in California. After we find our bags, we pick up our rental car and head down the Pacific Coastal Highway. In less than two hours, we'll be in Zanzibar Bay — gateway to the A.B.S.E.

Just like on the plane, Frankie lets me have the seat with the best view. I open the window and watch the ocean — a never-ending streak of bright blue and green. The mood in the car is a juxtaposition of excitement and sadness, alternating in waves of smiles and laughter as Frankie's family points out various sites and jokes at my bewilderment at the foreignness of it all, followed by silence — the unspoken melancholy pushing into the spaces Matt left behind.

Though I'd sat with them through sessions with the school counselor, through Frankie freak-outs in the living room, through awkward family meals and holidays where no one talked and all I could hear was the clinking of forks against plates, riding in the car with the Perinos as scenes sail along the highway triggering memory after memory after invisible, unsaid memory is the hardest thing I've done since Matt's funeral.

You'll have to be the strong one, Anna.

"You guys wanna pull over and get a better look?" Red asks after an hour on the road, changing lanes to exit at an overlook point. Ours is the only car there — a rocky patch of sand with a small parking area and picnic table.

Frankie and I walk to the edge of the cliff while Jayne pulls an assortment of airport donuts and juice boxes from a nylon cooler and sets them up on the picnic table. We lean over the wooden guardrails and drop rocks over the edge, each one shattering against the boulders below into tiny shards and dust that swirl and swoosh before dissolving into the ocean. If not for the dolomite boulders, according to the informational signpost behind us, the base of the cliff would have eroded in the ocean's tumult thousands of years ago, and Frankie and I would not be suspended so perfectly as we are above the water.

I wrap my hands around the rail and look down. The viscous churning below makes me so dizzy that I have to close my eyes and count backward from ten to recompose. I inhale deeply, smelling and tasting the ocean's salt on my skin and remembering how Matt had described this same feeling in so many of his postcards.

Anna, when you meet the ocean, you feel it more than you see it. If you're lucky, that wonderment never fades, and you feel it again every time you get back here. You'll feel it someday.

"Girls," Jayne calls from the picnic table. "Not so close to the edge! Come back and have something to drink. We have three more weeks to enjoy the view!"

I open my eyes and tug gently on Frankie's arm.

"Let's go," I say.

"Wait, Anna, do you hear it? Listen."

"What is it?" It sounds like barking.

"Look — seals." She points about thirty feet down the shore where a dozen or so brown lumps wriggle and play in the sand, barking like some kind of water dogs.

"Wow," I breathe. "I'm changing my answer."

Anna, what's the number one coolest thing you've ever seen in your life?

He asked me one night, about a week after my birthday, when we saw three shooting stars in a row behind his house. It was after midnight, and everyone was asleep but the crickets. I remember telling him about this crazy lightning storm I saw when I was ten. It was far away but I could see the rain billowing out in sails and sheets, all the dark blue-gray sky lit up in flash after flash after flash.

What's yours?

It's always been the ocean. But I'm thinking about changing my answer.

He didn't say anything after that. He just looked at my eyes for a long, long time, missing all the stars above us until it was too light to see them anyway.

"What answer?" Frankie asks.

"Seals. The seals are officially the number one coolest thing I've ever seen in my life."

She smiles, nodding. "Agreed."

After inhaling a few powdered donuts, we pose along the rail with Jayne as Red sets up his camera and tripod for our first official trip photo. Though they'll probably appear in the picture as indiscernible brown blobs on the distant shore, the seals seem to line up in their best group pose, just for us. Satisfied with the angle, Red sets the timer and runs to join us in front of the ocean, laughing with the seals as we wait for the click.

"That's going to be a great one, Twinkies," Red says. Though we long ago shed the yellow wardrobe associated with babies whose parents didn't know what sex we'd be, Frankie and I are still inseparable. Our childhood nickname sticks.

"You okay, Anna?" Frankie whispers in front of the seals as Red and Jayne get into the car.

"I think so," I say. "Just taking it all in." I kick at the ground with my toes, sending a pile of detritus cascading down the rock face. A new breeze sucks moist air over the cliff and coats our arms with a silver mist.

"He's here," she whispers across the ocean. I take her hand and close my eyes again, steadying myself with my other hand on the rail, floating.

Another forty minutes of drive time goes by quickly. After the pit stop, both Red and Jayne show renewed energy and excitement, telling stories from their first few trips to the beach, when the kids were little. Red drives most of the time with one hand on Jayne's knee, and once in a while, she puts her hand on top of his and smiles.

Just as I start to feel nostalgic for lunch, Frankie points out a weathered blue sign along the shoulder:

> **WELCOME TO ZANZIBAR BAY**
> **PARADISE LOST . . . AND FOUND AGAIN!**
> **POP: ~~945~~ 949**

"Breeze! Breeze! Breeze!" Frankie shouts, pumping her fist up and down. She told me about their favorite restaurant tradition on our way to the airport this morning.

After we leave the main highway, Red crawls and putters through Moonlight Boulevard, Pier 7, according to the sign welcoming us to the main strip. Jammed with tourists, hot dogs, and neon bathing suits, the pier is an assault on every one of the five senses — possibly the sixth as well.

It isn't the town itself, but the people. *Us.* Summer seems to arrive with us, as though the entire place has been asleep since last September, awakening only as taxis and rental cars line up to deposit us along the beach — families with toddlers, college kids on break, retirees seeking to warm themselves under the California sun, and our own motley crew. Together we break upon the pier like a tidal wave as she rubs her winter-sleepy eyes, stretches, and turns on the coffee for us.

After finding a parking space on our fifth tour down the strip, we put our name in for a table at Breeze, which has a twenty-minute wait, and wander to the edge of the pier to watch the boats in the Pacific. The smell of coconut oil wafts up from the sun worshippers down below, but the sound of the waves camouflages most of their laughter and music.

"Don't worry, Anna." Red shakes his head at the undulating tangle of people below. "The beach near the house doesn't get nearly as crowded as this. The rental community has a private lease, so only the folks using the houses can be on the beach."

"Yeah, the *old* folks," Frankie whispers.

"So what do you think?" Red asks me. "Pretty amazing, huh?"

"More than I imagined," I say.

"Present location aside, I like to pretend that we're mostly cut off from the rest of the world here. It's pretty quiet, other than the surfers. And the tourists. And the vendors. And all the screaming kids." Uncle Red sighs. "Remember when this place was still kind of a secret, Jayne?"

"That was a lifetime ago." Jayne stares out over the water as Red puts his arm around her and kisses her head. It makes her smile, just a little bit. I turn away, feeling like an intruder.

"Let's go see if our table is ready," Frankie says. "Anna, they have the best piña coladas here. Wait till you try them."

"Nonalcoholic, of course," Jayne says, pulling away from Red.

Frankie smiles. "Virgins. Of course."

After lunch, including two of the best piña coladas, Frankie and I get in line for ice cream at Sweet Caroline's Creamery stand next door, Ultra Quick-Skinny be damned. Jayne seems to be feeling better, but I learned soon after Matt died that even something as simple as ordering grilled cheese from a diner menu can unleash a flood of memories impossible to corral.

As Frankie and I wait in line, completely canceling out our

calorie-saving nonfat muffins and combined weight loss in just a few hours, we count thirty-seven sagging, sunburned old women who don't know that they've outlived the statute of limitations on wearing bikini tops. Frankie and I make a vow to never let the other out in public like that after thirty, no matter how good we think we look. The shock of lime and tangerine spandex against the backdrop of storefronts whose deep hues have been sucked gray and pale by years of warm ocean salt reminds me that we're an inconvenience, a passing fad the town endures each summer as she welcomes, sells, feeds, and exists solely for our entertainment. I picture all the shops boarding up their windows in the fall — the signs unplugged, the saltwater taffy spinners cleaned and stowed away — a whole town folding up into a tent and packed on the train with the elephants and fire-eaters.

Ice-cream cones in hand, we walk around the back of the stand along the pier where we waited for our table at Breeze. As I lick a runaway line of melted cherry chocolate ripple from my hand, I become hyperaware of our surroundings. The back-and-forth ancient lull of the tide. The cry of seagulls passing overhead. The smell of salt and fish carried on the warm breeze. With each step along the old wooden planks of the pier, tiny grains of sand that hitchhiked from the beach below are pulverized under our heels. Sand that traveled millions of miles over billions of years across shifting continents and churning oceans, surviving plate tectonics, erosion, and sedimentary deposition is crushed by our new sandals.

The cosmos can be so cruel.

"Frankie, look at this sand. Isn't it amazing that —"

"Shh — Anna, check it out. No, not *now*. Don't look yet."

"Don't look at what?" I turn my head to see.

"Guys. In the baseball hats. Over there. I said don't look! They are totally checking us out. Are my teeth okay?" She flashes a quick grin so I can confirm that all evidence of lunch and ice cream is gone.

I nod and chance a casual glance at the boys in question, waiting for my heart to skip or my palms to sweat or my tongue to become hopelessly tied. But all bodily functions remain intact. They look just like all the boys at home, only tanner.

"What's the big deal?" I ask, thinking that if this is as good as it gets, I'll be lugging around the old albatross for quite a while.

"The big deal, Anna, is that they're totally staring at us. And we aren't even done up or anything."

I look at her eyelashes and the fresh coat of glitter mascara she applied in the restroom at Breeze. "Mmm-hmm."

"I'm just saying. We've been here an hour and already there are prospects. We'll get to twenty easily. Maybe we should up it to thirty."

"*Maybe* we should introduce your new boyfriends to your parents," I say, "because here they come."

eight

*F*rankie immediately switches back to the Good Daughter, stowing the Seductress for a more appropriate, i.e., parent-free, time. The boys across the pier must have sensed her personality change — or the danger of an approaching father — as they're nowhere to be found when Red and Jayne reach us.

"Find something you like?" Red asks.

"Huh?" Frankie almost chokes on her ice cream.

"Mom and I got cookies-'n'-cream," he says, holding up his cone.

"Oh — right. We got cherry chocolate something."

"So when are we heading to the house?" I jump in to prevent an awkward situation from getting much worse. Because Red and Jayne have become relatively lax in their discipline of Frankie, she's less careful with her secrets than the laws of parent-child relations dictate. I don't think she'd say something *really* awful, like, "I just lost my virginity with the foreign exchange student, please pass the salt." But I don't want to take any chances with our contest and risk getting sent home on the first day. How embarrassing. What would Red and Jayne think if they knew their daughter and her best friend staged a manhunt — rather, a *twenty* manhunt — on the family vacation?

"We have to pick up a few basics for dinner tonight and breakfast tomorrow," Red says. "Then we'll go. House is about five miles up the hill from here."

From the main road out of town past the grocery store, we can only see the top of the house, the roof rising like the tip of a wooden iceberg. It sits on a long ridge overlooking the ocean, not too close to the other houses nearby.

Uncle Red and Aunt Jayne are silent as we make our way along the dirt side road to the top. As we wind around a grove of palm trees and crest the hill, the house appears all at once as though it had been waiting behind the trees to jump out at us.

"Wow," I whisper. There is nothing else I can say. The sight of it, live and up close, hushes me. It isn't gigantic or ultramodern or anything, but it's breathtaking to me — a fairy tale that lived in hundreds of photographs and stories finally coming to life. It's all wood and windows top to bottom. In the bright oranges of the sun, it looks like it's on fire, a giant glass triangle burning against the blue sky.

From the dirt road, we turn into the driveway on the north side of the house, the backyard facing west over the beach and the ocean and the wide-open sky beyond.

"Wow," I say again. "I can't believe I'm here."

"Welcome to our second favorite spot in the world." Uncle Red cuts the engine and squeezes Aunt Jayne's hand.

We all sit in the car for a few minutes, not saying anything.

"I'm gonna check out the view from the backyard," I say, extracting myself from the car and the silence.

"We'll be right behind you," Aunt Jayne says.

I head up the gradual hill to the backyard, looking down at the silver pod of the car from the top. The three of them are frozen, afraid to move. I can't tell if they're talking, but Frankie is leaning between the two front seats.

For a brief moment, I miss my parents. Dad in his Parkside Realty sport coat. Mom with her coupons. Calm. Predictable. Normal. I wonder if they miss me, too, thousands of miles away in their quiet normal house where seals don't bark and families don't cry in the car.

The backyard is about the size of our school swimming pool and has six wooden steps on the far edge leading down to the beach. I know there are six of them because Matt used to tell me about how he'd run out the back door, off the deck, across the lawn, and jump down to the sand, sailing right over the steps as Aunt Jayne yelled after him about breaking his neck.

I kick off my flip-flops and walk across the wet grass to the steps, sitting on the bottom one and digging a little tunnel in the sand with my feet. It's wet and cold under the hot surface, just like Matt said.

As the waves shush against the shore, I look out over the ocean and watch a few families scattered along the beach. In front of me, a mother stands knee-deep in the water, waving and calling for two little boys to come in for lunch.

When someone you love dies, people ask you how you're doing, but they don't really want to know. They seek affirmation that you're okay, that you appreciate their concern, that life goes on and so can they. Secretly they wonder when the statute of limitations on asking expires (it's three months, by the way. Written or unwritten, that's about all the time it takes for people to forget the one thing that you never will).

They don't want to know that you'll never again eat birthday cake because you don't want to erase the magical taste of the frosting on his lips. That you wake up every day wondering why you got to live and he didn't. That on the first afternoon of your first real vacation, you sit in front of the ocean, face hot under the giant sun, willing him to give you a sign that he's okay.

"There you are!"

I jump. It's Frankie, coming down the stairs. "You okay?"

"Yeah." I move over to make room for her on my stair and put my head on her shoulder. "I was just thinking about him."

"Me, too." Her eyes are red and glassy, but she's smiling. "I think the hard part's over. We're officially out of the car."

I laugh, pulling my feet out of their sand caves.

In the distance, tiny triangles — some white, some red, some rainbow — navigate along the rise and fall of a thousand saltwater peaks.

"Isn't it amazing, Anna?" She looks out across the water. "It makes you feel kind of small, huh?"

"Yeah." I don't want to say too much; to break the thin glass bubble spell, my head resting on her shoulder, my oldest friend reflective and serious and still capable of being amazed.

"You know what the best part about California is?" She puts her arm around me, her Matt-bracelet cool against my shoulder. "No one knows me here. No one knows that they're supposed to feel sorry for me."

I think about the faces at school as we passed through the halls — eyes looking away, mouths whispering. *There goes Matt's sister. Hey, isn't that the best friend?*

"Except for you," she says. "You're the only one who knows the big black secret. And you're a locked vault when it comes to keeping secrets." She laughs, kicking at the sand with her toes.

We dust off from the sandy steps and walk out to the shore. Up close, the water churns and rolls, shifting between hazy blues and grays. As each new wave slides up to our bare feet, the tide pulls it back, lifting the water like a blowing skirt to give us a peek at the colored stones beneath.

The water is cooler than I expect. It bites at my toes until I'm used to the temperature and can no longer tell the difference between air and water on my skin. I kneel and scoop up a handful of silt and rocks, staring into my cupped palm as dark, wet sand lightens in the air.

"Where do you think it came from?" I ask, dropping my hands into the water to let the waves wash over them.

Shhh, ahhh. Shhh, ahhh.

"Lots of places, I guess," Frankie says, crouching to pick up a smooth, plum-sized rock. "The ocean has a never-ending supply of cool stuff. In the morning, you find shells and glass, too. Check this out." She holds the rock in front of me. "You can see bands of color from other rocks and sand that were pressed together over millions of — what are you staring at?"

I smile. "You know, Miss Perino, for someone who almost failed earth science, you sure know a lot about the oceanic ecosystem."

"That's not science, Anna. It's nature. Big difference."

I open my mouth to argue, but she's kind of right. Science: a construct created by man to explain away all of life's mysteries. Nature: its own creation, its own mystery, existing long before we took our first breaths and long after we take our last.

Shhh, ahhh. Shhh, ahhh.

"Frankie, thanks for bringing me here."

She looks at me and smiles softly. Her body is here with me, her feet leaving wet imprints in the sand, but her eyes are a million years away, swimming with some prehistoric creatures as sand and stones and tiny bones press together and grind apart, nature moving slowly onward, unaffected by the insignificant comings and goings of human life. I suddenly feel very small, smaller and less important than the grains of sand under our feet, and I'm simultaneously comforted and humbled.

"Here, keep it." Frankie smiles again, pressing her striped stone into my hand. "It's the first official souvenir from the A.B.S.E."

We walk up and down the shore for another half hour, stopping every few feet to scoop up an empty shell or a square of green glass. My fingers and toes pucker and my hair blows into my eyes and mouth, but I want to spend the whole trip out here, with the ocean replenishing her treasures like an old shopkeeper as I sleep alongside her in the sand.

Frankie is still quiet, digging in the sand for her own treasures. The last time she was on this beach, she was helping Matt unearth glass for his jewelry creations. They were throwing each other in the water. Making dinner plans. Talking about how you could ride a wave all the way to shore with just your body if you caught it right.

Sometimes I think if she knew about Matt and me, it would bring us closer. If I could just make her understand how much I cared about him, she'd let me into the exclusive club where all the members have a right to be irrevocably sad. Instead, I'm an intruder. I look into the windows and see them crying, but I'm on the outside in the dark, and they can't see me.

"Frankie, can I ask you something?"

"What?"

"Do you remember my birthday party last year? When I turned fifteen?" I ignore the sound of Matt's voice whispering over the waves. *Shhh. It's our secret, Anna. You promised.*

"Sure, I guess." She rinses her hands and wipes them on her hips. "Hey, you ready to head back up? We can unpack and set up our room. Hopefully Mom and Dad are done unloading the car."

"Okay." I throw a handful of stones into the water and watch them fall like rain.

"So what were you gonna say about your birthday?" She smiles, and I don't want her to stop.

"Oh, never mind." I grab her hand. "I forget."

I don't say anything about him.

I just swallow hard.

Nod and smile.

One foot in front of the other.

I'm fine, thanks for not asking.

As I cross into the house from the deck, sand grinds beneath my bare feet, making a soft, scratching sound against the floor. I try not to track it inside, but Frankie assures me that sand on the floor is just part of the Zanzibar experience.

"It's like a moving decorative accent," Jayne says. "You know, bring a little outside in."

"Hon, you're not allowed to redecorate on vacation," Red says. "We didn't pack your fabric swatches and paint chips."

"Don't you worry." She laughs. "I'll find a way, if the mood strikes."

There is no sign of emotional tumult — no mascara-stained cheeks, no slammed doors, no long sighs or faraway faces. They've already put all of our bags in their appropriate rooms, unpacked their own luggage, opened all the windows, and confirmed that we have enough towels, dishes, and other essentials. Whatever ghosts of memory tried to hit them as they walked through the front door rushed right on outside, down the street, and out of sight, for Red and Jayne are the perfect eight-by-ten glossy of *normal.*

I allow myself a tiny sliver of hope that maybe this vacation is exactly what the family needs. Then, another ray of possibility sneaks into my thoughts. If the California sunshine can fix them, maybe, just *maybe,* it can fix me and Frankie, too.

I hold my breath as Aunt Jayne sets the table for dinner, knowing that if the slightest feather falls on this thin mist of peace, everything will shatter. Sometimes I think we all feel guilty for being happy, and as soon as we catch ourselves acting like everything is okay, someone remembers it's not.

Tonight, when Frankie sits at the table and innocently knocks over her glass of Diet Coke, Aunt Jayne starts to cry, and the translucent veil of general okayness evaporates to reveal the honest, ugly parts underneath.

nine

"*I*t's okay, Mom," Frankie says, jumping up to grab a sponge. "I got it."

"We haven't even been in this house one night and already you're making a mess!" She grabs the sponge from Frankie's hand and kneels below the table, blotting spilled soda with one hand and her tears with the other.

"I'll get that, Jayne." Red jumps to his feet, eager to prevent a complete meltdown.

Aunt Jayne waves his hand away. "Can't we just have *one* normal dinner together as a family, *please?*"

She's still unpredictable. Some days she clings to the word *normal* like it's the big orange life raft that will save the family from despair. "Normal" people go on summer vacations. "Normal" people eat dinner together. "Normal" people do *not* spill soda on the floor or have dead children.

Other days, it's like now. Like Matt just died all over again. Jayne took it harder than anyone, and right after the funeral, she basically locked herself in her room for weeks, barely eating, not talking. Mom and I were over there all the time last summer waiting for the day she'd finally come out of her room. After a while, she did. She went as far as Matt's room, where she sat on his bed and smelled the clothes he'd left there on his last day, never washing them or changing anything in there. A few months later, we were all having dinner when Uncle Red suggested they donate some of Matt's books and clothes. I tried to imagine what it would be like to see someone else in his clothes, like we'd be standing in line at the grocery store and suddenly, *Hey, isn't that Matt? No, it's just the neighbor who bought Matt's shirt, buying applesauce and English muffins for his mother.* I couldn't bear it. Apparently, neither could Aunt Jayne. Without answering, she got up from the table and retreated to her room. She didn't speak again for days, not even to my mom, her best friend. It was like Matt's death was about to swallow them all up like a big, sad whale, leaving behind a house full of sympathy flowers, chicken casseroles, and ghosts.

"Sorry, Mom," Frankie says. Her voice is a whisper. "It was an accident."

Jayne sighs, mopping up a spill that's no longer there. "It's fine, Frankie. Just try to be careful. This trip is hard enough without —"

"Hard *enough*?" Frankie suddenly finds her voice, shouting at her mother below the table. "I'm not the one who planned this — this — prepottemous vacation!"

Preposterous, Frankie. Preposterous.

Jayne is stunned as she rises from the floor, but she presses on, tears in her eyes as well as her voice. "I'm sorry, Frank, but you're not the only one hurting here."

Uncle Red seems frozen at the end of the table, powerless to stop the mother-daughter breakdown happening before us. I'm afraid to look anywhere but my empty plate.

Frankie slams her chair against the table and stomps out of the kitchen. Never leaving the last word to chance, she tosses a casual "Bitch!" over her shoulder and disappears upstairs.

"*That* went well." Aunt Jayne wipes her hands on a dish towel and takes the same route as Frankie, slamming her bedroom door.

After a few moments of silence, me still looking at my plate, Uncle Red moves to clear the table and apologizes.

"This trip, we just thought — ah, forget it. I don't know what to say, Anna. I'm sorry." He crinkles his eyebrows to keep his own tears back. It's really bad when dads cry. My whole life I've only seen my dad cry twice — once in the hospital and then at Matt's funeral. No matter what Matt and my dad said — *dads* are supposed to be the strong ones. That's probably why Red has so many lines on his forehead. All the hurt goes up there to hide.

He apologizes again and excuses himself upstairs, leaving me alone in the kitchen with the big, sad whale.

What are you cryin' about? the whale asks. *He wasn't your brother.*

I wait until there's no sound coming from upstairs before heading up with my best-friend face to find Frankie. When I don't see her in the yellow room with the twin beds — the room she always had as a kid and would be sharing with me on this trip — I know there's only one place she can be. I walk to the end of the hall farthest from Red and Jayne's room and open the old oak door that

Jayne asked us not to disturb, heading up the narrow stairs to the attic room.

Frankie is facedown on the double bed, crying quietly into the soft white pillows where her brother slept every summer but the last. Hours earlier, she was at Breeze, larger than life with her virgin piña colada and freshly applied mascara. Now, hiding in the blue-gray room with its dusty ocean view, she's a pale, broken flower that makes my heart hurt.

I wish more than anything that Matt was here, that he was laughing with us in his old attic room, that it was all some big mixup at the hospital like when they give people the wrong babies.

"Hi, Mr. and Mrs. Perino? This is Peg over at Mercy General. I was shredding some old files and found some discrepancies. Yes, you know how these things happen. In any case, about a year ago, due to a paperwork snafu, we inadvertently gave you someone else's bad news. Turns out Phillip was the one who died, not Matt. Matt's been living with a family in Toledo. Yes, I've called them, too. They are flying Matt home tomorrow. No hard feelings, right? You know how these things happen. Buh-bye."

I put my hand on Frankie's back until the sobs go quiet and her breathing becomes long and even.

An hour later, we hear Red and Jayne head downstairs and out the front door, closing themselves in the car and setting out down the long driveway. Certain the house is empty, Frankie and I scrounge the kitchen for something to eat.

"I can't believe she just freaked out like that," Frankie says, pulling a fresh Diet Coke from the fridge. "And Dad didn't even say anything!"

"I don't think he knew *what* to say, Frank."

"I think they're gonna split."

"What do you mean?" I ask. "Like, tonight?"

"No. I mean split *up*. Divorce."

"What are you talking about? Your parents are fine. They're just adjusting to the first night back since — well, it's just hard for them." *And you.*

"Please," she says above the *shhhhhp* of her soda can opening. "At home, they don't even sleep in the same room anymore."

"But I've *seen* them."

Frankie shakes her head. "They say good night and close the door, but Dad sneaks down to the den when he thinks we're asleep. As if I can't see what's going on."

Fear and sadness squeeze my insides as I replay my recent overnights with the Perinos like a movie, scrutinizing every frame in slow motion for a hole in the plot. Red put his hand on Jayne's knee the night they told us about going back to California. *Did she wince?* I've seen them close the bedroom door as they wished us good night. Now I imagine them getting into their fake bed together. Lying next to each other, backs turned, careful not to let a pinky toe touch the other's leg, waiting for us to fall asleep so they can stop the show.

I shake the image from my mind, feeling like I've barged into a room of adults engaged in Serious Conversation Not Meant for Young Ears.

There *was* a time when I thought Red and Jayne wouldn't make it — right after Matt died. They'd been married for twenty years, but in just two days they forgot why. They barely spoke to each other — even when my parents and I were around. An all-out fight would have been better than the silence that engulfed them, but it didn't come — not then. Quiet tension settled into the Perino house like drying cement.

A month passed, and they stayed together. Three months. Then six. His birthday. Christmas. Mother's Day. Father's Day. The first anniversary, just a couple of months ago. Talking. Eating together. Laughing sometimes. Every smile or joke starting a tiny crack in the concrete encasing them.

"But your parents are different, Frankie. I thought they — I mean, how come you never —" I can't find the words to complete my sentence. Frankie sighs and traces the lip of her soda can, broken eyebrow hunkered protectively over her left eye, holding back the tears.

"The last time we were all in Zanzibar," she says, "I didn't get it." Her voice is far away and thin, like a ghost howling from another dimension. It doesn't matter that I'm right next to her — I could walk away and she'd keep talking.

"He was older," she says, playing with her bracelet. "I didn't see the things he saw. I didn't love the things he loved. I just didn't get it, Anna. I thought I'd have more time. I thought he'd —"

Frankie has her reasons for not talking about Matt, and forgetting about them — even momentarily — is too much. She folds her arms around herself and sobs. I move closer, put my arms around her, and let go. Together we weep like we did in the weeks following the accident — big, shuddering sobs that claw their way out from the places inside where the light went out over a year ago.

I don't know how much time passes, me and Frankie sitting without words, heads pressed together, short and synchronized breaths, but when we come out of our sad-trance, the soda is warm.

Frankie lifts her head slowly and wipes her eyes. I push her matted hair from her face.

"Hi." She exhales. Her face is pale, eyes puffy, but that voodoo magic smile is waking up around the corners of her mouth.

"How I Spent My Summer Vacation," I say.

Frankie laughs. "Eating and crying. What's not to love?"

"Exactly." I squeeze her hand.

Outside, headlights roll across the lawn, announcing Red and Jayne's ascent up the long driveway. Frankie and I drop our soda cans into the sink and head upstairs before her parents get inside, anxious to put this evening behind us. We change quickly, crawl into our matching twin beds, turn off the bedside lamps, and pull the sheets up to our chins.

Once Frankie's asleep, my best-friend superstrength disappears. My breathing shatters, tears blur the stars in the overhead skylight, and all the old ghosts I tried to leave home float like dandelion seed wishes into our room.

ten

*F*rankie snores lightly beneath her yellow quilt, and I am consumed with thoughts of Matt. Of the first kiss. The shooting stars. The stolen looks over the family dinner table. Texting me quotes from his favorite books in the middle of the night. His hand brushing my cheek when no one was watching. The smell of his skin as he leaned in front of me to pay for our ice cream that last day at Custard's.

If I'd known he was going to die, my last words to him would have meant something. They certainly wouldn't have been my out-of-tune attempt at singing that old Grateful Dead song he loved so much. No, I would have told him how I felt about him, straight out. No more flirting, wild-eyed whispers in the grass outside. I would have looked at him harder to ensure his image was permanently seared in my mind. I'd have asked him a million more things so I could remember what mattered *before* I got in the car on the way home from Custard's. Because *after,* nothing mattered.

We didn't even have a chance to label it. Whatever it was we'd become in the last month before his death will remain a mystery. I could never ask out loud. I wondered alone in my bed at night what would happen if he met someone else at Cornell, or if Frankie freaked out about us and he decided it wasn't worth it. But when you're in the middle of being in love with someone, you just don't stop to ask, "Matt, listen, if you die before you tell your sister about us, should *I* tell her? And by the way, is there even an 'us' to tell about?"

When it happens, you're totally unprepared, fragmented and lost, looking for the hidden meaning in every little thing. I've replayed the events of that day a hundred thousand times, looking for clues. An alternate ending. The butterfly effect.

If Frankie and I hadn't wanted ice cream that stupid day, he'd still be alive.

If I hadn't gotten his heart all worked up kissing him every night since my birthday, he'd still be alive.

If I'd never been born, he'd still be alive.

If I could find the butterfly that flapped its wings before we got into the car that day, I would crush it.

"Can't sleep?"

Aunt Jayne startles me from the dark corner of the deck where I've wandered absently with my ghosts.

"I didn't think anyone else was awake," I say, catching my breath. "Sorry, I didn't mean to — I'll just —"

"Anna, don't go." Jayne shakes her head. "It's okay. I was just — remembering."

"Me, too." I immediately want to take it back, run into the house, and dive under my bed. "I mean, you know, the stories and everything."

Aunt Jayne nods, the pale light of the moon falling around her hair like a halo, casting her in a faint blue glow.

"Sit with me." She pushes out a chair with her foot. It reminds me of the old Jayne, the one who treated me more like a friend than a little kid. Before everything happened, she used to lie in the sun with us, trading iced tea for a bit of girl time. Of course, the gossip wasn't as good back then. Frankie was still a virgin. Blue frosting didn't make me cry. I wasn't keeping secrets about one best friend from the other.

We sit for a few minutes, listening to the gentle rhythm of the waves against the shore. *Shhh, ahhh. Shhh, ahhh.* They seem slower in the dark, but louder.

"Frankie and Matt used to walk up and down this beach looking for sea glass," she tells me. "It was a contest they had."

"They used to bring some back for me. I still have it, actually."

"Right, I remember the jars. Matt used to make things out of it, too. Frankie's red glass bracelet. And the blue one he used to wear around his neck — do you remember?"

Rising. Falling.

I blink back tears and nod.

"I don't know what happened to it," Jayne says. "I've tried to find it so many times — I'm convinced he just took it with him."

I reach up and touch the spot above my collarbone where I sometimes feel the weight of the missing necklace, as though Matt had given it to me like he joked about. *Nope, still not there.* It was probably dragged off in the wreckage of the car with the loose CDs, the one sneaker, some overdue library books, and our ice-cream spoons — all the little bits and pieces left at the end of a whole entire life.

"Anna." Jayne breaks the spell of the evening tide. "Can I ask you something in confidence?"

"Okay." I'm not entirely sure where this is going.

"I know I wasn't myself tonight, and I'm sorry. Sometimes I just can't predict what's going to set me off. I'm working on it, truly. But is Frankie — how is *she*? Really?"

I look into Jayne's earnest face and think about Johan. I think about all the glitter eye shadow, in-room cigarettes, failing grades, and slamming doors, and wonder how Jayne can really ask. Maybe she wants to hear a yes — permission to go on not noticing anything. But the severity of her face, the lines across her forehead and around her mouth, her knuckles white over her mug — she's a blind woman seeking sight. Somewhere in the back of my head, I hear Dad, far away and sad.

As long as you're around, Red and Jayne don't really have to worry about Frankie — you're doing it for them.

"I'm sorry, sweetheart," Jayne says. "I hope I'm not pushing. I just worry about you guys. Frankie doesn't talk to me like she used to. My own daughter is a stranger to me."

"Me, too." My mouth is off doing its own thing again while my brain is half asleep. *Stupid mouth.* "I mean —"

"Tell me." Jayne's hand is suddenly firm on my arm. "It's okay."

She looks into my eyes and gives me that moment, that one chance to tell her exactly how it is, how different Frankie's become, her faraway mind trips, Johan, the twenty boys, A.A., the frosting-covered first kiss, the promise, how I can't stop thinking about

Matt — *everything.* I want so badly to tell her — the broken mother who after all this time might finally be able to fix all of us.

"Frankie's — she's managing okay," I say, wanting to kick myself. All the things I could have shared, and that's what comes out. *Managing okay,* like I'm evaluating her performance at the office.

"No," Jayne says, pulling her hand back. "She isn't. None of us is. Level with me, Anna."

A combo punch of weird emotions rushes through me — a fierce and loyal need to protect Frankie, guilt over my inability to tell Jayne the truth, and a lingering anger that no one seems to know or care about what *I* lost.

"Aunt Jayne, listen." I'm almost flippant, as though spoon-feeding these observations to my best friend's mom is too much effort. "Frankie's still here. She's not suicidal or on drugs. She can still laugh at things most of the time. But she's not the same."

"Anna, I didn't mean to —"

"Come on, you've seen her. All makeup and attitude. And she's not exactly an honor roll student these days. And look at what happened at dinner with you guys! Frankie knows he's gone, Aunt Jayne. He's just gone, that's it, and nothing will bring him back."

I'm shaking. My hand flies up to cover my mouth almost as soon as the words escape it; the weight of what I said suddenly pressing in on me. Mean, hurtful things I never should have said. I am officially the number one worst person in the universe, and Jayne's frozen, confused face is all the punishment I can bear.

But then — a deep sniffle.

A smile.

A look.

An openmouthed grin.

Right here on the back deck in Zanzibar Bay, in the middle of the black night, the ocean our only witness, I vomited out the ugly truth and Aunt Jayne . . . *laughed.*

"Anna," she says, wiping tears from her eyes with the back of her sleeve, "that is the first time anyone has been completely honest with me since my son died."

"Oh my God, Aunt Jayne, I'm so sorry. I don't know where that came from." I get up to hug her, hoping to shield my scarlet face from her eyes.

"Mmm-hmm." She hugs me back. "And I didn't even shatter!"

I pull away from her and drop into my seat, still shaking inside from my outburst and her unexpected reaction. She watches me and sips her tea, a lifetime of sadness behind her eyes — Matt's lifetime. But she's still smiling.

"Anna, you miss him."

"All the time. I still can't believe he's gone." The words come out in a whoosh, tasting funny in my mouth. No matter how many times I say them, they still feel like a garbled, impossible language. My chest hurts, and I have to hold my breath to keep from inhaling a deep sob.

"He was more than your best friend."

I nod absently, forgetting myself for a moment, forgetting that I'm talking to Jayne and not my journal.

"I — I mean, he was like a brother to me. You know, like Frankie. Well, she's the sister. I mean —"

Jayne reaches for my hands across the table, shaking her head softly. "Sweetheart, when you say Matt's name, you have the same look in your eyes that he'd get whenever he'd say yours." Her voice breaks up at the end, but her hands are warm and firm.

What look? I want to ask, but the butterflies are back, mixed with a sadness that seems to stick and slow their wings as they climb into my throat. Beyond our corner on the deck, the ocean sighs, waiting for my response.

Shhh, ahhh. Shhh, ahhh.

"Frankie doesn't know," I say, though I'm not sure what I want her to do with this information. Tell Frankie? Keep my secret? My head and heart are entangled. I haven't really said anything, yet Jayne and I have just shared more about Matt than I've shared with anyone — my own mother included.

"I know she doesn't," Jayne says. "She wouldn't be able to keep a secret like that from me." I think about Johan, but dismiss it. This is my secret, not Frankie's.

"Aunt Jayne, I —"

"I can't sleep, either." Frankie startles us in her frog pajamas, pulling the sliding door shut behind her. "What are you guys talking about?"

An arrow of fear shoots straight up my spine, pushing me to my feet.

"It's, um, it's nothing, Frank. I couldn't sleep. I didn't want to wake you." I study her face for an indication that she overheard something, but I see only sleepy eyes and sideways bed-hair sticking to the pink sheet lines across her cheek.

"Well, I'm awake now," she says, pulling up a chair next to her mom. Jayne downs the rest of her tea and wipes her mouth with her hand, letting out a long sigh like the ocean. "Do-over?" she asks Frankie, point-blank.

Frankie nods and rests her head on Jayne's shoulder.

"All morning I was waiting for a breakdown," Jayne says. "But by the time we got here, and I was unpacking and getting the house ready, I really thought I'd be okay."

"Me, too," Frankie says.

"When I went up to my room after you stormed up to the attic, I figured we'd all be packing up and heading home tomorrow morning."

"And now?" Frankie asks.

Aunt Jayne reaches into the front pocket of her cardigan. "I think your brother wants us to stay. I found this in the back of the linen closet while digging around for a box of tissues."

She holds out her palm, displaying a faded metal car the size of a peanut shell. Her eyes well up as she rubs the red paint with her thumb, but then she smiles.

"He was always losing these things," she says, running it along the edge of the table. "Half the time Dad would slip on them and nearly break his neck. Remember?"

Frankie smiles. "But how do you know it's his? Other people rent this place."

"Look." Jayne turns the car wheels up, revealing the plain metal undercarriage and two tiny letters in black marker: *M.P.*

Frankie gasps, reaching for the toy.

"See?" Jayne says, stroking Frankie's cheek with her knuckles. "He wants us to stay."

It sounds crazy, but things like this happen all the time. For me, it's the pennies. Whenever we'd pass a penny on the sidewalk, Matt wouldn't touch it. "Let someone else have a lucky day," he'd say. I used to tease him and tell him that someday when he got to the great beyond, there'd be a room stuffed full of all the pennies he'd left for other people.

Now I find pennies everywhere. Not just on the sidewalk — which I leave alone, as he would have wanted — but in the strangest places. One in the shower. A few more in my shoes — that seems to be a favorite spot. Just yesterday, one dropped out of a book I brought. I put them in my pockets and drop them on the sidewalk the next chance I get. Let someone else have a lucky day, I say.

Jayne takes the car from Frankie and slides it back into her pocket, smiling. Is Aunt Jayne making her way back to us from the secluded island she'd been marooned on by Matt's death? I can never be certain. Just like at dinner, a smile can turn into a code five freak-out as quickly as a storm can break over a ship.

But for now, she seems okay.

The three of us sit at the dark table, retreating into our own silent memories until our breathing unites us with the waves against the shore. *Shhh, ahhh. Shhh, ahhh. Shhh, ahhh.* Many minutes pass this way, and as I look from Frankie to Jayne and back out to the water, I don't want it to end.

When the silence finally breaks, it's Jayne, jumping up from the chair and grabbing our hands.

"Come on, girls," she says. "Follow me."

Frankie and I follow her down to the beach, squealing as the icy water hits our toes. Jayne jumps back and lies down in the sand, just clear of the tide.

We stand above her, unsure whether we should join in or call for Uncle Red. Suddenly she's flapping her arms like a flipped-over butterfly stuck in the sand, and all we can do is laugh.

"Sand angels," she says, as though it's perfectly normal for a grown woman to run down to the beach at three in the morning to make them. "Come on."

We lie on either side of her and flap our arms and legs as hard as we can, tears streaking our cheeks, though from laughing or crying we can no longer tell.

"Do you think he sees them?" Jayne rolls over and asks after we've made three angels above the tide.

"If he does," Frankie says, "he's probably wondering why the women in this family are so certifiably nuts."

The women in this family. For now, I'm one of them. Not the neighbor kid. Not a barnacle. But a woman in this family, running back to the house in a fit of slumber party giggles, freezing cold with sand in my hair.

eleven

"What were you guys talking about last night, anyway?"

My sleep-sticky eyes blink open one at a time like a broken doll's, unable to piece together the images in front of me. Frankie, sitting on the edge of a bed that isn't mine. A strange room. Sherbet sunlight falling on my face at all the wrong angles. I sit up quickly, my memory kicking in late to remind me that we're in Zanzibar.

It's the morning of our first full day.

And Aunt Jayne *knows*. Not everything, but more than anyone else.

"Huh? Oh, nothing. Just a little bit about Matt." My heart beats faster.

"That's what I thought." Frankie slides off the bed. "Do you really think she's okay now?"

"Yeah, I think she's good. Last night was fun, wasn't it?" I run my hands through my tangled hair, shaking more sand out on the wood floor. "I mean, the beach part."

Frankie scratches her head. "Yeah, tell me about it. I have sand in my ears."

I check the white plastic clock on our shared night table — eight a.m. We didn't sleep more than four hours last night, but excitement for the day ahead overshadows any lingering sleepiness.

"Anna, thanks for staying with me last night when I freaked. I'm sorry about all that weirdness and yelling at dinner."

She looks at me and half smiles, and I think of the therapist guy Frankie's parents sent her to a few times last year. I went with her once. If he was here, he'd probably say something like, "It's okay, you needed to explore the memories triggered by your first vacation without your brother." But all that comes out of me is, "Don't worry, it's cool."

I slide off the bed and stretch, trying to rub the sleep from my eyes.

"Hungry?" I ask. "We could make chocolate chip pancakes." It's not psychotherapy, but chocolate chip pancakes work for a lot of things.

She nods. "Anna, can I ask you something?"

"I know what you're going to say. Yes, we can use strawberries, too."

Another smile — a hint of a laugh.

"No," she says. "Not that. It's . . . Why are my parents such *freaks?*"

"Because they're parents. It's in the job description. Must drive minivans. Must be immune to fashion. Must be freaks."

"I'm serious, Anna," she says, peeling a broken fingernail. "Mom is, like, yelling and crying one minute, then she finds an old toy car and she's running down to make sand angels on the beach. Why did they want to come here?"

I consider her question, one I asked myself a thousand times in the weeks after their initial invitation. "I think they just want to make things better, Frank. Maybe they thought it would get things back to normal."

"But it won't," she says. "They don't get it."

I open my mouth to say something in their defense, but Frankie shakes her head. "It's okay, Anna. I'm just a little out of it. I mean, last night was fun, but it's still kind of weird after Mom freaking out over my stupid spilled drink like that. Let's go downstairs — I think they're already cooking something."

We stretch and head for the stairs, slowly moving toward the breakfast smells floating up from the kitchen. I pick out Aunt Jayne's French toast from the vanilla and cinnamon in the "secret" recipe she learned from a cooking show, along with the usual coffee and bacon staples.

"Morning, my angels." Aunt Jayne kisses Frankie's cheek and gives me a wink that's quick and subtle like a secret handshake.

"Hi, Twinkies," Uncle Red says, a frying pan full of bacon in hand. "Hope you're hungry."

"I'm starving." Frankie sits at the table and reaches for the orange juice. "And still wondering what happened at dinner last night. If anyone cares. Which I'm sure they don't."

"Sweetheart, let's not talk about last night," Jayne says, patting Frankie's hand. "We called a do-over, right?"

"Mom, that's not the point."

"Okay, kids." Uncle Red joins the table with a dish towel on his shoulder and a platter of French toast at the ready. He's prepared to prevent another stomping, door-slamming incident at all costs. "Eggs are getting cold."

Frankie puts down her glass and takes a deep breath. "Dad, I was just surprised, okay?"

Red stands with the frying pan awkwardly balanced over the plates, waiting to dish up breakfast like he's the hired cook rather than a man embroiled in a conversation about his dead son.

Frankie continues. "You guys are the ones that wanted this trip in the first place. You didn't really ask me. Well, I'm scared, too, you know? All the things I remember about California — I just don't want — I'm scared I'll remember new stuff, and everything else will be — *erased*."

Jayne stands up from the table and moves to the sliding door, her back to us. Her shoulders shake lightly, but she doesn't make any sound. After a minute, she wipes her eyes and joins us again at the table. I've seen this movie a hundred times, but it never gets any easier. I want to crawl under the table and disappear.

Uncle Red gives up on the eggs and sits with us. My face is hot as I focus on the interlocking circle pattern along the edge of my blue plate. I can't stop thinking about the back door, and how good it would feel to run straight through it and down to the shore.

"Frankie." Jayne reaches again for Frankie's hand. "We aren't trying to erase memories or pretend that everything is okay."

"I *know* that, Mom. It's just —"

"My girls," Uncle Red says, voice soothing, eyebrows crinkled, "let's just get through breakfast, okay? We have to take it as it comes." He puts his hand on Jayne's cheek and smoothes it with his thumb.

Jayne nods and pats Frankie's hand.

Frankie sighs and touches her foot to mine under the table. "Sorry," she mouths.

"You girls were up late last night," Red says, resuming his position as head chef and dropping a healthy scoop of home fries on his plate. "Causing trouble?"

"Just a little girl talk." Aunt Jayne smiles at me as she passes the maple syrup. My eyes lock on hers for a moment, and I wonder whether she can read my thoughts: that I want to tell her more about Matt and me. That I don't know what to do about Frankie. That I'm not sure how I can compete in the Twenty Boy Summer contest when there's only one boy I ever think about.

A new wave of guilt laps at my toes, threatening to creep up into my heart with the rest of my regrets. Aunt Jayne was a great listener last night, and I'm glad I said what I did about Frankie, but maybe I shouldn't have let her believe that I cared about Matt as more than a friend. If she sees us talking to other guys on the beach, will she think I'm cheating on her dead son?

"Right, Anna?" Frankie kicks me under the table, shaking me from my thoughts.

"Right. Sorry, what was that?"

"Our plans today. We're just going to lie around the beach near the house, right?"

I know Frankie has no intention of staying anywhere near the house or its private, secluded beach and designated middle-aged lifeguard, but I nod. "I go where you go, Frank."

"Dad and I are going grocery shopping after," Jayne says. "We have to get stuff for the rest of the trip. Don't you want to come?"

"Let's see," Frankie says, holding her hands out to her sides like

Lady Justice. "Walk around in a grocery store for two hours while Dad evaluates the quality of the produce, or hang out on the beach where we can swim, get a tan, and meet — I mean, swim and get a tan. Tough choice, Mom, but we're gonna have to pass."

"Thought so," Aunt Jayne says. "Just make a list of anything you want. And make sure you wear sunscreen, and reapply after going in the water. And if you've been out there more than two hours, reapply again. Actually, you shouldn't be out there between twelve and two, so —"

"Got it covered." Frankie rolls her eyes. "You guys act like I've never been in the sun before."

"No," Red says, patting her shoulder, "we act like you get burned every time we come out here."

"Dad, that's not burning. That's getting a base tan."

Uncle Red shakes his head and smiles. "All right, you girls can wander down to the concessions area if you'd like, but I don't want you going near the alcove. There aren't any lifeguards. Okay?"

"Okay, Dad," Frankie says.

"Good." Uncle Red. So loving. So trusting. So naive. "Have fun, my lovelies." After seconds and a few thirds, he pushes his cleared plate away. "Mom and I are heading out soon. Call the cell if you need anything. Otherwise, be back before dinner. Mom wants to cook Chinese."

Such a normal family breakfast on such a normal family morning. If they had a dog, his name would be Spot, and he'd start barking outside until one of us tossed him a Frisbee.

After breakfast, we (and by we, I mean Frankie) spend over an hour getting ready to swim in the ocean. She switches between sandals a few times and agonizes over which earrings to wear. Hair and makeup are another discussion — hair casual and messy like always, or swept back with a classy headband? Waterproof mascara, or just a touch of lip gloss? Serious or playful?

"Listen," I say, standing ready in my bikini — which I'm still not used to — and sarong. "No one is going to notice what you're wearing. They're going to notice *you*. Everything else is just background noise." I twist my uncombed hair into a loose bun on top of my head.

"Anna, for your information, nothing you put on your face, hair, or body is *just* background noise. Speaking of which, why aren't you filming? We need to document these things." She pulls her camera from her backpack and hands it to me.

I almost laugh, but she isn't joking. Like the boy contest, this is a project for her, carefully planned and executed, recorded start to finish for posterity. Not even her toe rings will be left to chance.

I keep the camera on her as long as I can, discreetly turning it on and off to spare future audiences from the tedium of Frankie applying lip liner, Frankie blowing her nail polish, Frankie tweezing her eyebrows. I'm about to leave without her when she finally announces she's ready.

"Thank God," I say, closing the camera and sweeping my journal and two paperbacks into my bag. "Can we *please* get down to the water now?"

"Wait!" Frankie shrieks with such immediacy that I almost think there's a scorpion or tarantula on my head. "We still have to do *you*."

"Frank, I've been ready for an hour."

She laughs. She actually *laughs*. "Anna, you can't go out like that. Look at your *hair*!"

"*Please,* Frankie. We're going swimming. In the water. Remember?"

"Don't be lazy about your looks," she says, coming toward me with a comb and a few bobby pins in her mouth. She's one creepy step away from spitting on a tissue and wiping my face with it. "It won't take that long."

Be strong, Anna. Be strong.

twelve

By the time we get to the water, it's close to eleven and the water-proof mascara Frankie combed over my lashes feels heavy and goopy. I worry that all the good spots on the beach are gone, but Frankie assures me that there will be plenty of spots when we get down near the alcove and away from all the "old people."

The other end of the beach is actually a whole different beach — an entirely separate stretch of sand with no water buoys, hot dog vendors, lifeguards, or people.

It does have *one* thing conspicuously absent on our beach — a No Swimming sign.

"See?" Frankie asks. "Totally private. No screaming kids or annoying families."

"Or witnesses."

"Don't be a baby, Anna."

"Frankie, it says No Swimming for a reason. Sharp rocks? Sharks? Undercurrent?"

"It says No Swimming because it's not a public beach, so they don't have a lifeguard," she says, crouching to unfold the beach blanket. "It's the same water, Anna. If there are sharks here, there are sharks at our beach, too. It's not like they read signs."

"How do you even know about this place?" I ask, dropping my bag and with it, the shark debate.

"My brother," she says. "He used to come to the alcove sometimes."

The beach is always crowded, he told me last year, a few nights before their trip. We were alone in the living room, pretending to watch a movie while Frankie dozed on the chair next to us. *But there's this one spot I like farther down. Sometimes I just go there to read and think. The ocean is good for clearing your head.*

And for looking at girls, I said.

Well, sure. He laughed. *But not that part. No one goes there except for occasional surfers. There's no lifeguard. Just the water and the rocks. One time I sat there for three hours, just listening to the water and wondering what was underneath.*

I look out over the water and wonder the same thing, trying hard not to think about the fact that I might be standing in the exact same spot Matt stood, looking out at the same blue sea, wondering the same endless, unanswerable questions.

What would we see if they drained it like a giant bathtub?

I curl my toes into the sand, waiting for Frankie to say something else.

"Here, help me with the blanket." She hands me a corner and lies down on the other side.

"Okay, blanket is secure," I say, still fighting the image of Matt on the couch that night, telling me his favorite things about California. "Now what? Just lie here all day until something exciting happens to us?"

Frankie inches and wriggles until she is strategically positioned in her most flattering pose — stomach flat, parted lips glistening, legs bent slightly, bosom heaving. "You'll see."

"You're really just going to lie there?"

"That's why they invented the beach, Anna."

"What about the water?"

"Are you kidding? We just did our hair!"

She used to love swimming. She and Matt would tell me about it in their postcards — all the hours they'd spend in the water, skin pruned and eyes burning from the salt, swimming and riding waves and playing Frisbee with summer friends, or sometimes just floating out there on their backs.

"Frank, let's just go in the wa —"

"Oh my God, Anna. Hotties, ten o'clock."

"What?" I turn my head to see what she's looking at, which is more in the direction of two o'clock, but who's counting?

"Don't *look*!" She swats my thigh. "Just act natural. Here they come."

I lie beside her, trying to guess what "act natural" means. I decide on mimicking her position, only I keep my sarong securely fastened and my arms folded over my chest. To the average onlooker, if anyone other than the rapidly approaching boys is looking on, I probably look cold. Or extremely pissed off.

"Oh, Anna," Frankie says in an exaggerated voice when the guys are within earshot. "I'm *really* hot. Pass me a water?"

Is she kidding?

She looks at me expectantly, eyes bulging, bordering on annoyed.

She's not kidding.

I sit up and fish a bottled water from my bag. The boys are about twenty feet away, staring at us with open mouths as Frankie sucks on the water bottle in an entirely inappropriate manner.

"Hey," one of the guys says with a swift man-nod. "What's up?"

Frankie shrugs and waves, inviting them over to our previously undisturbed patch of sand.

They exchange glances like hungry lions that have just been invited into the zebra den for dinner and jog over to our blanket, introducing themselves as Warren and Todd (or is it Rod? I've forgotten already). After thirty seconds of conversation, I can summarize their entire raisons d'être.

Drink beer. Meet chicks. Get tan.

Lather, rinse, repeat.

At Frankie's insistence, they shake out their blanket and camp next to us, thankfully on her side. Rod or Todd or whatever is the loud one, unable to be serious, unable to focus on one subject for more than a minute. He's a freshman at Berkeley, studying marine biology, and what his on-campus girlfriend doesn't know won't hurt her, *wink wink*.

Do guys really think this crap works on girls?

Frankie giggles. I guess it works on *some* girls.

Warren isn't exactly the *quiet* one, but the fact that I'm pretending to be asleep while Frankie and RodTodd laugh at each other's banter and trade cell phone numbers doesn't leave him an entry.

"Dude," Warren says after about fifteen minutes of staring at the ocean. "I gotta jet. See you later." I open my eyes when he stands, his shadow falling on my face. Frankie is doing some sort of half-kiss thing with RodTodd — more than friends, but not quite a full-on lip-lock. I expect this sort of gratuitous behavior with foreign exchange students, but total strangers? Annoying strangers, at that? The whole scene is more than I can stomach.

"Frank, I think I see your parents."

"That's my cue," RodTodd says. "Call me later, sexy."

Call me later, sexy? I'm going to be ill. Frankie, on the other hand, is practically ready to move in with him.

The boys take off down the beach and Frankie scans the opposite shoreline for Red and Jayne.

"Where are they?" she asks. "I don't see them, Anna."

"I guess I was wrong. Can we go in the water now?" I'm hot, bored, and quickly getting cranky.

"Anna, that was two out of twenty already scratched off the list. Why didn't you talk to Warren?"

"He has backne, Frank. Not to mention he's about as interesting as wet sea kelp."

Frankie laughs. "All right. But I'm still counting them as two. With them and the boys checking us out at Caroline's yesterday, that makes four."

"Yesterday doesn't count," I say.

"Well, it would have, if my parents hadn't shown up." She digs her camera from her bag and zooms in on my face. "So, Miss Reiley, will you or will you not admit specimens A and B from Caroline's into the official count of the summer of twenty boys, per the original contract terms of the Absolute Best Summer Ever?"

I crinkle my forehead to appear serious. "After careful consideration, the court hereby consents to a compromise. We shall count yesterday's platonic and lackluster ice-cream duo as a single boy."

She agrees, holding up three fingers in front of the camera before turning it on herself. "Three down. Seventeen to go. Not bad for our first twenty-four hours."

I roll my eyes and untie my sarong, ready to get into the water. If reaching our twenty-boy goal takes precedence over the high standards of good hygiene, interesting personality, and a minimum sixth-grade IQ, I'm dropping out right now.

"Can we *please* go swimming?" I ask.

"Oh, all right." Frankie stashes the camera in her bag and follows me into the water, splashing and giggling in the sharkless waves near the shore.

We go in up to our shoulders, waiting to catch the stronger waves and ride them up to the shore. The water and air above it taste equally salty, stinging my eyes and coating my skin, just like Matt said in his postcards.

When you taste the water on your lips, it feels like you've been eating potato chips. But there's nothing else like it, Anna.

"Ready for lunch?" Frankie asks after two hours of wave jumping. "I'm starving."

We gather up our blanket and bags from the beach and head back toward the concession stands near the house for hot dogs and curly fries. After watching us eat, a leathery guy who looks old enough to be our father sits down next to me at the picnic table.

"Can I get you girls a milk shake? Or more fries?"

His breath smells like sour milk as it falls on my shoulder.

"Sure," Frankie says. "I'll have a chocolate shake."

He smiles. "What about you, honey?"

"I'm fine," I say, kicking Frankie under the table. I'm totally creeped out that she's encouraging this geriatric pedophile to spend any more time with us than he already has.

"Fine? You sure are. I'll get you a *cherry* shake, how's that?"

Frankie answers for me. "She *loves* cherries."

He winks at us and heads up to the stand to order our shakes.

"Frankie, grab your stuff," I say. "Let's go."

"No way. This is the most fun I've had all year."

"He's an old *man*!"

"We're getting free shakes, right?"

Her logic astounds me. "At what cost?" I ask.

"Calm down, *Mom*."

Leather Man returns before I can convince Frankie to leave. She brushes her fingers against his when she takes her shake, and his eyes linger on her boobs for a very long time before he returns to my side of the table.

Just when I can't take another shot of his alcohol breath on my skin, we're saved by an equally leathery woman in a bright pink tank dress.

"Harold, what the hell are you doing?" She stomps a half-spent cigarette into the sand with her flip-flop. Her voice is coarse and the loose, brown skin on her arms jiggles. "Marcia's waiting in the car."

"Coming, my darling." He rolls his eyes for our benefit and dislodges from the picnic table — quite a task when you're drunk. "Enjoy the shakes, cherries — I mean, *ladies.*"

Mrs. Harold grabs his arm and leads him to the car, nagging him all the way.

"We're not drinking these." I take Frankie's shake before she can get a sip and drop them both in the trash can. Frankie laughs.

"Okay, big brother," she says. I almost laugh, imagining what her real big brother would do if he'd witnessed this disturbing exchange.

"So Old Man Date Rape was number what?" she asks. "Four or five?"

"We're not counting him," I say. "This is the Twenty Boy Summer, not the Twenty Dirty Old Man Summer."

"Sounds like we already have a name for next year's trip," Frankie says, wiggling her one and a half eyebrows. She winks at me and heads up to the counter to order two new shakes, hold the roofies.

None of this makes it into the final report we present to Red and Jayne during dinner when they ask about our first day on the beach.

"We had the best day," Frankie says, showing her parents some carefully preselected footage of our fun in the sun. After lunch, we shot a bunch of stock video of the crowded part of the beach for just this purpose. "The beach was packed, but we still had fun in the water."

Red passes out plates of the Chinese food Jayne cooked for our first official dinner in the house after last night's freak-out, clueless and happy that his daughter and her best friend had such a wonderful first day on Zanzibar Beach.

"I'm glad we decided to stay," he says, beaming.

thirteen

*T*he next morning has all the makings of our first day in California, but this time I'm prepared. While Frankie takes her shower, I get dressed and throw on just enough sparkle and bling to shut her up before our grueling death march to the deserted other side of the beach.

"If you want to meet guys," I ask as we shake out our blanket for day two, "why are we out here like a couple of wandering nomads?" If yesterday was any indication of the caliber of boys available, I don't want to meet more of them. I just feel safer in a crowd — especially after our encounter with Harold the Milk Shake Man.

"Anna," she says, reconfiguring herself on the blanket like yesterday, "only the tourists hang out in the crowded part. This is where the locals come."

"Suit yourself," I say. "But I'm swimming, not sunning."

I unwrap my pale body from the sarong, still not used to showing so much skin in public. I apply another layer of sunscreen just to be safe and hope no one is watching as I plod down to the water.

It doesn't feel as warm as yesterday, but my feet adjust quickly, allowing me to inch in up to my waist. In the distance, vacationing families move up and down the shore from the water to the beach and back again, their laughter weaving softly through the moist air.

I look over my shoulder to check on Frankie. She smiles and waves, repositioning herself on the blanket so she can reach the trail mix without sitting up. "Stay where I can see you," she shouts. "I need to get some shots of this."

The alcove is quiet today. As the water moves back and forth over my thighs, my mind drifts to my conversation with Aunt Jayne the night we made sand angels. How much does she actually know? Did he ever tell *her* about us? Did she see us kissing over a sink full of dishes when we thought no one was watching? Did she just figure it out? And what did she mean when she said he got the same look in his eyes when he talked about me? Matt and I spent so much time talking about when and how and what he was going to tell Frankie — we never got to the part about telling anyone else.

A new wave of butterflies flutters in my chest as I consider this, and I have to close my eyes to beat them down. *Matt's gone, remember?* Those butterflies have nowhere to go but darkness, beating and tangling their tiny wings until they break.

"Hey, *virgin!*"

The appellation is so sharp and unexpected that it takes me several seconds to realize it's aimed at me. I whip around to find Frankie giggling on her blanket in the shadow of two tanned guys with stubby-looking surfboards — the perfect California cliché.

"Virgin, right?" the voice asks again. It comes from the tall one with white-blond hair falling into his eyes. Frankie is still giggling, and my entire body goes hot and red, despite the chill in the water. If Frankie thinks she's just going to auction me off, well . . . I don't know. It's kind of hard to be witty when you're trying to call forth a giant sea squid to swallow you up and drag you down to the depths of the ocean floor, never to be seen, heard from, or mocked again.

I drop down so the water covers my chest. "Excuse me?"

"Um, you guys have never boarded before?" Blondie sort of asks-says, holding out his arms like he's expecting applause for his cleverness.

"Come back, Anna!" Frankie waves me in. "Meet our new friends."

I look behind me to confirm that the aforementioned giant sea squid has ignored my telepathic plea, then refocus, willing my sarong to float itself over to the shore and drape around my body as I emerge from the surf. When that doesn't work, I think about faking a cramp and quickly decide against it, reasoning that if I look like I'm drowning, one of them might jump in and put his hands on me. Probably not Blondie, though. He's too busy cataloging Frankie's measurements with his eyes.

I trudge up to the shore, which looks really sexy other than that whole middle part when you've cleared your upper body and have to pick up and plunk down your legs like pistons to cut through the water. The giant squid may not be interested in *me,* but I'll make sure Frankie looks nice and juicy when I drag her out of bed tonight and sacrifice her to the sea gods.

"Hey," I say, trying to sound casual as I yank my towel from beneath Frankie's firm and purposely placed elbows. "I'm Anna." Towel secured tightly around my waist, I hold my hand out to Blondie, whose name is Jake.

"Why, Anna Abigail, you're so proper," Frankie teases with a slightly off-key southern accent. I am still angry at her for going along with the whole virgin joke, and wonder briefly if a more appropriate, less proper greeting would be for me to whip off my bikini top and twirl it around my head like a lasso. Before I can respond, Frankie's on her feet, dusting sand off her butt in slow motion. Jake stares. The other one — Sam, I learn — shakes his head and smiles at me.

"Forgive my mannerless cousin," he says, and his smile makes me momentarily forget how annoyed I am.

"So, where are you from?" Jake asks.

"New York," Frankie announces, not bothering to clarify that it's the lame, upstate part.

"Seriously?" Jake asks. "That's so cool."

"It's all right," she says, examining her nails and wearing that New York thing like a badge she never earned.

"What's it like in the summer?" Jake asks.

"Oh, you know," Frankie says. "Never a dull moment. That's why we came to Cali — to relax." She takes a sip of water and licks her lips, looking out over the ocean. Jake looks in awe at his newfound woman of mystery and intrigue: Frankie, New York heiress, dining with the stars, hobnobbing with the rich and famous, risking her life every day on the hardened streets. In reality, before coming to California two days ago, our summer activities included such exciting adventures as lying out in the sun doing *Cosmo* quizzes, making mock interviews with Frankie's camera, experimenting with facials made of oatmeal and mayonnaise, and going with Mom and Dad to a food festival where we made five-dollar bets trying to guess which of our crazy neighbors dressed as the ketchup and mustard combo.

"What about you guys?" she asks.

"We live here," Jake says. "Not, like, on the beach, but in town. Nothing like New York. That's awesome." I think about our neighbors zipping themselves into their giant condiment costumes. Awesome. Totally.

Ready to move on from our getting-to-know-you conversation, Jake turns to the water and announces loudly in Frankie's direction that it's "time to get wet." She lets out an "Oh, yeah!" that's overblown, even for her, and repositions the triangle of her bikini bottom, letting go with a sexy snap before following Jake into the water.

Sam turns to me and smiles. For a few seconds we do that awkward conversational tango where we're both trying to talk at the same time and just end up laughing and not saying anything at all. Frankie squeals from the water, and Sam shrugs, looking at me.

Despite my chilly demeanor on the subject of twenty boys yesterday, something about Sam gets me. With messy, dirty-blond hair streaked from the sun and green eyes, he's definitely good-looking. Backne-free. No creepy old man vibes. Seems smart.

In other words, totally wrong for me.

"All right, Anna Abby from New Yawk," he says, nodding at his board. "You wanna try?"

I must have said yes, because I drop my towel and follow him out to the water, paying absolutely no attention whatsoever to the way his well-defined muscles move down his back, the jagged white scar on the left side above his hip, or the weird feeling I have in my stomach when he looks over his shoulder and smiles at me.

Absolutely *no* attention. What. So. Ever.

In the water, Frankie's lying facedown on Jake's board, paddling with her arms as he explains the basics.

"This alcove is great for learning because the water's pretty calm," Jake says, his hand resting in the small of her back as though it's the only thing keeping her attached to the board. "Once you get into the public beach part, it gets crowded and choppy.

"Now, the first thing you want to do is get a feel for the weight of the board, and how it reacts to your body." His teaching skills seem so expert that I wonder if the two of them walk the length of the beach every day, body boards in tow for just such a girl-impressing occasion.

"He teaches," Sam tells me. *Oh, no! Did I say that out loud?* "He's actually a great teacher, despite the ego."

"Sam," Jake says, raising his eyebrows, "let's not confuse ego with confidence in one's abilities."

"Please, continue," Sam says with an exaggerated wave.

"As I was saying. You wanna get into a tight crawl, knees against the board with your body as close to it as possible, like you're gonna kiss it." He guides Frankie into position, moving his hands along her body like a sculptor.

Jake continues his lesson while Sam steadies his board for me. When I move around to climb on, my leg brushes his in the water, bare skin on the wet fabric of his board shorts, and I feel a jolt from my head down.

It just surprised me, that's all. I wasn't expecting his leg to be there. I thought it was a shark. Or something.

"You okay?" he asks as I navigate the wobbly board.

"I'm good." The part of my leg that touched him still tingles.

Sam is not as versed in teaching as Jake, and his hands kind of hover over me, waiting for my permission to proceed through each step. When I almost topple the board, he gently grabs my arm to balance me, and I have to look away, pretending he's my overweight, middle-aged, *female* gym teacher giving me a swimming lesson.

We spend an hour with them in the water, learning body-board basics, watching Jake show off, talking about high school's inherent lameness. They're a year older than us and getting ready for their senior year. They pass most of their free time on the beach. Jake teaches swimming and surfing to summer renters, and Sam works at Smoothie Shack, their older cousin's place on the next tourist beach, another half mile past the alcove.

"So do you guys just carry these boards around looking for girls?" Frankie asks as if she doesn't care.

"You found us out!" Jake pushes her off his board.

"Actually, Jake was going to show me some new tricks," Sam says. "People don't usually hang out in the alcove. What were you guys doing here, anyway? It says No Swimming."

"Please," Frankie says. "I've been coming here my whole life. I've been all over this beach, and I swim where I want to swim."

"How come we've never seen you before?" Jake asks.

"You weren't paying attention." She shrugs, leaving out the part about how she probably wasn't wearing a bikini and didn't have anything to hold it up, anyway. "Or I was busy talking to someone else."

Apparently, apathy is today's modus operandi. Act cute and flirtatious at first, then when they're hooked, turn down the temperature a bit, feigning indifference. Voodoo magic. It works every time.

"You wouldn't be talking to someone else if *I* was there," Jake says. "Who can resist this hair, this body?" Frankie splashes him. He tells her she's hot. I think she's in love. Again.

Meanwhile, back on the plane of reality, Sam has to go to work. "Stop by later if you want," he says. "If you like smoothies, I'm your hookup."

"What about our lesson?" Frankie asks. "We didn't get to do anything."

"That was one-oh-one," Jake says. "Two-oh-one starts tomorrow, same place, same time."

"We might have other plans," she says, but we don't. Not only will we be here fifteen minutes prior to the appointed time, but we'll spend two hours beforehand picking out Frankie's wardrobe and rehearsing her lines.

"Let's go, dude," Sam says to Jake. "I'm gonna be late."

We trudge through the water back to our blanket. Frankie hugs Jake, but Sam just smiles at me with a barely perceptible raise of the eyebrows — *hopeful? Curious? Clueless?*

"See you later, Anna Abby from New Yawk," he says, turning and disappearing down the beach with Jake.

"Oh. My. God," Frankie says, flopping on the blanket. "They are *so* hot!"

"Frank, it's only day two and a half. We're not going to get to twenty if you run off and get married tomorrow." I drape my towel over my head like a veil. "Do you? I do! Do you? I do! Oh, Jake! You must tell me who does your highlights!"

Frankie laughs and snaps her towel at me. "Oh, okay, Miss 'Sam, hold the board for me! Sam, how do you do that? Sam, I want to see you naked.'"

"Oh, God, stop," I say, laughing with Frankie. "What about poor RodTodd? Aren't you going to call him?"

"Are you kidding me? That guy was gross."

"Why did you kiss him?"

"That wasn't kissing!"

"Um, *right*. So why did you give him your number?"

"Anna, I swear, sometimes you can be so — so *chartreuse*."

"Did you give him a fake — wait, what did you call me?"

"Chartreuse. You know, dense. What?"

"Frankie, you just called me a shade of green. I think you mean *obtuse*."

"Well, you *are* looking a little pale."

I shake my head and laugh. "It's called sunscreen. Try some."

"No, thanks. At least we met some decent guys today," she says, flipping over on her stomach and untying her top. "And we both want separate ones."

I put on my sunglasses and rest my hand on my leg — the part that touched Sam's in the water. The part that's still tingling. "I don't want anyone."

"What's *wrong* with you?" she asks, as though she's a doctor who can't diagnose my weird combination of unlikely symptoms. "Sam was totally checking you out. And it looked like you were having fun."

I shrug, suddenly intent on digging through my bag for a book. There are probably a million different things I can say to her to get her to shut up. He's not cute enough. I don't like his hair. I saw someone else closer to the house I want to check out. But none of these things is true. The truth is the one thing I *can't* say — that if I can be interested in Sam, I'm forgetting about Matt.

fourteen

As Frankie drifts in and out of an afternoon sun-nap on the blanket beside me, I read the same paragraph in my book about a hundred times, absorbing nothing. I will myself to think about something else. *My book has three hundred and one pages. Where will we go for dinner? Wow, sand is sparkly!* But Sam invades my thoughts — thoughts that have become dangerous and need little encouragement toward misbehavior.

His smile. *Stop it, Anna!*

His green eyes. *Focus, focus!*

The way he says, "Anna Abby from New Yawk."

Do they have strawberry banana smoothies at the smoothie shop? I bet he's got that tan all year. Does he have a girlfriend? Maybe. Maybe one from every state. A collection of virgin tourists just waiting for it to be special.

I think about the girl in the mirror from when Frankie and I went bathing-suit shopping. When I agreed to the contest, I was half joking, all for Frankie's benefit. Besides, I can't get involved with anyone out here. Attached. All those words and feelings and intentions tangling into something more wild and confused than my windblown hair — *no,* thank you. The last boy who got me tangled up that way died.

The thought of Matt squeezes my insides again. I rub my eyes and stare at the water in front of our secluded, off-limits beach where sharks, undercurrents, and boys may or may not be waiting to drag us out to sea.

Shhh, ahhh. Shhh, ahhh.

I concentrate. I clear my head. I am the master of my thoughts. My head is empty. I am floating. I am a masterful, empty-headed, floating feather on the wind.

Shhh, ahhh.

Did Sam say we should come by for smoothies tonight, or tomorrow?

I give up.

I need to get off this beach, back to the quiet cool of the house. I shove my book back into the bag and wake up Frankie.

"Let's go back. I'm hungry." I rub her shoulder gently, feeling heat rise fast from her pink skin. "Frank, wake up. You're really hot."

She stirs and reaches up to tie her top. "I know," she says. "I think this suit was the best idea I had all year."

"No, I mean, you're *really* hot. Your skin is burning up."

When she sits up, her back looks spray-painted hot pink.

"Didn't you put on sunblock before we left the house?" I ask.

"Mom made me do it yesterday. But why would I want to block out the sun two days in a row?" She twists back and forth like a fish on the shore to get a look at her back. "I need to get a base going so I don't burn later in the week."

"You're already burned," I say. "I can't believe you're not in pain."

"I'm fine." She stands to shake the sand from our blanket. "Quit being so paranoid. You could use a little color yourself, Casper."

We walk the beach back to the house, taking a few videos of the sights and vendors closer to the property in case Red and Jayne want to see more.

They're reading on the back porch when we get back.

"Tough day?" Red asks as we drop our stuff on the floor and kick off our flip-flops. "I didn't expect you guys back until — *Frankie,* what did you do to yourself?"

"I fell asleep," she says, shrugging. "But I'm totally fine. Just tired." She flops on the couch and closes her eyes before Jayne can fully inspect the damage and regurgitate another sun safety lecture.

"It's the same thing every year," Jayne says, shaking her head. "Anna, I'm putting this lidocaine gel in the fridge. She won't ask me, but you can give it to her later when she can't even get into her pajamas." Jayne holds up a family-size bottle of blue goo.

"Should we cancel our reservations and eat at home tonight?" Red asks. But Jayne says Frankie wouldn't pass up lobster for anything, so we spend an hour playing cards in the kitchen before waking her up for dinner.

Frankie's clearly suffering but, as Jayne predicted, unwilling to miss out on lobster. She can barely walk but somehow manages a cold shower and an hour of makeup and hair. She can't show anyone how much it hurts, fearing Red and Jayne will forbid her from leaving the house without long sleeves and pants for the rest of the trip. If I were a better friend, I'd probably sympathize and offer to carry her purse or something, but watching the drama queen try to hide every wince is just too amusing.

She does okay with the physical fakery, but she's cranky and short-tempered the entire evening, whining about nonsensical things in place of the real issue of tenth-degree burns all over her back and legs.

"How long do we have to wait for a table, Dad? This is taking forever." And . . .

"How can a place be out of ginger ale? How can you run a restaurant and not have enough ginger ale?" And . . .

"Our waiter seems like he's in training. Who doesn't know how to describe the mahimahi sauce?" And . . .

"It's so hot in here. What kind of place doesn't have the air conditioner on in the middle of summer?" And . . .

"I *said* I don't want any water, thank you." At this, she holds up her hand to the busboy pouring ice water from his plastic pitcher. Whether it's Frankie's looks, her sunburn, or her attitude, *something* distracts him. He drops the entire pitcher in her lap, fumbling in slow motion to stop the force of gravity from taking that water to its final destination down her shirt and into her lap.

Frankie squeals and shoots up from the table, soaked from the middle down. The poor busboy jumps into awkward action, grabbing at cloth napkins from the unseated table behind us and attempting to blot at the air in front of her without actually touching her body, lest he cause any more of a scene. Red, Jayne, and I are stunned, each of us holding back a flood of well-deserved laughter. One wrong move and we'll lose it, I know we will. The busboy, probably fearing for his life, excuses himself to find the manager.

"I'm so sorry, sir," the manager says. "Your family's dinner will be on the house tonight. Dessert, too."

"Don't worry about it," Red says, blotting at his face with his napkin to hide a smile. "She was just saying how hot she was. Perfect timing."

With that, Jayne and I can no longer contain ourselves. Our laughter confuses the manager, who pretends to have a sudden culinary emergency and implores us to call on him if there's anything else he can do to enhance our dining experience.

Frankie pushes away from the table and storms toward the ladies' room like an angry tornado.

I'd much rather stay at the table with Red and Jayne and enjoy the whipped-cream-topped strawberry daiquiris (nonalcoholic, of course) the waiter brought (on the house, of course), but after ten minutes, I'm compelled to check on our angry diva.

In the ladies' room, she's standing at the sink, blotting her face with a wet paper towel.

"Come on, Frankie," I say. "Come back to the table — they brought us strawberry daiquiris."

She ignores me and tosses out the paper towel.

"You have to admit it was kinda funny," I say.

"Great. I'll ask the busboy to come by and drop a gallon of ice water on *you,* then we'll see if it's still funny."

"Frankie, you were complaining about the heat. It's kind of like an answer from the universe."

She tries to act offended, but I can see a smile creeping onto her face.

"You look great, anyway," I say, appealing to her most susceptible side. "That's probably why he dropped the water. He was stunned into clumsiness by your ravishing beauty. Technically, you should take it as a compliment."

"True." She shrugs her shoulders and wipes some stray eyeliner from her lower lids.

"Let's go back," I say. "Your dad ordered the lobsters."

She pushes open the door. "Perfect. More jokes at my expense."

Back at the table, Red and Jayne apologize for laughing at Frankie and offer to take us miniature golfing after dinner.

After gorging ourselves on seafood and decadent desserts, not to mention those daiquiris, we waddle down to Moonlight Boulevard in search of the best mini golf, which turns out to be a themed place called Pirate's Cove. The course is packed with old people who move too slowly and actually keep score, kids who abandon their clubs and stuff the balls into the holes with their sticky little hands, and people like Frankie and me, who would much rather be at Sam's smoothie shop than spending quality time with parents.

Frankie is practically limping from her sunburn, but Red and Jayne are so excited that it would be cruel to bail early on them. Besides, it's nice to see them laughing so much.

"Hole in one!" Red pumps his club in the air after putting his ball successfully off the plank into the mouth of a plastic crocodile. "Write that down on the card, honey. One shot. It's the score to beat!"

Red and Jayne move on to the sunken treasure chest as Frankie tees up for the crocodile. As she's lining up her shot, I spot the boys from our first day on the pier paying for a game up front.

"Frankie, look." I nod in their direction. "Your boyfriends from Caroline's."

She turns to look, then ducks behind me. "I thought you were kidding. Hide!"

"The other day you were practically posing for them."

"Anna, I don't want anyone to see me like this."

"So you're actually admitting that you look like a fried lobster?" I hobble ahead of her, imitating her slow-motion sunburn limp.

"For the last time, this is just a base! I'm talking about being seen with *them*." She nods toward Red and Jayne, high-fiving each other under a black skull-and-crossbones flag two holes ahead.

"Come on, yeh scalawags!" Red shouts at us, eliciting sympathetic looks from the patrons at holes five through seven. "Catch up, or it's off the plank with yeh."

Okay, Frankie has a point. I grab her hand and lead us to the second-to-last hole, far away from the pirate parents we arrived with and, more importantly, the guys from Caroline's. Upon further examination, they're not so bad. Still. Sam is way better.

Anna! You were on a roll. Almost ten whole minutes without thinking about him!

We finish out the last two holes with little effort and return our equipment, waiting at the snack bar for Red and Jayne to complete the course in their own pirate revelry.

"What are we doing after?" I ask.

Frankie hovers over an iron bench, trying to lower herself without causing additional pain to her burned backside. "Probably nothing," she says. "You know Mom and Dad are early people. Why?"

"I'm kind of craving a smoothie."

*   *   *

"I don't get you," I say, back at the house. "You're the one trying to get me to drop the A.A., and you don't even want to meet them tonight? They totally invited us!"

It's after ten, Red and Jayne have long since gone to bed, and I'm trying to convince Frankie to sneak out. *Me.* Trying to convince *her.* In just three days, I barely recognize myself.

"God, Anna. You'd think you never hooked up with a boy before. Oh, that's right, you haven't!" Frankie throws a pillow in my general direction.

"Oh, shut up." It's lame, but I can't exactly correct her.

"Go if you want," she says. "But I'm staying right here." She winces as she crawls between the cool of her sheets.

"Admit it." I sit on the edge of her bed. "Admit that you're embarrassed about this stupid sunburn, and that's the only reason you won't go."

"Anna, I just don't feel like breaking the rules, okay?" She looks at me with feigned severity, starting a chain reaction of hysterical laughter. I lean over her, palms outstretched, and threaten a good slap to the tender skin on the back of her arms if she doesn't relent.

"Okay, you win!" she says, still laughing. "It burns! It burns!"

"And?" I say, looming closer with my stinging hand.

"And I look like a tourist!"

Satisfied with Frankie's newfound humility, I fetch the giant blue bottle of lidocaine from the fridge, granting her temporary relief from her own stupidity.

Later, after we've settled into bed and accepted our fate as wholesome, rule-abiding beach community citizens for at least one more night, Frankie advises me to play it cool with Sam.

"Sam and Jake are only four and five on the list. We don't want them to think we're actually *interested,* Anna," she says, probably scanning her memory for another Johan reference with which to demonstrate her sexual expertise.

"Right," I say. "Because I'm not. Interested, I mean. I'm just saying, is all."

fifteen

*T*hanks to Frankie's ultraviolet oversight, we're forced to hole up inside the house playing card games and eating ice cream out of the carton the entire next day. Even Uncle Red and Aunt Jayne are having more fun than us, running in the morning, swimming in the afternoon, sitting out back and reading in the last hours of sunlight. I'm going a little stir-crazy.

I don't want to mention it to Frankie again, lest she accuse me of being overeager, but I can't stop thinking about Sam (who by now has probably found some other tourist girlfriend who doesn't blow off his invitations for surf lessons and smoothies. Mental note: if Frankie survives tenth-degree sunburn, kill her).

Frankie finally announces her triumphant return to civilization at eight the following morning, waking me up to begin the long and painful process of primping for a dip in the ocean.

Maybe it's the sunshine, or the salty ocean air, or the laid-backness of California, or thoughts of winning Sam back from the beautiful new beach princess he probably found in my absence yesterday, but this time, I'm all Frankie's. I check my regular self at the door and let her work her voodoo magic. I pay attention. I watch and listen and ask questions on her hair-blowing and makeup-mixing techniques as though my entire future depends on it. I let her gel me and tease me and color me up until I look at least ten years older. We paint our nails, select our sandals carefully, and even coordinate our beach bags with our blanket. No mortal boy can resist coordination and cuteness like *this*!

We practice our strut up and down the back deck until Red and Jayne leave for a day of *real* golf, promising to meet back at the house for a late lunch together.

"Remember, Anna," Frankie says as we cross the yard to the stairs and the beach below. "Shoulders back, stomach in, boobs out." I do as she instructs, sucking and pulling and contorting the right parts at the right times as I follow her down to the alcove and pray to the God of Most Embarrassing Moments that I don't trip.

As we approach the curve in the shore that curls around to our spot, I'm momentarily relieved to see two guys goofing around in the water. But as we get closer, I realize our spot in the alcove has been completely overrun with other tourists, Sam and Jake not among them.

"I knew it," I say, dropping my bag before we get close. "They gave up on us."

Frankie picks up my bag and hands it back to me. "Come on, Anna. It was one guy. Get over yourself."

But even she can't hide her disappointment as she scans the water and shore for her beloved California blond.

"Should we go back?" I ask, trying hard not to sound too deflated. I know we only just met them, but still.

"I guess."

"Wait!" I practically shout. "Maybe they're at the smoothie place? Sam said it's not far from here. We could —"

"You and your smoothies!" Frankie laughs. "I thought you weren't interested."

"I'm not. I just — I mean — don't you want to learn how to surf?"

She looks hard at me, trying to gauge the lameness of my thinly disguised argument. Then, laughing, she grabs up the rest of her beach stuff and leads us onward, past the alcove, farther than we've ventured before.

"Operation Smoothie in full force," she announces, digging out her camera. "Let the lost albatross countdown begin."

We walk side by side, weaving our way through increasingly dense crowds of oiled-up tourists, keeping a running commentary for the video. Just when I've seen all the pasty old men in Speedos I can handle, Frankie spots the sign for Smoothie Shack.

We charge up the sand, energy and hopes renewed by the fading wooden sign with its chipped green-and-yellow lettering. Sam is standing behind the counter and he smiles when he sees us, making the entire hike totally worth it.

"I'm done in ten," he shouts across the counter. "Hang out, okay?"

Frankie stashes the camera in her bag and we find a booth near the counter. After the long walk through all the pasty people and soggy-diapered little kids, we'll camp out here all night if we have to.

Ten minutes later, Sam joins us with three banana coconut something-or-others — his favorite. He sets down the drinks and slides into the booth next to me.

"Hey. What did you do to your — I mean, you look different."

My cheeks go immediately hot. Not that your average onlooker can tell, given all the makeup I'm wearing. "Frankie and I were just messing around this morning."

"Oh," he says, tying the paper from his straw into little knots. "It looks nice, I mean. I just can't see you, that's all."

I make a mental note to ditch the makeup tomorrow.

Then I get mad at myself for letting some boy that I just met dictate what I do with my own face.

Then I get mad at myself for getting mad at myself and remember that I, too, prefer the natural look.

See? This is exactly why I don't want to get involved with anyone.

"Where's Jake?" Frankie asks, trying to sound as if she doesn't care. I make a kissy face across the table when Sam isn't looking. She *totally* cares.

"He's teaching today. We're supposed to meet up in an hour. Come with me." He nods as though it's already settled. "We thought you ditched us."

I want to set the record straight. "Frankie had a —"

"Anna," Frankie cuts in, shooting a severe stare my way. "You don't have to report our whereabouts to him."

"Let me guess," Sam says. "Sunburn?" He laughs, thankfully impervious to her attitude. I imagine he's seen his share of girls like Frankie. Most guys dismiss the less appealing parts of her external personality in favor of the much more appealing parts of her body, but every once in a while there's a guy like Sam. To Frankie, it's truly vexing.

"It's a *base*," she announces. "Anyway, we had other plans."

"Right, Pinkie," Sam says. "I wasn't really asking. Just pointing out that you ditched us."

Frankie opens her mouth to rebut, but Sam's too quick. He tells us about the stretch of beach where we're meeting Jake, and how the water's a little rougher there than at the alcove, but it's close enough to the public part of the beach that the lifeguards can still get to you in an emergency.

"Don't worry," he says. "I have a feeling you two can handle it."

Back in Frankie's good graces, Sam clears our table and drops his apron behind the counter. "Let's go," he says, holding the door for us.

Outside, he grabs his body board from where he stashed it behind the restaurant and leads us about ten minutes farther down the beach.

The spot where we meet Jake is on the outer edge of the touristy part. It's more open than the alcove, so there are a few other surfers in the water, but we have plenty of room to spread out.

Jake is near the water, waxing his board. When he sees us coming, he runs up to Frankie and picks her up in just the sort of attention-doling hug Frankie expects.

"Damn, girl!" he says as he sets her down. "Did you fall asleep in the sun?"

"It's a — you know what? Yes," Frankie says. "I fell asleep in the sun. Can we move on now?"

I toss Frankie a bottle of sunblock as we get ready for Surfing,

Part Deux. This time we kneel on the boards and ride a few waves to the shore with Sam and Jake close behind. The water is much choppier than the alcove — mostly because of the speedboats racing through just a few hundred yards away. I half expect Frankie to fake an undertow incident, just so she can be gallantly rescued, but she's so focused on Jake and surfing and laughing with her mouth open and head thrown back that she all but forgets most of her standard Frankie tricks. I even catch a few glimpses of the old Frankie. Sure, she still exudes the confidence of a girl who could attract a swarm of lifeguards and medical personnel with a broken nail, but she's not doing it on purpose.

Unfortunately for me, by the end of our lesson, Sam has gotten neither less attractive nor less attentive. Against my better judgment, which seems to be conspicuously absent these days, I accept the hard reality that I maybe might possibly be just the slightest tiniest littlest bit kinda sorta interested in him.

Which means of course that he's hereby *off* the list of contenders for Last Boy to See My Virginity Alive. I certainly can't endure the kind of impossible embarrassment required during the ditching of one's albatross with someone I might actually *like*.

We have to meet up with Red and Jayne for lunch but agree to find Sam and Jake again tomorrow.

Tomorrow quickly turns into the next day, which turns into the next one, and the next one after that. Soon, Frankie and I are running back and forth every day between morning and afternoon surf sessions for long lunches with Uncle Red and Aunt Jayne. I think Frankie's parents appreciate the time alone, but it's also important that we don't give them any reason not to trust our daily reports about the nonexistent, really friendly local girls that we supposedly hang out with all day, just down the beach.

By the end of the first week, we settle into a routine. Meals and other random activities with Red and Jayne, as required of the good daughter and her angelic best friend, and mornings and late afternoons with Sam and Jake. In our short time together, the four of us become the kind of impossibly close that only happens with people you barely know — people who live hundreds of miles and entire states away from you.

People who don't know your secrets.

Frankie and Jake are all over each other in a sickening sort of way that makes old married people visibly uncomfortable. The only thing keeping them from venturing into the final frontier — Johan-soccer-field-style — is lack of opportunity. Even with Frankie's penchant for public spaces, daylight hours on the beach are just too crowded.

Sam wants to kiss me, I can feel it. It's that look he gives me sometimes — a look I've seen before, and one I'm not sure I'm ready to see again — not wholly. My body is composed of various parts and nerve endings that would love to see it again. But thankfully, my logical side keeps winning out, reminding me how good ideas can quickly turn bad, helping me change the subject or turn away whenever that look starts to creep into Sam's eyes.

Frankie thinks I'm crazy.

"I don't get you, Anna. I really don't," she says at the end of our first week with Sam and Jake. We watch them do tricks in the water as we lie on our blanket in the hot sand. "Don't you like him?"

"Yeah, but . . ."

"But what? Don't you want to ditch the A.A.?" She looks concerned, as though my response might impact the outcome of her entire life.

"I guess, but . . ."

"You *guess*?"

"Frankie, I really do like Sam." I keep my voice low so he can't hear. "It's just not something you can force."

She stares at me. "Then I can't help you, Anna. You're going to have to lose your virginity all by yourself."

I look at her and laugh. "If only it were that simple."

Sam and Jake join us on the blanket, dripping cold water on our legs. Before Sam can ask if I want a soda from his cooler, Frankie and Jake are locked at the mouth.

"Prisoners of lust," Sam says, handing me a Coke.

Prisoners — oh, no!

"Frankie, shit! Alcatraz!" We totally forgot that we promised Uncle Red we'd take the afternoon tour. According to Sam's watch, we're already twenty minutes late.

"Shit!" Frankie unsticks herself from Jake and ties up her sarong.

We say quick goodbyes, shove all of our stuff into our bags, and take off down the beach, running through the sweaty, undulating mob of tourists on the stretch between Smoothie Shack and our rental house.

We show up for the Alcatraz outing forty minutes after the previously agreed upon meeting time, apologetic and out of breath. Red and Jayne are sitting at the kitchen table, keys in hand, camera bag packed, waiting. Frankie makes up some story about having lunch with "Jackie" and "Samantha" at Jackie's beach house and totally losing track of time, which was easy to do considering both our cell phones sat idly on the bedside table all morning. My face burns as she expertly weaves our tale. I focus on my pink toenail polish, waiting for Red and Jayne to tell us how worried they've been and how disappointed they are that we've taken advantage of their leniency on this trip.

They don't, though. They just kind of shrug, tell us we can still make it, and ask us next time to try to stick to the plans. I would have preferred the standard parent lecture about learning to be young adults and proving our capacity for responsibility and why do we pay for cell phones if you're not going to carry them? — the one my parents wrote many years ago and have relied on throughout the difficult teenage years. But Red and Jayne seem genuinely okay with it.

"Don't worry about it, girls," Aunt Jayne says. "We're glad you're making friends on this trip."

Because somehow that means everything is going to be okay.

"But I wouldn't mind spending some girl time alone with you two tomorrow, if that's okay," Jayne says. "That is, if you don't mind being seen on the beach with an old fossil!"

"Sure," we say, smiling like the little cherubs we are, making a simultaneous mental note to notify Jackie and Samantha that they don't exist, that we don't exist, and, should they discover us lounging around with aforementioned old fossil on the beach tomorrow, they should just keep on walking as though we've never met.

We apologize again, change into shorts, pile into the car for Alcatraz, and promise Red that next time, we'll stick to the plans.

Of course, Uncle Red's plans don't include the part about his two little Twinkies making a break for it as soon as he and Jayne are asleep, but come eleven o'clock tonight, that's the only plan on our agenda.

sixteen

"*I*t's time." Frankie tiptoes into our room from her recon mission down the hall. "They're totally out."

As the longtime and only voice of reason in this operation, I'm compelled to resist. "Are you sure we should do this?" I ask. "What if we get caught? What if we get all the way out there and they're not even there?"

"Anna, they told us they hang out there every night. Besides, we're not gonna get caught. Mom and Dad sleep like rocks, especially after being out in the sun all day."

"They might wake up for water or something."

"Don't be ridiculous. Even if they do, they won't come in here. Just do what I do."

Frankie pulls the extra pillows and blankets from the closet in our room and stuffs half of them under her blankets, motioning for me to do the same.

"Even if they open the door, they'll think we're sound asleep."

Voice of Reason tries to chirp up again, but when I think of Sam hanging out on the beach at night in front of a campfire, Voice of Reason, along with his close cousin, Voice of Logic, go hoarse.

"Okay," I say. "Let's do it."

Frankie does one more recon and gives the thumbs-up from outside Red and Jayne's door. We tiptoe down the stairs, avoiding the third one that always creaks, and go, leaving the door unlocked for our return.

Meet me out back again later, okay? Matt pulled me into the hall closet before anyone else could see us.

What if my parents hear?

Anna, we've been doing this every night for weeks. They're not going to hear. Besides, I can't wait another twelve hours to see you.

His mouth was hot on mine, sealing our promise before I could think of any more excuses.

Okay, I'll be there.

Better be.

"Anna, you with me?"

The memory of my last sneak-out attempt with Matt fades into the salty sea air.

"Huh?" I look at Frankie, trying to read her expression in the dark. We can't turn the flashlight on until we're down the stairs, safely out of visual range from Red and Jayne's bedroom.

"I said, watch out for rocks in the grass. You're totally spacing out."

"No, I'm with you. Come on." I grab her hand and lead us down the stairs, watching our steps carefully. Once we're on the beach, it's easy to navigate our way down the shore. The sound of water stays solid on our left, and the beach is glowing with the lights of roaring campfires. We can still faintly smell the hot dogs and cocoa butter from the afternoon sunbathers, but now it's mixed with cigarettes and beer and the gentle melodies of random acoustic guitars — underage base camp. Every other gang whistles and yells as we pass, inviting us to sit by the fire and stay for a drink. Frankie loves the attention, waving and smiling at everyone, taking random video shots, but we're on a Sam and Jake mission, not to be dissuaded from our course.

The boys are hanging out in front of the Shack, just like they said they'd be when we rushed through our goodbyes earlier this afternoon. Like the other groups, Jake and Sam have a fire going and a small cooler of beer. My stomach goes a little fizzy when Sam smiles at me. "Missed you," he says, handing me a bottle. "We didn't know if you'd actually risk it."

"I had to convince her," Frankie says. "Anna can be sort of a baby sometimes."

I try to choke her to death with my eyes, but she throws her arm around me and laughs. "We love her anyway," she says.

The four of us stand around sipping the beers and digging holes in the sand with our toes. We tell them about our trip to Alcatraz with Red and Jayne.

"That's actually a pretty cool tour," Jake says. "I took my little sister there last year."

"You have a sister?" I ask, suddenly realizing that in all of our lengthy discussions on best and worst school subjects, potential careers, favorite foods, and music, we haven't talked much about family.

"Three, actually," he says. "Katie is thirteen. And I have twin older sisters, Marisa and Carrie. They're in North Carolina for college. You?"

I tell them I'm an only child and realize with a sharp tingle in my stomach that I've just set up a perfectly awkward and agonizing moment. I look at Frankie and make a quick scrunched-up face that hopefully conveys how stupid I feel for getting us into this territory.

"Me, too," Frankie says, setting down her empty bottle in the cooler. "Jake, let's go in the water." She wipes the back of her hand across her mouth and turns toward the ocean.

"Are you crazy?" he asks. "We can't see anything."

"Exactly." Frankie takes off her shirt to reveal her bikini and throws it in the sand by the cooler, settling the "to swim or not to swim" debate once and for all.

"In the water we go!" Jake hands his beer to Sam and tosses his T-shirt on top of Frankie's, chasing her along the shore.

The space of our conversation goes quiet in their absence, but not empty. The fire is warm and so is the air around us.

"Frankie is, um, a *fun* girl." Sam shakes a red-and-white-striped blanket out and spreads it on the sand.

"She used to be really shy, believe it or not." I join him on the blanket, glad to have something to do besides pretend to like beer.

"Why, was she fat or something?"

I laugh at the idea. "Fat? God, no. She — well, her — you know, let's not talk about Frankie now." There's no reason for me to invite Matt here tonight. Frankie said she didn't want to bring that piece of her life to the beach this summer, and so far, despite my close call with the sibling conversation, she hasn't. It's her tragedy, and whatever thoughts torment my head, I have no right to conjure him up at my whim.

"That's cool." Sam slips off his sandals and leans back on the blanket with his hands behind his head. "Lie back," he says. "Trust me."

I kick off my flip-flops and lie on my back like Sam, keeping a good foot and a half between us, lest a stray toe touch a stray leg and spontaneously combust. Unfortunately (or fortunately, I'm not sure), he turns to face me. I keep my face pointed up, focused on the stars. I'm *not* thinking about him. I'm not measuring the super-charged particles of air between us, willing them to become smaller and closer. I can't smell the boy-soap and sea salt on his skin. I can't hear his soft, measured breaths, or the beating of his heart, opposite mine.

"What do you see?" he asks.

I tell him about the shapes I find in the stars, the all-encompassing blackness of the sky. A gray, smoky wisp of clouds backlit by the halo of the moon.

"Mmm," he says softly. "Now close your eyes." His palm is over my face, fingers closing my eyelids. Heat falls in waves off his hand and onto my skin, simultaneously frightening and exhilarating.

"Okay." He resumes his position on his back, leaving cold in the spaces where he touched me. "Focus on all the things you *can't* see with your eyes."

I take a deep breath and try to concentrate on the task at hand. I don't want to disappoint him. I don't want him to mistake my childish nerves for shallowness.

"*Now* tell me what you see," he whispers.

"Well, there's a fascinating view of my eyelids."

"That's not what I mean, Anna Abby," he says, his breath crossing the space between us to reach my ear. "Tell me again."

I take and hold another deep breath.

In the darkness, I see the way the breeze floats over my skin. I see every grain of sand pressing into my back beneath the blanket. The crackling sparks of the fires, sputtering and fading around us. The music drifting into my ears and into my heart from a cluster of people farther down the beach, playing guitars and singing and laughing. And I see the ocean, the sounds of the waves rushing up against the shore, only to fall back down again — a never-ending race.

My heart is full, but I'm shivering. I open my eyes and look toward Sam. He's staring at me with such intensity that my whole body reacts to it like a magnet to iron, no choice but the natural order of things, moving closer, surprising me. I'm afraid. Afraid something will break his stare. Afraid something won't.

Frankie and Jake have disappeared down the shore, the faint line of Frankie's laughter trailing behind them like breadcrumbs in the air. I hear her far away, but it doesn't fully register. Nothing registers. I want to say something, but my lips can't seem to remember how to make words.

"Anna, you're shivering," Sam says, breaking the trance. "Here." He sits up partway to pull off his hooded red sweatshirt and hands it to me.

I sit up and pull it over my head, grateful for the soft fabric against the bare skin of my arms. As I pull it on, I'm instantly and uncontrollably overwhelmed. It's like Sam has wrapped himself around me, close and warm and safe. It's *him,* the smell of his skin and something clean and the smoky campfire, hot and familiar inside as though he's in here with me.

Everything stops mattering. The cold is gone. Time is gone. The ocean stops whispering. I turn my face to his, his eyes unmoving, and everything around me stops, suspended. Sam grabs hold of the front of his sweatshirt with me inside and pulls it to him. My arms move around him, his around me, and he kisses me, so hot and severe that I feel it all the way in my toes. We fall back to the blanket and I'm outside of myself, twisting my legs with his to get closer, closer, closer. He moves on top of me, the weight of his body pressing me into the sand, kissing my lips, my neck, his hands tangled in my hair, then reaching under my shirt, and I'm floating, all the old, tired heartsickness evaporating. My whole entire heart evaporating.

"Anna Abby from New Yawk," he whispers. He's shaking, still on top of me. I move to unzip the sweatshirt and let him in, wrapping us both up, pushing him over and draping an arm and leg over him lazily. My head rests tight in the groove between his chin and shoulder. I breathe in his skin and hold him there, right in my lungs, where nothing can get to him.

My whole life can end right now and nothing else will ever matter, not now and not again.

Moments later, Frankie and Jake walk up the shore and Sam and I untangle. That's when I feel it. Like trying to hold water; that old slipping away. The cold air on my skin where he pressed against me just moments ago. The smell of his hair fading from my breath. The gentleness of his hands, gone. Sadness rolls over me like a wave, but Sam is still next to me, smiling. His eyes are content. His hand reaches to brush against mine. Frankie and Jake run up from the water, breathless and laughing. Sam moves a stray curl out of my eyes and kisses my eyebrow.

I can't stop thinking about what he felt like against my body, against my lips. I can't remember anything else, anything before that. And I realize in this moment that I've finally done it. That horrible, awful thing I swore I would never do.

The frosting. The cigarettes. The blue glass triangle. The shooting stars. The taste of his mouth on mine in the hall closet.

Gone.

All I can think about is Sam. Matt is — erased.

My whole body is warm and buzzing.

Sam is smiling next to me, *because* of me.

And I've never felt so lonely in all my life.

seventeen

Dear Matt,

What is the statute of limitations on feeling guilty for cheating on a ghost?

The words are black and messy like ants in my journal and look about as ridiculous as they sound. It's been almost twenty-four hours, and I can't shake the hot, prickly feeling that's settled in my stomach. It's not so much that I kissed him — romantic night on the beach, stars, campfire, beer — these things happen, according to Frankie.

It's that I want it to happen *again*.

We didn't see them today. We promised to spend the morning with Jayne on the beach, which quickly turned into lunch, then dinner, then game night with Uncle Red. By then it was too late to go back to the beach — the sun was down, and somehow we'd managed to spend the whole day with Frankie's parents doing wholesome family vacation things involving neither boys nor guilt nor things that shiver in the night.

Part of me doesn't want to go. Matt and I were walking through the neighborhood, whispering in the middle of the street at two in the morning. They were set to leave for California in two days, and after that, we'd have about a month before Matt moved to Cornell. I tried not to think about it; tried not to count the days until he left or the days until we'd visit him or the days until he was home for break. An hour wasn't that far away, but we'd all have school and it's not like we could just go up there whenever we wanted. No more text messages to sneak out in the middle of the night. No more dumping out all the sugar just to have an excuse to run next door for something after dinner.

You've been talking about college since we were kids, Matt.

I know, but you won't be there. Everything will be different.

Not here. We'll be the same.

What if I come back and I'm different, Anna? Sometimes you go to a place where everything is different, and everything you ever know changes, and no one ever looks at you the same.

No way. It's all I could say. And then I kissed him.

I didn't know what he meant back then. I thought he was being sentimental, just worried about leaving home for the first time. To Frankie, Red, and Jayne, he was confident and ready, born for college, born for reading and writing and achieving great things. But I knew he was scared. It was such a change for him — being away from me and Frankie, away from our inseparable triune, away from his family. Truthfully, I was just as scared to see him go as he was to leave, but in those vulnerable moments when he confessed his insecurities under the stars, I couldn't agree with him. I couldn't do anything but stare at him and hold his hand and hope that he knew what I was thinking — that I could never, ever look at him differently, or feel anything other than what I felt in those shared and fleeting moments.

Now, curled up under my sheets and writing to a ghost in my journal, I know what he meant. I've been in California for just over a week, and I'm already different. Everything about me feels different. It hurts to remember Matt, to relive his postcards, to try to simultaneously remember and forget his voice. I'm fighting it every day.

I can't stop thinking about Sam.

And Frankie has absolutely no clue about any of it.

It's ten-thirty, and Red and Jayne are finally asleep. The sneak-out witching hour approaches. Frankie is anxious to get back to Jake, but I'm not ready to see Sam tonight.

"What's up?" Frankie asks, surprisingly gentle. "You were all over him last night. You don't want to go?"

I close my journal and shrug, not quite sure how to explain it.

She sits on her feet at the end of my bed. "Anna, did something happen?"

I consider her question. *Yes, something did happen. Sam kissed me, and it was crazy and intense, and even more amazing than it was with Matt, and now I want it to happen again.* There, I said it. Only I didn't really say it.

"No, not like that. I don't want to freak them out, that's all." I conveniently omit the rest. "If we keep showing up every single day and night, right on schedule, they're going to think we're desperate."

"Aren't you?" she teases, broken eyebrow arching hopefully toward the sky.

"Sure." I smile. "Just not tonight."

Frankie nods, playing with the red glass bracelet on her wrist. This buys me the night, but another day wouldn't hurt, either.

"Frank, we haven't really spent any time alone together on this trip. Why don't we get up early tomorrow and go somewhere without the guys? San Francisco, maybe?"

"Wow, you *really* don't want to seem desperate."

"I just thought it would be nice to get off the beach for once. We still have two more weeks to hang out with Jake and Sam." His name catches in my throat, and I hope that Frankie doesn't notice my skin flush.

She considers my idea and nods.

"There's a bus down the street that goes into the city," she says. "But my parents would never let us go alone, and I don't really feel like spending the whole day with them. I had enough family bonding today to last the rest of the trip."

"So. They don't let us sneak out at night, either, but we do that."

"Excellent point," Frankie says.

"Isn't it time Jackie invites us out on her boat for the day? With her parents, of course."

It's probably the one and only time Frankie will ever call me brilliant, but she does, and as we turn off our matching lights and pull up our matching blankets, the wheels of Operation San Francisco are in motion.

The next morning, I wake up at seven as Red and Jayne leave for their morning walk. I grab my journal and tiptoe down to the kitchen, hoping to finish writing about the past few nights and work out the remaining bits of guilt still jolting my stomach before Frankie wakes up.

I make myself a cup of green tea as quietly as possible, dig around for a granola bar, and head out to the deck in my bare feet, carefully sliding the door closed behind me.

The morning is perfect. It's early enough that only the runners are out, affording me a relatively unspoiled view of the ocean. I peel open my granola bar and prop my feet up on the adjacent chair, making a mental note to get out of bed early more often.

The earthy smell of the tea reminds me of Mom and Dad in their garden, quietly working side by side on steadfast soil invaders, not talking yet still somehow communicating — kind of like seeing with my eyes closed last night with Sam. I can't picture Mom and Dad in the same thought with me and Sam, so I dismiss it entirely, wondering instead what they're doing two thousand miles east and three hours into the future. I sent them a postcard from Alcatraz and talked to them a few days ago on the phone. Their voices were light and faraway as they told me about Dad's latest sale and ongoing progress in the garden, real estate deals closing and weeds growing and life moving on without me.

I close my eyes and sip the tea, allowing Sam to creep back into my thoughts. The sun falls warm on my face in orange and lemon rays, reminding me of his hands as he closed my eyelids and taught me to see in a whole new way. It's simultaneously painful and exhilarating, but I make myself go back there in my head, replaying every instant, every touch, every breath. I can almost feel his lips on my mouth again, when —

"*There* you are!" Frankie startles me, stomping all over my quiet reverie like an impossible elephant. "Why didn't you wake me up?"

"I thought you heard me get out of bed," I lie, hoping I don't sound too irritated.

"Anna," she says, pulling hairs off her shirt and letting them drop to the floor. "You have to shake me, otherwise I'm dead to the world and look what happens. You have to spend your morning alone."

"Right." I close the unfinished story in my journal. "Tragic."

"What are you wearing today?"

"For what?"

"Anna!" She sighs. "You really exacerbate me sometimes!"

"You mean exasperate."

"Huh?"

"I *exasperate* you."

"That's what I *said*! Anyway, San Francisco, remember?"

Oh, that. While I was off on my pre-Frankie morning mind trip, I kind of forgot about my idea. My San Francisco Sam diversion.

"I'm sure you'll pick out something cool for me," I say as she heads back into the kitchen to look for breakfast.

I watch her through the open sliding door. Beneath the clang of her hands searching the silverware drawer, the clink of a spoon tossed into a cereal bowl, the bang of the cupboard door responding to her careless hand, Frankie softly hums a song from our shared childhood. She pulls a box of Cheerios from the pantry, a carton of milk and a can of Diet Coke from the fridge, and sings quietly, unaware of her audience.

"If you could, would you ask
for moonbeams in a heart of glass?
For sun rays on the silver sea?
Or would you ask for me?"

I haven't thought of that song in forever. When we were in fourth grade and Matt was in sixth, we all went to see him perform in the school show, *Music Moves Me.* My parents and I sat with Frankie and Jayne while Red stood in the back row with all the other dads videoing the musical for future hours of family torture.

Now I remember it as if we'd just left the auditorium. Matt had a solo for "Ask for Me." He wore a tuxedo with a silver-sequined cummerbund. Kids from the younger class dressed as mermaids and fish. Matt sang the chorus and led the kids center stage to sing their own verses. Most of them forgot their lines, so Matt just kept on singing as if it were scripted that way.

Sometimes looking at Frankie is like seeing Matt through a glass of water — a distorted composition of him with all the right parts, but mixed up and in the wrong order. As I watch her sing his old song, I can't shake the feeling that he just stopped by to say hello.

Frankie scoops up the dishes and food and continues humming. When she finally catches me spying, she stops and giggles, and for a moment I see her — not the distorted Matt composition but the real Frankie, the one who used to bake cookies for me when I was sad, the one who picked dandelions for her mother on the way home from school, the one who's embarrassed to get caught singing.

"Don't listen to me," she says softly, letting out a fake cough.

"I wasn't," I lie. "I just heard you coming out."

She sets her breakfast staples on the table and begins the meal by reaching into the box for a handful of little beige Os. Satisfied with the magnitude of their crunch, she pours a bowl full and drowns them in milk.

I hate milk slurping more than all other breakfast idiosyncrasies combined, but Frankie is unable to enjoy her breakfast any other way.

"I'm pretty sure the San Fran bus leaves every two hours on Sundays." Milk pools in the corners of her mouth as her spoon dives for another lot of Os like a heron for fish. "It's, like, a two-and-a-half-hour ride. We can catch the ten and spend the whole day there."

Over the course of our vacation I'd become quite comfortable with lying to Red and Jayne in two- or three-hour increments so that we could spend more time on Sam and Jake's side of the beach. It wasn't really lying, anyway. We were still on the same beach, just a few hundred feet from where they thought.

The San Francisco trip was my idea, but lying to Red and Jayne for the entire day seems much worse than our previous tales, especially since we'll be sixty or seventy *miles* from where we're supposed to be.

"Why don't we come back before dinner?" I ask. "Then your parents won't be so suspicious."

Frankie almost drops her spoon at my suggestion.

"God, Anna. You're so *provokial* sometimes!"

"Parochial — and no, I'm not. I just don't think we should —"

"Look, telling them about Jackie's boat was your idea. If we come back for dinner it will look fake. Boating is an all-day thing, plus I'm sure Jackie's parents will invite us to stay for dinner."

"I guess."

"Come on, Anna. You were right. We need some girl time. Now finish up here and go get ready — we've got to look *good* today."

I pick up my journal, mug, and granola bar wrapper, look up to the sky, and curse the God of Summer Vacations for getting me into this whole albatross-ditching, Sam-avoiding, aiding-and-abetting mess in the first place.

eighteen

Since the Perinos are under the illusion that we've proven our capacity for responsibility by coming home before curfew, avoiding alcohol and boys, and being all-around nice girls, it's not difficult for us to secure an all-day freedom pass when they return from their run. Frankie tells them about nonexistent Jackie's nonexistent parents inviting us out on their nonexistent boat, throws in a well-placed "I love you," and we're good until bedtime.

Getting ready for a day at sea is rather different from getting ready for an unsupervised jaunt to the city, so we quickly shower, throw on casual shorts and T-shirts, and stuff everything else into backpacks so we can get ready for real in the locker room at the community pool down the street.

Uncomfortably coiffed, dressed, accessorized, and stuffed into strappy black sandals that weren't made for walking, we lock our "boat clothes" in a locker for later and walk down to the bus stop, camera rolling. Men and women in khaki shorts and appliquéd golf shirts stare as we approach.

"Is this the bus to San Francisco?" Frankie asks one of the women. "We're making a documentary."

"Yes," the woman says firmly, trying to smile for the camera but unable to stop her eyes from their natural path to the slit in Frankie's denim skirt. I love watching older women react to Frankie. They either stare disapprovingly as if to question what kind of mother would let her daughter out of the house like that, or they look at her longingly from their little white Keds, realizing that their husbands — consumed with thoughts of car insurance and prostate monitoring — will never again sneak in through their unlocked windows or kiss them on the mouth in the middle of the day for no reason.

Men, of course, always look at her the same.

Hungry dogs, whimpering for a scrap of food from the table.

The ride to the city takes forever, the bus stopping every few blocks to drop off and pick up passengers. Like Frankie and me, the tourists sit still the entire ride, our worlds composed solely of the resort town and downtown. To us, the little gray villages in the middle are largely invisible. Haggard people board and disembark in between, a constant exchange of strangers carrying groceries or children or heartbreak or some other unknown weight with every step.

Frankie and I don't talk much on the trip, taking turns watching and aiming the camera out the window as buildings and cars and patches of another world sail by. It's like we really *are* on Jackie's boat, heading toward the horizon at a constant speed while everyone else sits bobbing and listless on the water.

When the diesel engine finally cuts out at the downtown station, I'm startled from my daydreaming by the driver's final announcement.

"Last stop — San Francisco. All passengers must exit."

We hop off the bus and head toward a diner on Market Street. Cars rush past as though we're not even there, splashing heat and exhaust over my bare legs and arms. I'm surrounded by people and colors and sounds and smells unlike any I've ever seen.

If the bus made me feel like I was in a speedboat, the city streets are the ocean, full of the flotsam and jetsam of every race and culture in the natural world, bobbing and weaving along the sidewalks toward an unknown end.

Even Frankie is unnerved, and I realize that she hasn't been here in two years, and never without Red and Jayne and her brother.

"Let's just get lunch," she says, pulling me into the diner once we're across the street. "We'll figure out what we want to see after."

From the safety of a sparkly red pleather booth, we order veggie burgers, fries, strawberry shakes, and an extra paper place mat, noticing a map printed on the back. Typical of tourist attractions listed on a place mat, nothing sounds interesting, and we switch to plan B, which involves finishing lunch and wandering up, down, and sideways through the city streets until something jumps out at us.

We find plenty of fresh vegetable stands and hippie stores with lots of handmade jewelry and blankets and sweaters we can't afford, even when Frankie offers to put the hippies in our movie in exchange for a discount. We film in Chinatown, Frankie flirting with the men wrapping salmon as all the leftover fish heads fall into the gutter and slide down the street. Next to the fish market, an old woman sells postcards and magnets and little green statues in the shape of Buddha.

"I could live here forever," I say, enamored by the bright blue sky and the ocean sleeping in the distance.

"Not me," Frankie says as we wander toward our next unknown destination. "Too crowded. Too expensive. And not to mention, too smelly."

Frankie laughs, and suddenly, right behind her, there it is — City Lights. I've seen the old bookstore so many times in Matt's pictures, I'd recognize it anywhere. He loved to come here on day trips with Red, Jayne, and Frankie — but she doesn't seem to notice it.

"Frankie, look — City Lights! Come on!" I grab her hand and drag her toward the doorway.

"What's the big deal, Anna? It's just an old bookstore. It doesn't even have a coffee place. Let's go somewhere else."

"Frankie, not all of us equate great literature with nonfat caramel lattes. Don't you know this place? It's where Matt used to —"

"I *know* what it is, Anna. Go ahead," she snips. "I'm going next door for a drink. Meet me over there when you're done." She disappears across the street into a place called Vesuvio. It looks like a bar, but when she doesn't come back out the door, I assume they gave her a table.

Five minutes. I'll just take five minutes.

I pull open the glass door and walk to the middle of the store, letting the smell of old books soak into my lungs. It's different than I expect; it feels more like a library than a store, and I can totally picture Matt hanging out here. He loved to read. He loved words, the way they string together into sentences and stories. He wanted to study them, to know and create them, to share them with the world. Often, Frankie and I would sit on his bed while he read passages from his favorite books, pacing frantically as he turned the pages for the best parts of a story. He read with intensity and was passionately in love with every character, every turn of plot or twist of language. He made the characters come alive for us, like he wasn't reading a work of fiction but telling stories about his own friends.

Frankie liked hearing his stories, but she was never much for reading. I've always enjoyed books, and Matt would pass along his favorites, including those he'd picked up here — Jack Kerouac's *On the Road,* a book that sparked a restlessness in me that was unrequited until this trip. *Howl* by Allen Ginsberg. *Dharma Bums* — another Kerouac book that left me equally longing to travel, to discover, to feel.

After my birthday last summer, in our short weeks together, Matt would whisper passages to me as I lay sideways across his bed with my feet up, waiting for Frankie to change or shower or whatever it was that gave me and Matt a few moments alone.

It's my mission in life to make you care about these words, Anna. About these people and everything they say and everything they were. He traced the lines of my face with his fingers as he spoke. *Every story is part of a whole, entire life, you know? Happy and sad and tragic and whatever, but an entire life. And books let you know them.*

The sun would fall on his face as he read, lighting up the whole room. That's how much he loved words.

Frankie privately collects her memories of Matt, but this one is all mine — a connection she can't share, a memory she can't hold in her hands or put in the tightly closed jar with the others. Love of reading was something I shared with him alone, *because* of him alone. It was everything to him.

I walk up and down the aisles and run my hands along the spines of books, old and new. An undisturbed layer of dust on one particular shelf makes me think that Matt may have touched the same books the last time he was here. I crouch down to read some of the titles on the faded spines, remembering a description of this exact scene from one of Matt's postcards.

> *Books line the shelves in no particular order, waiting to be discovered. It's like the spirits of Kerouac, Ginsberg, and Ferlinghetti haunt the aisles, calling me to pick them. To read their stories. To let them be heard. You would love it, Anna.*

He was right. I love it. And soon I can no longer tell the difference between my own real experiences here in Matt's favorite bookstore and the ghost stories that have imprinted themselves in my mind from years of postcards.

I buy a book of poetry about the ocean by local writers from the seventies, thank the cashier, and take one final look around before crossing the street to find Frankie.

Inside Vesuvio, I move through the tables and bar area looking for Frankie's auburn hair, but she's not here.

"Have you seen a girl my age?" I ask the bartender. "She came in, like, a half hour ago? Short skirt?"

"Nah," he says. "I just started my shift. Sorry."

My heart pounds in my chest. I can't believe I lost her. I dig in my bag for my cell phone, hoping she's not too mad at me to answer.

"Try the second floor," the bartender says.

Upstairs, there she is. Sitting at a two-top with some guy, stirring her drink with a straw, laughing with her head back at something her newfound companion says.

"Frank?"

"Oh, there you are." She's wearing her grown-up voice. "I'd like you to meet Jeremy."

"It's Jarred," he says, standing to offer me his chair. He looks about our age but acts much older. "Frankie has told me much about you, Anna."

"Jarred left high school to pursue his music in the city."

"What kind of music?" I ask, wondering if Jarred has what it takes to break the Jake spell.

"I play drums for a few bands," he says. "Mad Rabbit and Hex?"

"Cool." I nod like I've been listening to his bands my whole life.

"Speaking of which," he says, "I have rehearsal now. I should go." Frankie smiles over her soda. "Thanks for the drink," she says.

"Don't mention it. So, see you at the show later?"

"Definitely."

"Sweet." Jarred smiles and heads to rehearsal, practicing to win the heart of his dream girl at tonight's show — the one we're apparently attending.

"What show?" I ask. "Or was it just to get a free drink?"

She smiles, no longer mad at me. "You're learning fast."

"All right," I say. "We're up to six." I'm glad she's the one growing and grooming the list. The last thing I need is more boy confusion.

"Get anything?"

"A poetry book." I sit down across from her. "Mostly I just wanted to check it out."

Frankie nods, sighs, sips her soda, sighs again, and then, as if possessed, apologizes.

"Sorry, Anna. I didn't mean to ditch you. I got hit with this Matt-wave or something."

"No," I say. "It's me. I should have been more sensitive. I just got really excited when I saw the bookstore."

"It's okay." She gives me a sip of her drink. "I was just thinking about how he used to read to us," she says. "Remember? He'd get so into it, it was like he was acting out the play or something."

I smile and watch her closely, waiting for her to get that faraway look again. But she stays right here with me on the second floor of Vesuvio, wearing her short jean skirt with the slit up the thigh, drinking Diet Coke with lemon on our big sneaky trip into the city.

"I took some of his books," she tells me. "Before Mom started freaking out and not letting anyone in his room. I don't know why — I'm not a reader."

I nod, trying to remember what his room looks like. I haven't been in there since the day before he died, when he played Frankie and me this HP rehearsal bootleg he found online. Jayne keeps the door shut now, like the attic room at the beach house, confident in our silent understanding that no one will enter.

"You should take them," she says, and for a moment I forget what she's talking about.

"What?"

"You always liked to read his books. If he were here, he'd have given them to you already."

"Frankie, I can't. I mean, I —"

"He would want you to have them."

I reach across the table and squeeze her hand and she closes her eyes against a single tear. In typical ridiculous Anna fashion, I still can't find the words to break my promise and tell Frankie about everything that happened, but the lid on *her* memory jar has loosened, and for the moment, I'm grateful.

It's after three when we leave Vesuvio. Since the Cartoon Museum is closed for renovation and neither of us can think of anything else we'd like to see in the city, we decide to take a bus to the Golden Gate Bridge and walk partway across, stopping every few feet to film the sailboats below.

It's windy on the bridge. By the time we cross back and catch the bus downtown, fog and rain have rolled in, stamping out the sun and chilling the air around us.

Neither of us feels particularly enterprising, so we head back to the same Market Street diner to share an order of fries before we go home. Our server is wearing a Blade Surf Shop T-shirt that reminds me of Sam, and as he sets down two waters and takes our order, I realize that I haven't really thought about Sam all day. Now, when I let him back into my thoughts, the prickly feeling that occupied my stomach for the past two days is gone, a few wandering butterflies bumping around in its place.

The rain picks up as we leave the diner — cold, wet sheets that come hard and fast. We wrap our arms around each other and run toward the bus shelter, freezing and laughing and breathing hard. Along the road, cars speed past, drenching our feet. By the time we reach the Plexiglas shelter, we're shivering and very aware of the weight of our wet clothes and backpacks as the electric glow of the city fades behind us.

This morning, Frankie said we'd catch the seven o'clock bus to be back before ten, perfect timing for the end of a long boat ride and late dinner with Jackie and Samantha. But as she repeatedly runs her fingers along the schedule posted in the shelter, I feel a tinge of concern.

"We didn't miss the seven, right?" I ask. "It's only ten till."

"No, it's worse."

"What?"

"It's Sunday."

"So?"

"The buses back to Zanzibar stop running at five on Sundays."

nineteen

*P*anic starts at my toes in little pinpricks that quickly move across my feet and into my knees so that I have to sit on the wet metal bench in the shelter. Before the fear reaches my already overworked stomach, I take a deep breath, pull out my cell phone, and dial information.

"Smoothie Shack," I say. "In Zanzibar Bay."

Frankie and I duck into a coffee shop behind the bus stop to wait. Two hours later, a car slows in front of us and pulls over, hazards flashing. Sam opens the passenger door and runs toward us, holding one hand above his face to shield himself from the rain that's now falling kind of sideways. His green Smoothie Shack apron sticks out the bottom of that red sweatshirt, and I feel a little jolt when I think about unzipping it and climbing in there with him. His hair curls up in the rain, like it does when he's in the ocean, and when he grabs me into a wet hug, I can't remember why I was avoiding him.

Sam ushers us into the car, giving up the front seat for Frankie and climbing in the back with me.

"We were wondering about you two," Jake says as he pulls onto the street.

Before Frankie says anything to embarrass me, I tell them we were just busy doing family stuff and wanted to meet them out tonight, but since we got stuck in San Francisco later than we'd planned we might not be able to risk sneaking out.

They laugh as we recount our day, mock witness-style for Frankie's camera, starting with the presto-change-o act in the locker room and ending with our bus schedule oversight and frantic phone call to the Shack. Thankfully, Sam's friend could cover his shift.

"You should still come out tonight," Jake says. "Even if the rain doesn't stop. We'll just hang out on the deck at the Shack — no one will be around."

"We probably will," Frankie says. As Sam's leg brushes against mine in the backseat, I agree. She could promise them we'll help kill someone and hide the body — as long as Sam keeps me warm, I'll go along with anything.

After almost two hours on the road, we reach the Welcome to Zanzibar sign. Jake pulls up in front of the community pool so we can change back into our boating ensembles.

Unfortunately, the fickle old universe wants to teach us another Important Lesson About Secrets and Lies, and the community pool — along with its locker room — is closed. Locked. Lights out, thank you, please come back tomorrow.

"You could tell them that you hit a big wave and soaked all your clothes, so you had to change into your friends' clothes," Jake says.

"Even better," Sam says. "Tell them someone went overboard, and you had to jump in to save them."

"Or that the boat tipped, and you had to use your backpacks as flotation devices until the coast guard showed up."

"*Or —*"

"Or," Frankie holds up her hand to shut them up before they start talking about bombs or drug enforcement agents or any other James Bond boy fantasies, "we'll just tell them we came back early because of the rain, changed at Jackie's house to hang out for a barbecue, and left our clothes there accidentally."

We rehearse the story again before Jake and Sam drop us off a few houses from ours. Otherwise, Red and Jayne might spot us getting out of a car full of strange boys and want to invite them in for tea and lemon cookies. We'd have to pretend that they were Jackie and Samantha's older, super responsible, super gay brothers who dislike girls and coincidentally have almost the same exact names as their sisters. *Those crazy parents!*

The guys pull over and get out of the car to say goodbye. We make tentative plans to meet up at midnight at the Shack, assuming we can get away without incident. This time, after Sam kisses me and we unhook, the warmth of his body lingers against me, blocking out the cold like a blanket on a snowy Saturday morning back East.

I will see him tonight, no matter what.

The car pulls away and we watch the brake lights brighten at the stop sign before turning the corner. Frankie and I walk the last fifty feet or so to the house, rehearsing our story one last time for consistency. There's no way Red and Jayne are already in bed — they'd never fall asleep until Frankie and I got home safe. But if tonight's a good television night, there's a chance we can sneak in unnoticed, make our way upstairs, and hide out in the bathroom taking showers and changing into our pajamas without Red and Jayne asking too many questions. I blow a wish up to the God of Broadcasting and open the door to the kitchen.

I should have known better than to invoke the universe when it's so clearly in the mood to dole out lessons. Tonight turns out to be a horrible television night in the Bay area, for Red and Jayne are waiting for us in the kitchen, drinking tea, playing cards, and eager to hear about our wild pirate-girl adventures at sea.

"Wow, did you fall in?" Red asks. Bathed in the fluorescent light of the kitchen, we look like two sea creatures dragged to shore by a fishnet. The only things missing are renegade starfish, old seaweed, and a few well-placed barnacles.

"We walked back from Jackie's," Frankie says. "We wanted to be in the rain."

"Did you guys still go out on the water today? Even with the weather?" Jayne asks.

Frankie shrugs in her voodoo cool way. "Partly. We didn't stay out as long as we wanted. But her dad invited us back to the house for an indoor barbecue, so it was still fun."

"Where are your clothes from this morning?" Jayne asks, eyeing us suspiciously.

Why do mothers always notice things? Uncle Red's just sitting there with his tea, holding his cards, patiently waiting for Aunt Jayne to get her head back in the game. But Jayne's on to us. Any minute now, she'll cluck her tongue, let out a long sigh, and pick up the phone to call my mother and remind her what a horrible daughter she raised.

Frankie stays cool under pressure and repeats the whole story, just like we practiced it. Boat ride prematurely interrupted by the weather. Back to the house for dinner. Changed out of boat clothes that got wet when the rain came in. Jackie's parents offered to drive us back (because they're reallyreallyreally great, concerned, responsible people), but we refused, insisting that we wanted to walk in the rain since it's still so warm out. We had such a fun day with Jackie, Samantha, and their families that we totally forgot our clothes — but we'll get them tomorrow morning. And by the way, if those are indeed lemon cookies on that plate in front of Dad, can we have some?

Jayne reaches across the table to pass the cookies and expresses sympathy that our boat trip was preempted by a storm. "Sounds like you still had a fun day, though."

We assure them that we did, grab a few more cookies for the road, and make haste for the bedroom, where we close the door and explode in laughter.

"Parents," Frankie says, mouth full of lemon dust. "They believe just about *anything.*"

"Maybe yours do." I pull off my wet clothes and get into shorts and a sweatshirt, chasing away the last of the soggy chill from the rain. "You know Helen and Carl would never leave us alone in the first place. And a boat ride with strange girls? They'd demand their phone number so they could call in advance and secure the facts of our story with a responsible adult, get an accurate count of the available life jackets and flotation devices on board, then call the coast guard to make sure someone would be watching us."

"Don't remind me," Frankie shrugs. "So, how long till we break out?"

"Maybe two hours," I say. "We need to go downstairs and appear extremely tired until your parents go to bed. You know, being out on a boat most of the day can be very draining."

"Anna, you're turning into a rather naughty girl."

"Oh, that's not regular Anna," I assure her. "It's Crazy Anna from the dressing room mirror. Totally your fault."

Frankie laughs. I think we both like Crazy Anna a little more than regular Anna. It's like magic — while I was trying on the bathing suit last month, it rubbed against my butt and unleashed the A.B.S.E. Bikini Genie, granting all my wishes.

"That reminds me," Frankie says, changing out of her clothes. "I think we should alter the contest rules. Our vacation is almost half over and we haven't gotten very far."

"We didn't plan on Sam and Jake." I sit on the end of her bed as she touches up her makeup for our big date on the couch downstairs.

"No. I mean, I could still find my own ten, but I don't want to get ahead of you. You *really* like Sam, don't you? I can tell these things." She dabs at her smudged eyeliner with a Q-tip.

"Maybe." I shrug. "But so what? You *really* like Jake."

"He's okay, I guess. I think we're gonna — *you* know. *Tonight.*" She tosses her mascara on the dresser and flips her head over to shake out her hair as though making this decision is no more taxing or important than choosing between the powdered sugar and the glazed from the morning donut box.

"Frankie, are you *serious*?"

"Maybe." She half grins, the devil that sits on shoulders in all the old cartoons. The one that's way more cute than scary and therefore causes infinitely more destruction and chaos.

I stare at her with my mouth open, but additional details aren't forthcoming. Instead, she does a final face-check in the dresser mirror, blots her lips with a tissue, and leads us downstairs for Act Two, in which doting daughter and friend give an Oscar-worthy performance as the two sleepiest girls on the planet, putting all fears of illicit behavior to rest.

But two hours later, as we tiptoe off the deck and into the back-yard with the camera, beach blankets, and the trusty turned-off flashlight, we uncover a previously unresolved and potentially dangerous hole in the plot.

"Can't sleep, girls?" Aunt Jayne calls from the dark and lonely shadows of the sea, wrapping a crocheted shawl around her shoulders against the breeze.

twenty

*F*rankie crashes into me at the sound of her mother's voice and I yelp, though from the shock of Frankie stepping on me or Aunt Jayne wandering up the shore to meet us, I can't decide.

"Going somewhere?" Jayne asks, surveying our gear.

I've become quite adept at lying on this vacation but still haven't mastered the skill of instantaneous fabrication under extreme pressure. That's more Frankie's specialty. Unfortunately, the queen of far-fetched fairy tales is cocooned in a state of shock behind me, unmoving and silent.

"We were just, um, we were going to — we wanted to —" I hope my stammering snaps Frankie back to reality, since Jayne is too close for me to give Frankie the swift mule-kick-in-the-shin she deserves.

It works. Frankie drops her blanket and heads down the stairs with purpose to meet her mother.

"Anna and I wanted to come out to the water to get some night shots," she says. "You know, for the trip documentary."

Aunt Jayne eyes her closely. "In full makeup?"

"Mom, we don't want to look all *hideous* on camera."

"I thought you two were exhausted?"

"We were," Frankie says, twisting her bracelet around her wrist. "But now we're rejudevated."

"Rejuvenated," I say, translating for Jayne.

"Right. And you need blankets because . . ."

"Because we might want to lie down and look at the stars." Frankie has an answer for everything.

Aunt Jayne looks from her daughter to me, to the blankets at my feet, and back to Frankie before letting out a long sigh and shaking her head. "Frankie, I —"

"Mom, why are you out here alone, anyway?"

If you can't afford an attorney, Frankie "Teflon" Perino will be appointed to you by a court of law.

Aunt Jayne opens her mouth, but Frankie counters again before any sound comes out. "Do you want to be in our movie?"

Jayne laughs as Frankie heads back to the stairs to pull her camera out of its bag, adding credibility to our threadbare tapestry of lies.

"All right, all right." Aunt Jayne throws up her hands and ushers us back across the lawn. "But let's do it on the deck. It's freezing out here tonight."

Tonight? As opposed to other nights you've been hiding out in the shadows as your doting daughter and I slipped away into the darkness? My heart is thumping its way up my esophagus and into my throat. I swallow it back down and shoot Frankie a sideways look that translates to, "Did your mom see us sneak out the other night, and if so, why hasn't she said anything?"

Frankie responds with a lift of her eyebrow. "Doubt it," the broken little wings tell me.

On the deck, we interview Jayne, asking her how she'd redecorate the beach house, the lawn, and the entire shoreline if given the opportunity. This amuses her, and as she plays along with our silly questions, I relax, convincing myself that she doesn't know about our previous boy-filled escapades and, by some inexplicable break in tonight's chain of horrific events, accepts our documentary cover-up story.

"That's a wrap," Frankie says. "We have to do some editing before we can show it to you, though. We want it to be a surprise when we get back from the trip."

By editing she means transferring all the parts with Sam, Jake, and our secret life in the shadow realm to a separate DVD and slicing in the loop of random shots she and I took of us splashing, swimming, reading, and generally behaving ourselves on the beach, sans boys. We filmed it all in about twenty minutes the first day, but that's the beauty of swimsuits. No one expects a change of clothes to indicate the passage of time.

After Aunt Jayne goes to bed (at least, after she *tells* us she's going to bed), I turn to Frankie. "Okay, I know you're good. I've seen you snow teachers and security guards and my parents and all manner of responsible adults, but your mom isn't *that* stupid. There's no way she believes us."

Frankie shrugs. "Whatever."

"Forgive me, o great one. I should not have doubted you." I bow in admiration.

Frankie is unaffected, her eyes far away and glassy.

"Frank, what's wrong?" I ask. "Do you think we're busted and she's just waiting to tell your dad?"

Nothing.

"Frankie?" I'm getting concerned. The last thing I want is for the trip to be cut short because of our stupidity.

"It doesn't matter, Anna," she finally says. "She sees what she wants to see."

"What are you talking about?"

"I know you think she's so cool and everything, but sometimes I wish she'd just — I don't know, get *mad*. Yell. Call me out on my lies. Be disappointed. She doesn't even care."

I picture Aunt Jayne on the deck that first night, red-eyed and severe, pressing me for the truth about her only daughter. Her only living child.

"Yes, she does, Frank. You can't say that."

"Whatever. I'm not her precious dead son. I'll always be second."

"I don't think it's like that, Frank."

"You have no idea what it's like."

I look at my feet and don't talk for what feels like a long time. Frankie sighs, breaking the silence. "Sorry — it's not you. I don't know what my deal is tonight. We're not busted. That's the main thing. Let's go."

Some invisible force — the Force of Sam — wants to pull me back to Smoothie Shack, but I resist. We can't risk getting caught again, and it's way too late.

"No, Frank. We're, like, two hours late. They won't even be there."

"Fine. Tomorrow, then."

"Tomorrow."

I watch her face for another opening, another chance to convince her that her mom really does care, but her eyes are set against the chill coming in off the ocean.

End of discussion.

Tomorrow comes quickly, the sun falling through the window and warming my feet like a hot bath. Frankie's awake and smiling at me from her bed across the room, the sourness of last night evaporating in the new light. We shower and dress as fast as Frankie's glamour routine allows, inhale some cereal and juice for breakfast, and run outside before Red and Jayne invite us on another family tourist trip. After a quick stop at the community pool for our fake boat clothes, we head down the beach.

We don't need to go all the way to the Shack — we find Sam and Jake in the alcove, laughing it up with a hideous, frightening, evil, super-cute girl. My heart sinks into my stomach, and in an instant I turn into a bad friend, secretly hoping that the cutie belongs to Jake and not to Sam. It's all we can do not to turn back before they notice us.

"Hey! Over here!" Jake sees us and waves us out to the water.

She must be with Sam. For a moment I don't think my legs will work, but Frankie nudges me to set our stuff down and drop our beach cover-ups. I follow her out of numb obligation, angry that he's already with someone else, and angry that I let myself care.

We get into the water, and Sam runs up to hug me. My first response is entirely physical, acting before my mind can process the situation and prepare a more appropriate — that is, bitchy — reaction. His bare legs and chest are warm against me in the water, and I know if I stay like this it won't matter how many other girls he has.

I pull away just as Jake introduces the girl. Now that I see her body — rather, lack of body — I think I'm almost old enough to be her mother. At least her older sister.

"This is Katie," Jake says. "My kid sister — the one I told you about."

"Whatever," she says. "I'm not a kid."

Katie. I totally forget about his sister. I'm so relieved and embarrassed that I almost laugh out loud. She's only three years younger than me, but it feels like there's a lifetime between us. When I look at her easy smile and happy eyes, I can't remember the last time I felt that way — probably back when Frankie still had two whole eyebrows.

We spend the morning with the surfing trio until just before lunch, when a group of girls clad in pink beckons Katie to join them for ice cream. Before she ditches us, Katie hugs me and Frankie goodbye in the BFF way of kid sisters. She's sweet, and I feel bad for wishing evil things on her when we first arrived.

Whether I like Sam is no longer a question — at least not one that I can lie about. It's all I can do not to count down the remaining twelve days of the vacation, after which I won't see him again.

But I can't think about that right now.

Once Katie's gone, Frankie and Jake become an undulating, kissing, indistinguishable mass of flesh and highlights sticking out of the water. If things progress any further, I'm going to have to upgrade the rating on this public spectacle from PG-13 to R.

Thankfully, Sam is nothing like Jake. Just his foot brushing against mine under our secret layer of ocean is enough to drive me crazy, and within five minutes I know I'll meet him out here tonight, even if I have to leave a ransom note to fake my own kidnapping.

Several hours later, Frankie and I cautiously test our new escape route, hoping to avoid the ransom note plan. This time, we wait until Aunt Jayne is definitely in her room and definitely not making any sounds. Then we stuff the beds, tiptoe downstairs, exit through the front door, and cut back to the beach through a neighbor's yard several houses down. It adds five extra minutes to our arduous journey, but it's better than running into a renegade parent out for a midnight stroll in the sand.

The next week passes quickly, our days filled with swimming and sunning and catching up on sleep in the sand, our evenings spent hiking the length of the beach to the Shack. Each night I'm with Sam, things get more intense, closer and closer to the ultimate end.

Sometimes when I'm with him, something will remind me of Matt. A shooting star, the smell of someone's shampoo, a long laugh, a turn of phrase from someone passing by along the shore. When it happens, I close my eyes, count to ten, and will him to go away. To leave me. To give me back my memories so that something as simple as a song floating out from behind a bonfire doesn't bring me all the way back to him every time.

It never works.

twenty-one

"So, did you or didn't you?" On the way back from our ninth successful moonlight mission, I laugh and grab Frankie's shoulders. She started telling the story ten minutes ago, and she's only to the part where they went skinny-dipping. She's way too starry-eyed, and frankly, this uncharacteristically romantic version of my best friend is freaking me out.

"Frankie, yes or no? You've been debating it all week. Come on!"

She looks at me sideways, letting her dancing broken eyebrow do all the talking.

"You dirty girl!" I tease. "So?"

"I was trying to tell you before, but you just wanted the punch line."

"Come on!"

"Sorry, I guess you'll just have to find out what it's like for yourself."

I look at her hard, forcing my smile into hiding. "How do you know I haven't?"

The weight of the potentially devastating news that I actually had sex without telling her hits her like a wrecking ball. She simultaneously drops her bag and her jaw, cocking her head sideways to begin the scolding. She really knows how to make torture fun.

I work up my best devilish smile and walk past her on the shore. "Let's go, Sloppy Seconds," I say.

"Aaaa-nnaaaa!" She whines behind me, kicking at the sand and refusing to move until I acknowledge her discomfort, sympathize for the appropriate length of time (it varies by offense), apologize for said offense (even if it isn't mine), and spill every detail.

"All right!" I've built up a relatively high FPT (Frankie Pout Tolerance), but this is getting out of hand. "We didn't do anything yet. Not like *that*. I would have told you."

"I guess." She picks up her backpack, only partially convinced.

"Come on, Frankie. You know I tell you everything."

She smiles, and I wonder if there will ever be a time when those words don't burn on their way out.

"Too bad," she says, Queen of Everything, her little Anna still bumbling down the beach with the big fat albatross. "I guess you'll have to wait till the party tomorrow night to join the big-girls' club. Did he tell you about it?"

One of Jake's surf students has this huge house near Moonlight Bay. His rich parents are supposedly up north all weekend with their rich friends doing rich-people things like polo or something, and he'd probably never be able to face his friends again (what respectable young man *would*?) if he didn't take full advantage of the opportunity by throwing a giant beach party, complete with half-naked girls in a hot tub and plenty of underage drinking. I can picture it now — just like the parties on TV where too many people show up, something expensive gets broken, and the poor little hot girl cries about how hard life is, gets drunk, and throws up on herself.

Frankie and I have never been to *those* parties. Historically, our parties have been more like small gatherings — Frankie, me, and one or two other girls trying to concoct something out of the cooking sherry and orange juice. Since Matt died, our party crowd is even smaller — me and Frankie sneaking drops of rum into our Diet Cokes from the sample-sized bottle stashed in her sock drawer.

"Yeah," I say. "We won't be able to stay long or drink too much, though." Since our run-in with Aunt Jayne, Lady of the Night, we've been extra cautious. Extra quiet. Never too late, just in case Jayne is wandering around outside again. Making up a story about filming a moonlit documentary is one thing. Stumbling drunk and deflowered through the front door is quite another.

"Right," Frankie sighs. "I wish there was some way we could just come back in the morning. I'm sick of sneaking around in the dark."

"No kidding. More importantly, I believe you were about to tell me the rest of the Jake story?"

Frankie laughs, louder than the ocean. "Okay, okay. Listen and learn, my friend. Listen and learn."

By the time she finishes her story, which is patchy and romanticized in parts but seems at least fifty percent true, we're at the front door, peering into the windows for signs of life. Seeing none, we slowly turn the knob and tiptoe back to our room, mission accomplished.

Lying in my twin bed watching the moon through the skylight, I listen to Frankie breathe, deep and happy. The air around her is charged and hopeful and reminds me of summers past, when she and Matt would come home carefree, exhausted, and sun-filled from their annual trip to Zanzibar Bay.

California is good for her. Even Uncle Red and Aunt Jayne seem happy, despite Jayne's late-night wanderings. They've spent most of the trip together, laughing with us at dinner in their old, uncomplicated way. Maybe we've gone back in time. Frankie and I are fourteen again. Matt is asleep in his blue-gray attic room. And Frankie hasn't already been with two different guys — *really* been with them. . . .

But no — we're sixteen.

Matt's not in the attic. Frankie crossed into the realm of "experienced" months ago, and I'm still a little freaked out about Sam's hands on me, the big scarlet letter V forever emblazoned on my forehead. When I'm with him, I imagine it blinking and sputtering like a neon sign, just before it sparks into its final bright sizzle and then — black. All I have to do is sleep with him, and the embarrassing glow of the big V will be extinguished.

The whole idea of losing one's virginity is kind of ridiculous. To lose something implies carelessness. A mistake that you can fix simply by recovering the lost object, like your cell phone or your glasses. Virginity is more like *shedding* something than losing it. As in, "Don't worry, Mom. You can call off the helicopters and police dogs. Turns out — get this — I didn't actually *lose* my virginity. I just cast it off somewhere between here and Monterey. Can you believe it? It could be anywhere by now, what with all that wind."

I imagine some kids happening upon the cast-off virginity on the shore. They'd have to close down the beach and put up a sign. *Danger! Wild virginity found here! Swim at your own risk!*

Why does it have to be so special? Frankie says the first time isn't special. It's a minor inconvenience, an act no more significant than going to the dentist. You schedule the appointment at a mutually convenient time and lie as motionless as possible to expedite the process. The next time — and all subsequent next times — can be special, but not the first.

The only problem is that with Sam, I *want* it to be special. I mean, if it happens with Sam. Not that I'm planning it or anything. Other than shaving my legs. Just in case.

It's almost five in the morning, according to the glowing numbers on my bedside clock. I roll over on my stomach and shove my hands under my pillow, soaking in the cool clean of the sheet.

It's great that we can vote and go to college and wear pants and all *that,* but if anyone *really* wants to make a difference in the lives of women, they should invent a magic pill you swallow with a glass of water before bed, and when you wake up — presto! No longer a virgin! No agonizing over expensive-yet-uncomfortable undergarments! No worrying about how your boobs disappear when you lie on your back to make your stomach look flat! And certainly no lying awake all night trying to figure out a way to sleep over at some stupid party tomorrow just so I can finally have sex with a guy I've known just a couple of weeks — a guy I may never see again.

But when I think about him touching me, my whole body feels electrified and I know that there's only one thing left to do. Go to the party and sleep with —

Wait — sleep! Sleepover! That's it!

They say true genius often strikes in the pale moments between awake and asleep. *This* is one of those moments. Whether it's the neon V or thoughts of Sam's hands on my body, the right combination of carbon and oxygen comes together in a single, brilliant spark, a firecracker on the horizon of hopelessness.

It's my most ingenious idea so far this vacation — possibly *ever.*

"Frankie? Frank?" I call her name until she shakes out of her peaceful slumber. She yawns and sits up in bed, stunned and confused beside the blinding light of such a true mastermind.

"Jackie and Samantha called," I say. "Jackie's mom said she can have a slumber party tomorrow night."

The room is suddenly bathed in light, though from the sputtering neon V, my creative genius, the moon through the skylight, or Frankie's beaming smile, I cannot discern.

twenty-two

*W*e spend the next day with Red and Jayne, walking around Moonlight Boulevard pretending to be fascinated with beach-themed paintings, handmade wind chimes, and myriad other artsy trinkets without which no family vacation is complete.

Somewhere during the postlunch key lime pie course at Breeze, Frankie mentions Jackie's all-girls, parent-supervised, ultrachaste night of fun, which starts after dinner (of course we want to eat dinner with you, Mom! The party's not till later!). She has no trouble securing permission. Red and Jayne don't even ask to *meet* the fictitious Jackie and the fabled Samantha. They just nod and smile, thrilled that Frankie is so normal and well adjusted.

With the pier packed and Jayne's trinket-quota satisfied, we head back to the house for a cutthroat game of Frisbee on the beach with Red. The family fun continues through dinner, and soon enough, it's time to start prepping for the party.

Frankie and I spend an hour trying on clothes that will fit

smoothly over our bikinis and convey just the right kind of mixed messages: casual but not sloppy. Hot but not trashy. Fun but not easy (well, not *that* easy, anyway). Hair and makeup take another hour — a delicate dance of various chemicals applied with just the right amount of pressure for shading, highlighting, and contouring without caking, flaking, or smudging. Sam prefers the natural look, but Frankie's right — looking natural takes a lot of science.

We pack our backpacks for our "girls' night" (cute boxer shorts, matching pink T-shirts, sweatshirts, camera, makeup, nail polish, fuzzy socks, a copy of *Celeb Style* featuring a two-page spread of Helicopter Pilot's hot, blue-eyed singer Joe Donohue and Apollo, his dachshund, and the journal I never leave home without), kiss Red and Jayne goodbye, and make our way down the beach, arriving at the Shack precisely ten minutes later than we'd promised, so as not to appear overeager.

Sam and Jake are waiting on the deck in cargo shorts and T-shirts undoubtedly yanked from piles of laundry on their bedroom floors. Sam's hair is ungelled. His cheekbones — unblushed. His eyebrows are not tweezed, and I don't think he spent any time curling his lashes.

Despite his ignorance of haute couture, he makes my whole body buzz.

"Wow, you — *wow*." He pulls me close to him and smells my neck, his hands finding their way into my hair. "Maybe we shouldn't go to a party. I mean, there will be other people there. Other guys. *Looking* at you."

I wait for a smartass comment from Frankie or Jake, but they appear to be vapor-locked at the mouth, unable to communicate.

"Okay, then," Sam says loudly. "We'll just start heading over to the party. You guys can catch up later."

I follow him down to the beach. The sky is dark, but there are still streaks of orange and pink, fading leftovers from the sunset.

"The key to a great party is the music," Sam says, scrolling through his iPod as we tramp through the sand. Eddie — the guy having the party — put Sam in charge of the playlist. "If it's too intense, no one will be able to hang out and talk. But if it's too mellow, it will turn into a snoozefest. You also have to consider timing. There's a particular kind of music appropriate for each stage of the party — intro, warm-up, full swing, wind down, and outro."

I didn't know there was a whole science behind party music, but when Sam talks, I *want* to know. In these moments along the shore, I don't care about anything as much as I care about the melodic string of words and breath passing from his lips to my ears, and when I nod and ask questions and laugh, his eyes light up as he looks at me and I think I could quite possibly love him forever.

I mean, not that I *do* love him.

Just that I could *possibly*.

Love him.

Forever.

"Outro?" I ask.

He smiles. "The opposite of intro."

"Right. So how do you know when to switch?"

"You just gotta feel it. I'll show you later. We'll start with some ambient techno and see when the energy of the crowd calls for something else. Here — check it out."

When I take his iPod to scroll through his songs, Sam puts his arm around me, strong and protective and tan and a little banged up. The heat from his skin seeps into my shoulders, and I am so suddenly alive that if I don't kiss him right this second, we will both burst into flames and die. I turn around beneath the weight of his arm and pull him into a desperate kiss, pressing as much of myself against him as I can.

We get to Eddie's around nine-thirty, Jake and Frankie arriving just after us. The sky is indigo and the moon lights up the backyard like a spotlight, erasing the remnants of sunset. Crowds of people arrive behind us, chattering and whooping and bearing various gifts of an alcoholic nature. Based on the number of times Eddie says, "Cool, nice to meet ya," I guess each person he invited brought about three or four extras, coolers and pizza in tow. The house fills up fast with noise, bodies, and clanking glass bottles. At times I feel intimidated, afraid that things will get out of control, and I'm careful to stay close to Sam and Frankie. But soon Frankie hands me a fruity drink with a paper umbrella, and everything seems a little less intense.

Sam is right about the music. By eleven, his ambient techno vibe blends gracefully and seamlessly into an all-out reggae dance club, packed wall to wall with more people than the entire off-season population of Zanzibar Bay, gyrating and bouncing to Jamaican kettledrums.

The house can take it. It's like a dance hall in and of itself. Huge floor-to-ceiling windows looking out over the ocean. Gigantic, in-ground swimming pool. Pool tables in more than one room. Stainless steel kitchen appliances. The place probably has ten bedrooms, too. It's like it was built for entertaining — like one of those celebrity houses where a bunch of famous people sit around and do coke all day, whining about their lives. I half expect them to walk in any minute with their drugs and their fantasyland problems, and Eddie will just shrug and smile and say it's cool, nice to meet ya.

Sam goes to check on the music situation, and in all the commotion and space, I lose Frankie. I wander through the crowds, get lost down various corridors, and finally find her in the kitchen, camera in hand, filming Jake as he takes the door to the side entrance off its hinges.

"Frankie, what are you guys doing?"

"We need a beer pong table," she says without further explanation, zooming in on my face as if it's perfectly normal to deconstruct a house for such a noble purpose.

"Remind me again how you play beer pong?"

"Oh, you remember," she says as if we're regular pong champs. She slings the camera strap over her shoulder, still filming, and rummages through the stacks of open coolers on the counter for a pack of red plastic cups. "You set up six cups on each side like bowling pins and fill them with beer. Then you have to try to bounce the Ping-Pong ball into the other team's cups to make them drink. If you miss, you drink."

"See, Anna," Jake says over a gathering fan base lining each side of the room, "the thing about beer pong is that even when you lose, you win!" He pulls a pair of yellow Ping-Pong balls from his pocket that he apparently carries around for just such an occasion. "You in?"

I nod. "Only if we can do teams."

Frankie grabs me. "She's mine. Girls against guys."

Jake calls for Eddie to join him at the helm of the side door, which is now flat and horizontal atop two barstools, six red cups arranged in triangles at each end.

"Girls rule!" She raises her hand up for a high five.

I slap her palm and take a chug of beer.

"You two are about to get housed," Jake says, but not before coming back to our side of the door to kiss Frankie one last time before the big game, eliciting a cacophony of catcalls from the fans on the sidelines.

Jake returns to home field and bounces a ball in Frankie's direction, missing completely, finishing out his turn with an overdrawn pout.

Frankie returns, surprising me as she sinks her first shot in the lead cup right in front of Eddie. He dips his fingers in to remove the ball and downs the beer.

I turn to her and stare, unable to hide my shock. "Practice, or magic?" I ask.

"I've played a few times, Anna. Remember the parties?"

"Not exactly." I must have been in the bathroom during that part of the nonexistent parties, hiding out from the vomiting hot girl while Frankie completed her beer pong apprenticeship.

The game lasts about ten minutes. Thanks to a strange combination of Frankie's dead-on skill at sinking Ping-Pong balls into cups of beer and Jake's distraction over Frankie's boobs bubbling out the top of her camisole, we win.

Unfortunately, the celebration is short-lived. Our championship title is yanked ruthlessly from beneath our overconfident feet during round two. Jake and Eddie sink every ball, forcing us to chug in record time.

"Sam's girl drinks!" Eddie shouts as he sinks the final ball in front of me, splashing my shirt.

Sam's girl. The sound of it hits me hard and fast, spinning my head around. Suddenly, I can't feel my feet. I'm floating. I'm content.

"Sam's girl! Sam's girl! Sam's girl!" the entire kitchen chants, and I realize in that moment how many people a raucous game of beer pong can attract. I take the ball out of the cup and chug it down, letting out a loud hiccup that I'd probably regret if I was so-ber, which for the record I'm not.

"Don't worry, girls," Eddie says, putting his arm around me. "The good thing about beer pong is, even when you lose, you win."

Jake peels Eddie's arm from my shoulders. "Anna," he says, "where's that boyfriend of yours, anyway?"

"He's not my —"

"Here." Sam sneaks up and wraps his arms around me from be-hind. My hair is up and he's breathing on the back of my neck, moaning softly so no one else can hear. If I was content before, now I'm effervescent. I'm an empty-headed floating feather again, a feather who is also effervescent. *Hiccup.* Someone could douse me with beer and I wouldn't even know it.

I turn and kiss him, eliciting another round of catcalls.

"I see you've been losing at beer pong," he says, smiling in front of the cups scattered all over the sticky table.

"Yeah," I say. "But the thing about beer pong is that even when you win, you win. I mean, even when you win, you — oh, never mind. We totally lost." I wriggle loose to grab another beer, which has somehow become suddenly not so disgusting.

Frankie and Jake grab the cups off the table and restack them for the next match.

"Anna, you're up," Frankie says.

"Sorry, guys." Sam takes the beer from my hand and sets it on the table. "I'm kidnapping your MVP. She needs a time-out."

I smile and wave to Frankie as she disappears into another match. Sam navigates us through the mob in the house, which has become even more tangled in the last hour. Lots of people are still dancing, while others are strewn across various couches and floor space, some laughing, others making out, a web of arms and legs and pedicured toes with tiny silver rings.

We make our way outside, past the pool, and across the lawn. The backyard is packed but not as noisy. Surprisingly, no one is on the steps that lead down to the beach, and no one seems to be *on* the beach, either.

We sit on the bottom step listening to the ocean, my legs outstretched and draped over Sam's. In the dark, reflected only by the near-full moon overhead, the water is black and frothy like licorice soup. As we sit in silence, the party noise fades behind us and I start to regain some of the brain cells I sacrificed during beer pong.

"It's weird," Sam finally says, one hand rubbing my bare (and thankfully shaved) leg. "I've lived here my whole life, but I never stop being amazed at how different the water looks at night."

I squint and try to see beyond the immediate shoreline, past where the waves crest and foam and crash against the sand. Everything is black. If I try to walk in the water beyond the moon's sheen on the surface, I'll drop right off the earth into outer space.

"I know what you mean," I say. "I've only been here a couple weeks and already I can't imagine not waking up to this."

It's the first time I've allowed myself to go beyond the happy bubble of our vacation, beyond our lazy days on the beach and secret nights at the Shack. Beyond the ocean and the sand and the Perinos being happy and, most importantly, Sam. I think briefly about my life back home. Anna, daughter of real estate deal-closer. Anna, sad yet supportive neighbor kid. Anna, haunted by secrets.

I rest my head against Sam's chest and know as his heart pounds softly in my ear that Zanzibar is my time capsule. I want to seal myself in this place, locked in this moment with Sam on the rickety sea-washed stairs in front of the ocean, not to be opened, examined, or otherwise disturbed for a hundred million years.

"Can we go somewhere?" I ask. I don't want to think ahead of this night and am suddenly overcome with the urgent need to cram as much as possible into it.

"Sure," he says, shifting my legs so he can get up. "Want to walk out to the Vista?"

Artists' Vista is a narrow curve of shoreline that juts out on the other side of the pier beyond Moonlight Boulevard. Frankie showed it to me our first day here when we were waiting for Red and Jayne to get ice cream, but we haven't gone out there on our midnight missions. I imagine at this time of night, there's only one reason *to* go out there.

"Yes." I answer immediately, standing to brush the sand from my shorts. "Let me go tell Frankie so she doesn't freak out later."

"Good idea," he says. "And put your sweatshirt on. I'm going to grab a blanket, too."

I've lost track of time, but it must be close to two in the morning. I'm not tired, and judging from the sound bouncing out of the house as I approach, neither are the beautiful party people.

Frankie's where I left her in the kitchen, except that now she's sitting on a barstool in front of the beer pong table with her arm around another girl, both in bikini tops and shorts, interviewing her companion for the camera about the loss of her clothing.

"Heyyyyyy," she says when she sees me, stumbling from her perch in front of the door-slash-table. "Look who's back!"

"Frankie, where's your shirt?" I ask.

"I lost it in strip beer pong." She speaks slowly, making an exaggerated frown.

"Sounds like this game went downhill fast," Sam says, coming in behind me.

"Hey, look who showed up!" Jake comes in from one of the mysterious corridors of the house with a bottle of Jägermeister. "Who wants to do a belly shot?"

"Off your hairy gut?" Sam asks. "No thanks."

"No, silly!" Frankie hops off the stool and nearly drags down the other beer pong shirt-loser in the process. "Me and Lisa — I mean Leah — are the shot glasses."

"Right," Sam says. "Anyway, no thanks."

"More for us!" Jake pulls Frankie back to her spot on the table next to Lisa/Leah, who still hasn't said more than two words but releases a dopey giggle whenever Frankie speaks or moves and, for the record, looks like she's about Katie's age — not that it matters to Jake.

I don't know how long it will take us to get to the Vista or how long we'll hang out, so I tell Frankie not to wait up. After confirming that Jake is planning to stay the night with her, I hug her goodbye and ask her not to drink any more unless she wants to spend the whole next day throwing up.

"Don't worry, *Mom,*" she says, leaning her whole body against mine from her position in front of the door-slash-table. "I won't.

And also, I love you, Anna. You are my best friend in the world. I'm not just saying that because I'm drunk, either. I mean, I am drunk, but I still love you even when I'm not."

"I love you, too, Frankie," I say. "Now please get off of me."

She laughs and leans back on the stool, her long, tanned legs dangling over the edge next to laughing Leah, the pong-turned-Frankie fan club awaiting her next move.

I grab my backpack from an out-of-the-way closet Eddie tucked it in earlier and dig out my sweatshirt, leaving my fake slumber party gear, journal, and toothbrush in the bag and dropping it next to Frankie's on the closet floor.

I locate a bathroom along the hallway back to the kitchen and duck inside to put on my sweatshirt and do a quick hair and face check. As if by magic, I even find some lotion for my legs and a bowl of mints on the sink.

Butterflies are batting their wings against my rib cage as I take a final look in the mirror.

The next time I see you, Crazy Anna, you won't recognize me.

C

twenty-three

*I*t doesn't take long to reach the Vista, and when we arrive I recognize the view immediately. All of California's beach towns light up the coast like fireworks, just as I'd seen in Matt's picture-perfect postcards a thousand times.

"We used to come here a lot for picnics when I was a kid," Sam says, shaking out a blanket for us on the sand. "I haven't been here in a while."

I sit on the blanket next to him. "Tell me a story," I say. "I just want to listen."

"Sure. Come here." He lies down and pulls me against his chest, stroking my hair. He tells me about growing up in California, and how it's so hard to make friends because everyone you meet leaves at the end of the summer. His voice is low and soft, muffled through his chest against my ear.

"The most tragic thing about California is that nothing is permanent or real here," he says. "It gets to you, you know?"

"No. I wish I could stay here forever."

"But you can't, Anna. That's the point." He lifts my chin and looks at my face. "You're like this beautiful, crazy ghost, and when I wake up, you'll be gone, and I'll wonder if any of this really happened."

"I know what you mean," I say, wishing I didn't.

Sam asks me about New York, rubbing my back lightly as I talk. I tell him about our childhood, carefully skirting the tragedy that so defines me. But all my real childhood stories — the important ones — reach the same inevitable end.

Before — together.

After — apart.

Before — happy.

After — sad.

Being with Sam on this trip has been like a vacation from sorrow, but now I can't talk about growing up without thinking about Matt. The effort of pushing him from my thoughts and words drains me. Finally, his memory wins out, creeping into my mind and making me go quiet against the sound of the ocean and Sam's breathing.

Right after Matt died, I was afraid to do basically everything. I couldn't even bite my nails or sniff my shirt to see if I needed deodorant without feeling like he was watching me. I willed and prayed and begged him to give me a sign that he *was* watching, that he *was* with me, so I would know.

But he never did. Time moved on. And I stopped being afraid.

Until right now, vulnerable and insecure and a little bit drunk. Lying in the sand and falling in crazy love with someone I just met. Matt is watching me. Observing. Possibly judging. And the worst part of it is, I don't *want* to wake up under his landslide of sad rocks anymore. I don't want to taste the marzipan frosting and the clove cigarettes. I don't want to think about the blue glass necklace or the books he read to me on his bed or the piles of college stuff or some random boy in the grocery store wearing his donated clothes.

I don't want to be the dead boy's best-friend-turned-something-else.

Or the really supportive neighbor friend.

Or the lifelong keeper of broken-hearted secrets.

I just want to be floating, suspended here in my California time capsule with neither yesterday's dusk nor tomorrow's dawn anywhere on the horizon.

Erased.

What's your earliest memory? I asked Matt. We were washing his car while Frankie made sandwiches in the kitchen.

Most of them are in California. The ocean. I don't really remember the first time I saw it, just how I felt.

How?

Impossibly small. Impossibly insignificant. And completely safe. Sounds crazy, right?

No.

What's yours?

I wanted to tell him it was my fifteenth birthday party two weeks earlier, because everything that came before that night was a pale moon behind the sunshine of that kiss. Instead, I told him about sitting in the garden with my dad while Matt caught caterpillars and tried to feed them oak leaves from the tree in our backyard. I must have been about three.

I wanted to make a caterpillar farm. I can't believe you remember that, Anna. Matt smiled, rinsing the car soap from his hands.

Not as cool as seeing the ocean for the first time, but it still makes me smile.

I promise I'll take you there someday. I want to see it with you. I want to see everything with you.

Sam looks at me hard and serious, like he's trying to read my mind. I can't find the words for this conversation and even if I could, I'd probably just cry. So I do the next best thing and kiss him.

Erased.

He kisses me back, deeper and more intense, and moves on top of me, pulling off my sweatshirt, his hips pressing against mine, harder and closer than ever before. I feel things that I've never felt, in places I didn't know existed, like a hundred hungry little flowers waking up and blooming in the sun after a long, harsh winter.

Somewhere beneath my newly tanned skin I know that I should wait, that it should be special, that it should be with someone I can wake up with in the morning, tomorrow and always.

What if he thinks I'm a tourist girl looking for some romantic long-distance love affair just so she can share his gushing, beach-stained post-cards with her friends?

No — after this vacation, that's it. Sam and I will no longer exist in the context of *Sam and I.* I will lose him, just like Matt. Whether by death or the impossible distance between New York and California, soon I will wake up, and Sam will be gone.

Sam, whose sea locks fall in soft waves on my cheeks as he kisses me.

Sam, whose wild green eyes are on me like his hands, searching and finding, hot and intense.

Sam, whose skin tastes like salt and summer.

Sam, whose last name is — a total mystery.

"Wait!" I pull away from him as he fumbles with the ties on my bikini top. "I just realized that we don't know each other's last names. Mine's Reiley." I look at him with a sense of urgency, as though this new piece of information will sway the forward momentum of this crazy night.

He laughs. "Macintosh."

"Like the apple?" I ask.

"Like the computer."

"Same thing, right?"

"Um, Anna?"

"Yeah?"

"No more talking." He smiles.

"Okay," I whisper, running my fingers along his lower lip. My mind is racing faster than my heart, but I'm not sure how to stop it. I don't want to stop it. I want to devour everything about him. I want to taste his mouth and smell his shampoo and then die with this memory, immediate and swift, before anything can take it away.

He moves close to kiss me again, but I push my hand against his chest. "Sam, I mean, it's *okay*. Do you have something?" I wait for the glimmer of recognition to rise on his face.

"Yeah," he says, nodding and reaching for his sweatshirt beside me. I hear the crinkling of paper as he tears open the condom.

"Are you sure?" he asks.

"Yes."

Sam kisses me hard, breathing through his nose as he unzips, unties, unbuttons, and pulls our clothes down, kissing my stomach as he goes. His mouth moves slowly back to my lips, murmuring softly as I wrap my legs around him and pull him inside.

It doesn't hurt exactly — it's just kind of — *strange.* At first I hold my breath, my shorts and bikini bottoms clinging limply around one of my ankles like they didn't run off in time and now have to sit through the whole act without making any noise, lest they be discovered.

Sam tangles his hands up in my hair, pushing back and forth against my body like the waves in front of us. I sense his rhythm and relax as my shoulders and hips dig trenches in the sand beneath our blanket. Through the silk of his hair, I watch the low, orange moon, tasting the salt of his skin on my mouth, breathing hard, waiting for the stars to fall down around us.

But they don't fall.

They just fade, looking on in silence, lingering over the rushing waves until Sam disentangles from my body and I sit up, pulling my clothes back on.

The sparkle of the night sky pales with the receding tide, evaporating in the pink dawn along with the albatross I've at long last abandoned.

Somehow, I don't feel any different than I felt in front of the mirror back at the party. I'm not older. I'm not smarter. Nothing in the murky waters of my life has been suddenly clarified or demystified now that I'm a member of the secret club.

Sam lies with his eyes closed, arms crossed over his chest. "Stay with me, Anna Reiley," he whispers sleepily, smiling. I reach down and touch his stomach with light fingers.

"I'm just going to rinse my feet off. I'll be right back." I hook my flip-flops through one finger and walk barefoot to the edge of the water, my unbuttoned jean shorts slung loose over my bikini bottoms. Clumped with sand, the fringe clings to my thighs like wet spiderwebs.

I let the water lick my feet and wait for a sign that I'll be okay, that what I did is okay, that *everything* is okay. I look out over the licorice-soup ocean and wait.

The waves whisper against the shore as they have all night, knowing and ancient and unchanged.

The sand and the vanishing moon and the hotel beach umbrellas closed like flowers at dusk sit still, unaltered, unaffected.

The sea surges forward over my toes, only to recede, her opalescent slick on the sand evaporating instantly.

I took the magic pill, and now it's done.

I rinse my hands in the water and turn back toward Sam. It must be after five. He's sitting up now, watching me with his hazy green eyes, shivering and smiling.

"What?" I ask, digging in the sand with my toe, hiding my own smile.

"Don't move, Anna Reiley," he says. "Right now, everything is perfect."

twenty-four

*W*e walk along the shore at dawn, arms locked, heads down, scanning the damp sand as it passes below our feet. My pockets grow heavier with each piece of sea glass I collect — greens, blues, whites, ambers. After three weeks on the beach, I'm still amazed that pieces of things that were once whole, once part of something else, can break and fall into the ocean, traveling thousands of miles and years only to end up here, passengers in the pockets of my white sweatshirt.

The rest of the beach comes to life, preparing for the morning tourists. Hotel staff scuttle along the strip like tiny ants in khaki shorts and pastel polo shirts, cleaning, straightening, anticipating. As the umbrellas yawn and stretch and open their white-and-yellow petals against the sun, Sam smiles at me.

"You okay, Anna?" he asks.

I stick my hands in my pockets, feeling the cold, smooth glass between my fingers, remembering something I'd read in one of the trinket stores on Moonlight Boulevard with Frankie and Jayne.

"Pieces of sea glass are supposedly the tears of a lovesick mermaid," I tell Sam. "She was banished to the bottom of the ocean for all eternity by King Neptune because she fell in love with a ship's captain and saved him from a storm."

Sam nods. "Yeah, I've heard that before. There are all kinds of sayings like that around here. But sometimes you gotta just take things for what they are and appreciate them, not try to label it or explain it. Explanations take the mystery out of it, you know?"

"I guess." I crouch down to scoop up a square of turquoise glass I spot beneath my toes, and that's when I see it, dark and deep, poking out of the wet sand. "Oh my God, look!"

I stand and hold out my hand for Sam to inspect.

"Wow," he says, taking the glass and holding it up to the sun. "Red is, like, the rarest color there is. You're totally lucky you even saw it."

I take the deep red, half-dollar-sized piece from him and smile, looking out across the ocean. I told Matt in my letter before we left that I'd find a piece just for him, but now that it's actually here, sparkling in my hand, I know he'd want me to do something else with it.

I raise it above my head and throw it as hard and as far as I can into the sea.

Let someone else have a lucky day, Anna.

Sam laughs. "Hey, crazy, what'd you do *that* for? You'll probably never see something like that again in your entire life."

"Right. But I *did* see it. And now someone else can, too."

"I don't get it."

I shrug and smile. "Explanations take the mystery out of things, right?"

"Um, right." Sam laughs and wraps me up in a warm hug.

We walk the rest of the way to Eddie's house with our arms around each other, a happy exhaustion threatening to overtake us. My skin has goose bumps from the morning chill, but I'm warm and buoyant on the inside, giddy from lack of sleep, the way I feel next to Sam, and the red sea glass — sign from the universe or not.

As we approach the house, a shock of shimmering auburn hair shines from the stairs leading up to the backyard. When I see the light blue camisole, I know.

"It's Frankie. She must have waited up for me or something. I wonder where Jake is?"

"He has an early class — he probably had to leave. Speaking of which, I have to be at work in three hours myself. I'm on a double tonight."

"You can barely stand up!" I shove him lightly, knocking him off balance to prove my point.

"Nah. I just need like an hour's sleep, then I'll have some coffee. I'll be fine."

"Okay." I wave to Frankie. She's sitting on the stairs watching us, waiting for me to pay attention to her.

"Will we see you guys later?" Sam asks.

"Maybe we'll come for smoothies. Otherwise, definitely tonight."

He smiles and hugs me close, kissing me on the lips and fore-head before jogging down the beach, and I catch myself smiling.

Just that I could possibly.
Love him.
Forever.

Judging by the state of pollution at the bottom of the stairs, the party migrated from the backyard to the beach after we left. I pick my way through a debris field of bottles and paper plates to reach Frankie. Her head rests against her hand on the railing and she looks like she got about as much sleep as I did.

"Hey," I say, waiting for her to notice something different about me. "What are you —"

"*You.*" She doesn't move when she speaks, and there is nothing warm or happy in her tone. "You need to stay *far* away from me."

"Frankie, what are you talking about?" I try to remember anything I might have done or said last night to upset her, but nothing comes. She was fine when I left with Sam. And getting me to ditch the A.A. was her mission, anyway. "What's going on with you?"

She stands to face me. Her expression, like her voice, is empty and flat. Black, dried mascara streaks the skin below her eyes. Immediately, my heart seizes.

"Frankie, what happened? Is it Jake? Did something happen with him? Did he hurt you?"

She stares hard, unblinking, her breathing even and calm. Her eyes are beyond angry. Beyond hurt. Beyond caring.

I've only seen her like this one other time — in the hospital lobby when the doctor came out with the chaplain to tell us they couldn't save Matt. Jayne just fainted, and Red, holding a plastic bag full of Matt's things, screamed, "No! No! No!" over and over.

Frankie just stared at her parents, the same ghostly face, no sound, tears spilling out over her cheeks.

"Frankie, talk to me. Did something happen at the party? What's going on? Should we call someone?" My voice is shaky, moving fast. If I touch her, she could shatter. I wish Sam was still here. "*Please* talk to me."

I take a chance and put my hand on her shoulder, triggering an invisible switch. She flinches, coming back into her body from wherever she was visiting. Her eyes go wild, raging. Her face turns red and her shoulders shake violently, barely containing the fight in her.

"Talk to you? *Talk* to you?" she asks. "Okay, I'll talk to you, Anna Reiley. So, where *were* you last night?" Her voice is high and forced, mocking.

"Frankie, I was with Sam at the Vista. I told you that before I left. Remember?"

"With him? As in, *with* him, with him?"

I'm suddenly embarrassed and ashamed. I did not expect my best friend to react like this when I told her about last night. "I was trying to tell you —"

"Oh, *please*. Save it. You weren't gonna tell me *shit*."

"Frankie, you know I wouldn't keep something like this from you."

"Is that so," she says, rather than asks. "Just like you told me about *this*?" She reaches back to the steps behind her and pulls something up to my face, her hand white-knuckled and shaking. When I see the purple rectangle, it takes a minute for me to realize what it is, to put the pieces together. It's like when Aunt Jayne rearranged Frankie's room last time. All her stuff was still there, but it wasn't where it was supposed to be. We kept waking up and forgetting where we were.

The image of Frankie's tan fingers wrapped around my journal is something out of a science fiction movie. Those are her real fingers. That is my real journal. But the juxtaposition of two formerly unconnected objects doesn't belong in this dimension.

"That's my — my —" I can't speak. My knees go wobbly. That old hot, prickly feeling runs up my back and neck. The sound of the waves on the shore is amplified. I can feel the blood running from my heart through my veins and back again. I am hyperaware. Slow motion. Guilty and mad.

I lunge at her, reaching for the journal, but she's quick on her feet, backing away toward the water.

"Here's a good one," she reads from a random entry. "'Dear Matt, There is so much I want to say to you. Every day something happens at school that I want to come home and tell you about, but I can't.' Or how about this one. 'Dear Matt, Sometimes I wonder if it's ever going to stop hurting.'"

Frankie's flipping through the pages, shouting my fears and dreams and memories across the vast ocean, releasing them from their flat paper prisons and breaking me into little bits.

"Frankie, please stop!" It's barely a whisper.

"'Dear Matt, Your sister is out of control. I wish you were here — I don't know how to help her. Last night she went out with this guy from school to the soccer field and . . .'"

"Stop it!" I try to shout, but it still comes out as a whisper.

"You think you know everything?" she yells. "For your information, I didn't even sleep with Johan! We got all the way out there, and he didn't even want to be with me!"

"What?"

"It didn't happen! I didn't sleep with him! And while we're on the subject of truth, I didn't sleep with Jake, either. Happy now? You wanna put that in your little book report?"

I can't believe what I'm hearing. I open my mouth to say something cold and angry, but no sound comes out. All I can do is claw at the air for my journal, my written thoughts like the lost children of my soul.

Frankie takes another step back, still thumbing through pages. "'Dear Matt, We finally made it to California, and it's just like you told me. I feel you here with us — I think Frankie does, too.' How *dare* you write about me in here! How dare you write to my brother! You think just because you fooled around a few times he cared about you? You think he wouldn't have ditched you the second he found some new girl at Cornell? Get *over* yourself!"

Tears are hot on my cheeks. My throat has closed up. My heart is broken, and I am utterly paralyzed.

Frankie yanks on the cover and tries to tear it from its metal spirals, succeeding only partially. The cover flops sideways in the breeze like a broken wing, revealing the picture I've looked at every night since he died. *Matt's arm around my shoulders, bits of cake and colored chips and grass clinging to our clothes and hair, everything warm and pink in the glow of the setting sun, the whole summer stretched out before us.*

After he died, I spent hours staring at that picture, replaying the party in my mind, willing the two-dimensional images to come back to life, to bring us back there. We could tell Frankie right away. We could be together. We could skip Custard's and go straight to the hospital and tell them to fix Matt before anything bad ever happened.

I clear my throat and find my voice again, stronger this time. "Give it back, Frankie. You had no right to read it, and you have no right to rip it apart. Give it to me."

She looks at me with crazed, lost eyes. "No, I don't think so."

I'm desperate. "Frankie, *please* give it back to me. Please. I'm sorry I didn't tell you, but it's all I have left of —"

"Anna, he was *my* brother. *Mine.* You have no right to have *any-thing* left of him!" As the declaration leaves her mouth, she turns her back to me and runs to the shoreline, arching her arm behind her, the rarest-red mermaid tear sparkling in her bracelet like the stone I gave back to the ocean only heartbeats ago.

"Frankie, *don't!*" I run toward her, but my legs feel weighted, like I'm stuck in a horrible nightmare. I catch her and snag the bottom of her camisole, knocking her down to the sand.

But the journal is no longer attached to her fingers.

It's sailing through the air overhead, landing flat on the water with an uninspiring *plop.*

It floats for a moment, lolling back and forth in the current, giving me one last chance to retrieve it. I scramble to my feet and run into the water after it, pulling through the tide with heavy arms and heavy legs, willing myself to swim and stretch and reach it.

"Anna! Leave it! Let it go!" Frankie shouts from the shore, up to her knees in water.

I keep swimming toward it, but the current is too strong, pulling on my legs and arms and burning my lungs until I can no longer keep my head above it without fighting. As I kick and yank myself back toward shallower water, the tide moves the journal completely out of reach, encircling it, giving me one last look at the warped pages before it pulls them down to the depths of the ocean.

My heart pounds in a thousand shattered-glass pieces, each beating separately, painfully.

I've lost him all over again.

When I get out of the water, I sit down hard on the shore, put my head in my hands, and weep until I don't have any bones. I don't care what Frankie thinks. I don't care if the party guests or the hotel staff see me out here. I don't even care if Sam comes back and finds me here, eyes puffy and nose running and heart broken.

My best friend is crumpled in the sand next to me like a wet paper doll.

My virginity is gone.

The ocean has swallowed up my journal.

And it takes all the strength I have left not to dive back in and follow it down, down, deep to the bottom of the sea, lost for all eternity like the broken, banished mermaid.

twenty-five

The guilt of not telling Frankie about Matt and me is overwhelming, but it's a pale second to the violation I feel that she read my most private, raw thoughts and destroyed them. She broke into my carefully guarded heart, stole the only remaining connection I had to Matt, and turned it into a monstrosity. To make things worse, during all the time she spent educating me on first times and undress rehearsals like the Queen of Love, she was carrying an equally heavy and awkward albatross; she was no more experienced than I.

I can't even look at her.

For Frankie's part, she can't look at me, either. After we spill all of our silent tears on the beach, she heads back into Eddie's house alone.

We told Red and Jayne we'd be back just before lunch. If we show up before breakfast soaking wet and puffy-eyed, they'll know something's wrong. We have to wait it out here.

I climb the stairs up to the backyard, legs and heart pressed with sadness and fatigue. A few people are camped out on the deck chairs that line the pool, passed out cold, unaffected by my and Frankie's earlier battle cries. Through the back entrance, I step over the crumpled, sleeping pile of a guy whose clothes I recognize from the beer pong fan club last night. I take a few more steps into the kitchen before I'm stopped cold by a wall of funk and filth. The smell of someone's puke announces itself proudly, reaching up and trying to choke me. Open pizza boxes and loose crusts litter the entire kitchen, the door-turned-table has been knocked off its barstools, and a layer of sand mixed with a sticky film of spilled beer coats every flat surface in sight.

I've never smelled a decomposing corpse, but I imagine this house comes pretty close.

The place is silent, save for the dissonance of a collective snore and the soft hum of stereo speakers all out of music. A ragtag bunch of last night's Beautiful People are curled up in various states of disarray on the living room floor, stinky and hungover and smudged with makeup and beer.

I find my way back to the hallway, opening three doors before finding the closet where I left my backpack next to Frankie's. Hers is gone, but mine is there. I unzip it slowly, hoping beyond hope that the last few hours were just an illusion induced by a euphoric Sam-haze.

The front pouch is empty. The middle part holds everything I packed in it last night, save for the one thing I actually care about.

With my bag, I lock myself in the bathroom I discovered last night. Fortunately, no one is passed out in the tub, so I take a quick, searing hot shower, helping myself to the luxurious bath and body products lining the shower wall.

After the shower, I pull on the boxers and pink T-shirt I brought to sleep in, shoving my soaked clothes in the middle pocket. As I wipe the steam off the mirror, my face comes into focus and looks, much to my surprise and disappointment, exactly as I remember it. Other than the newly acquired emotional hangover, complete with puffy bloodshot eyes and tired frown, it's the regular old Anna face, same as last night — nothing new or improved about it.

Back in the main part of the house, I scan the perimeter to determine that Frankie isn't in the vicinity and find a spot of floor space near the den off main living room. Across the room, Eddie is passed out on a leather couch, wearing a black lace bra stuffed with napkins over his green T-shirt.

I listen to the ocean and the soft rattling snores around me. I close my eyes and slow my breathing, but sleep eludes me. Two hours ago, I imagined this moment very differently — lying on the floor next to Frankie, giggling softly as I recounted my evening for her, planning our activities for the final days of the A.B.S.E.

Instead, thoughts of Frankie tighten my chest and pierce me with angry black arrows.

My mind drifts between peaceful memories of Sam's lips against mine and the intolerable sadness of being betrayed by someone I've loved and trusted my entire life.

I think I hear someone calling from the front door and wonder briefly where Frankie ended up. Before I can shake it off as my imagination, I hear it a second and third time.

"Housekeeping! Housekeeping!"

The announcement precedes a few swift knocks and the unmistakable jangle of keys in the lock.

"Mr. and Mrs. Donovan? Anyone home?" The door opens, ushering in rays of sunlight that fall harsh on Eddie's face, but he's undisturbed. I scoot farther into the den so I can safely watch someone else's drama unfold without getting sucked into it.

"What the — good God, boy! Did someone *die* in here?" The housekeeper props open the front door with her industrial-strength vacuum cleaner and moves to the sofa where Eddie finally stirs.

"Hi," he yawns, a lone survivor in the aftermath of the party storm, stranded in the middle of a war zone strewn with bodies, bottles, cigarette butts, random articles of clothing, pizza crusts, plastic cups, shards of the obligatory expensive broken sculpture, and sand.

"Edward, where are your parents?" she asks, folding her puffy arms across her chest.

Eddie sits up slowly and surveys the damage. "Don't worry, Maggie," he tells her in his groggy voice. "You don't have to clean this up. I'll take care of it."

"Mmm-hmm. When do they get back?"

"Tomorrow, I think."

"Must have been some kinda party," she says, grabbing her chest with both hands and nodding at Eddie's lingerie.

"What the . . . ?" Eddie reaches up to feel the lace against his body and shakes his head, clearly not remembering how it got there.

"Okay then. You just call us if you need anything, *Edward*." She kicks a bottle out of the doorway, drags away the vacuum, and lets the door slam shut. The bottle rolls across the floor and comes to rest against a pizza box near Eddie's feet.

"Shit." He leans forward on the couch with his head in his hands, not making any effort to remove the bra.

"Busted?" I ask, crawling out from my nest on the side of the room.

"Nah, just a headache."

"Won't the housekeeper tell your parents?"

"Probably. But it doesn't matter, as long as I clean everything up. Same thing every summer. They don't have time to care."

I turn to tell Frankie. *See? There's a whole world of parents who don't care.* But then I remember that Frankie isn't next to me and, by the way, I hate her.

I offer to help Eddie start the cleanup effort, but he declines.

"Maggie will come back," he says. "It's this little game we play. She pretends to be all surprised and concerned, then she leaves. I wake up and kick everyone out. Then she comes back and helps me put it all back to normal."

"She must like you."

"Not really. She likes the hundred bucks I'll tip her later."

Eddie puts on some coffee and starts the task of waking the dead who are laid up around the house, pool deck, and yard. I ask him if he saw Frankie come in earlier.

"Yeah, she's upstairs. You two musta *drank* last night. You both look like shit!"

I force a smile. "I've been called worse." *Just a few hours ago, actually.*

I help myself to a cup of black coffee in the kitchen and wait for Princess Perino. I can probably name a good seven *thousand* people I'd rather walk down the beach with this morning, but we can't risk showing up at the house separately. As far as Uncle Red and Aunt Jayne know, we had a super-fun time at Jackie and Samantha's super-great sleepover, staying up so late giggling and pillow-fighting and *Cosmo*-quizzing that we need a few hours in our own beds to catch up on sleep.

An hour later, Frankie stomps down the stairs, full makeup covering up any evidence of turmoil. For my benefit, she makes a big show of hugging Eddie goodbye and thanking him for the "rockin'" party. Then, without turning her head even remotely in my direction, she hefts her backpack over her shoulder and heads out the back door and down to the beach, chin up, stomach in, shoulders back, chest out — a ferocious auburn-haired phoenix rising from the ashes of her best-friend breakup.

twenty-six

I keep pace a safe distance behind her, my twisted-up feelings wavering between sorry and angry, spending more time in the latter camp. Frankie doesn't look over her shoulder once, confident that I won't let her get too far ahead. She knows as well as I do that if we don't show up together acting natural, we're going to have a lot more explaining to do.

I sprint the last thirty feet to ensure we walk up the stairs to the backyard together, smiling, picture-perfect rays of sunshine coming home from our girls' night. Red and Jayne are in the kitchen chopping up something for lunch, right on cue.

"Hey, girls!" Aunt Jayne says, drying her hands on her shorts. "How was the slumber party?"

"Good." We both answer in dead monotone.

"Doesn't look like you got much sleep," Uncle Red says from behind his newspaper.

"Dad, you don't actually sleep at a sleepover."

"Forgive my ignorance," he says, folding up the paper and dropping it on the table. "What *do* you do?"

"*Tons* of stuff. Right, Anna?" Frankie's voice is high and contemptuous.

"Oh, you know," I say, grabbing an apple from the counter and taking a huge, exaggerated bite. "Booze. Boys. The usual."

Frankie's eyes bulge, but Red and Jayne just laugh. It would never occur to them that I'm telling the truth.

"In that case, I'm coming with you next time." Aunt Jayne winks and sets out sandwiches and tortilla chips on the table, looking at me a second too long. After that first night on the porch, we didn't talk about Matt and Frankie again. I wonder if she can see the distance between her daughter and me now, blowing in like dizzy seagulls after another all-night bender — another failed attempt at forgetting.

We drop our bags in the living room and take our places around the table, striking the most natural poses we can manage. I'm so tired that I may start hallucinating. My heart feels like it's pumping molasses in my veins, and my neck is hot as I wait for Frankie's next biting comment.

It doesn't come, though. She shoots me a few nasty looks when Red and Jayne aren't paying attention, which I wholeheartedly return, but her mouth is shut. I force myself to eat most of my sandwich and a few chips before excusing myself to our bedroom for a much-needed nap.

"All right," Uncle Red says. "We'll wake you up later for dinner. You two decide where we're going — anywhere you want."

"Thanks, Uncle Red." I put my dishes in the sink and head upstairs. Coming down with a sudden deadly illness to avoid faking my way through an evening with Frankie is probably out of the question, so I resign myself to it, force it out of my mind, and crawl between the cool white sheets of my bed, temporarily erasing the last few hours from existence. *Poof!*

A few hours later, Frankie wakes me up by kicking the side of my bed.

"What?" I snap.

"Get up. We're going to dinner in fifteen minutes."

"Oh, thanks for the advance notice."

"Whatever."

After the lovefest, Frankie and I get ready for dinner in silence, working around each other as though the next person to speak or make direct eye contact will turn to stone. Every few minutes she looks in my direction, and I in hers, waiting for an opening, a smile, a sympathetic tilt of the head — any indication that we will ever speak again.

But none come.

Not from Frankie, who would probably forgive the events of the universe for taking Matt before she'd consider forgiving me for not telling her about what happened between us.

And certainly not from me. As much fun as I've had with Frankie, as much as I loved her and wanted to spend all the summers of tomorrow with her, as much as I wanted to take care of her for Matt — I know it will never be that way again.

After several uncomfortable minutes, Frankie finally breaks the silence, tears welling up with scratchy whispers.

"I just don't see how you could *not* tell me about that!"

"Oh, really?" I shout-whisper back, yanking a comb through my hair. "I should have told you about Matt, but it's okay for you to lie about Johan *and* Jake?"

"That's totally different and you know it!"

"Quit trying to justify your bullshit, Frankie! I'm sick of it!"

"Girls, let's go!" Red calls from downstairs. "We're going to dinner, not to the prom!"

"Five minutes, Dad!" Frankie yells, turning back to me. "Oh, so I suppose I'm just a *horrible* monster of a friend, huh? I *made* you come on this trip and I *made* you lose your stupid virginity and I *made* you lie about Matt?"

I grab her wrist and meet her eyes, almost nose to nose. "You know something, Frankie? I'm *done*." I throw her arm away and quickly check my face in the mirror.

"Don't bother," she says to my reflection. "No one will notice."

All night, Frankie is a picture of good times and sunshine, telling Red and Jayne about girls who don't exist, games we never played, and movies we didn't watch, occasionally looking to me to add a supporting detail or an "Oh, I remember that! That was so funny!" Red and Jayne look on amused, a perfect snapshot of a normal summer vacation with their normal daughter and her normal best friend. What could be better?

"I'm so glad we took this trip together," Aunt Jayne says, reaching for Frankie's hand across the table at Shelly's Seaside Bistro. "We might just have to come back again next year."

"Maybe we can even get Helen and Carl to come," Uncle Red says.

"That sounds great, Mom!" Frankie shoots me another nasty stare. "Too bad we can't stay another few weeks, huh, Anna?"

I think about Sam and smile. "Yeah, it *is* too bad."

After dinner, the Perinos take us down to the pier. It must be everyone's last weekend on the beach — the place is packed.

"Crowded tonight." Red sidesteps to avoid colliding with a baby stroller. "Why don't we cross over to the other side of the beach. We haven't been down that way yet."

Well, maybe you *haven't. But your daughter and I are practically natives by now.*

We walk up the boulevard slowly, Frankie and I a few steps behind with clenched fists, our forced smiles betraying none of our private drama.

Aunt Jayne asks if we'd like to stop somewhere for dessert, and since nodding and smiling is easier than shaking our heads and inventing a reason for *not* wanting dessert, we okay it without thinking.

And since the universe has worked in its own mysterious way all vacation, tonight shouldn't be any different, which is why neither of us is particularly surprised to discover that Jayne is craving a smoothie.

twenty-seven

A jolt of simultaneous panic and excitement shoots through my body. At the moment, my head and my heart are duking it out, trying to decide whether I should be happy to see Sam or severely freaked out that if we don't execute some sort of rapid-fire planning in the next fifteen seconds, our entire Jackie-slash-Samantha cover will be blown. Frankie turns to me in utter fright, the first her expression has changed all night, and I curse myself for not thinking to lay the ground rules with Jake and Sam in advance.

Good evening, ladies and gentlemen! Welcome to Anna and Frankie's Hour of Lying Liars! We hope you've enjoyed our show thus far. In the unlikely event that we should happen upon you at your place of employ with Red and Jayne Perino in tow, simply pretend that you do not know us, or that you are the gay older brothers of our new best friends, Jackie and Samantha. Thank you, and good night!

Frankie's baby-bird eyebrow is all twisted up and afraid, and all I can do is shrug.

There's a long line to get a table at the Shack tonight but that doesn't deter Jayne. Thinking fast, I announce that I need to use the bathroom and push my way to the front of the line amid an angry series of "The line starts back there!" and "No cutting!"

Sam is at the counter, turning out smoothies in record time. It takes a few minutes for him to notice me, and I keep looking over my shoulder to make sure Red and Jayne can't see me from their spot at the back of the line.

"Anna!" He finally sees me as he sets two gigantic Strawberry Short-Shakes on a tray for an impatient waitress with a platinum blond ponytail and way too much eyeliner. "How'd you get out so early?"

He wipes his hands on his green Shack apron and comes around the counter to wrap me in a hug. I feel that same frightened-yet-thrilled electricity again and force my brain to quiet its emotional counterpart long enough for me to break free of Sam's embrace and tell him the five-second version of why he can't know I exist.

"Got it," he says, laughing. "But it's gonna cost you. You *better* come back tonight." I promise him that I will and head back through the line to find the Perinos, hoping the color in my cheeks returns to normal before they notice.

After telling twenty minutes of made-up stories about our chaste adventures on the beach, we're sitting in a cozy little booth, carefully examining the two-page smoothie and shake menu.

Frankie catches me staring at Sam and rolls her eyes at me above the menu.

I'm thinking about killing her.

The impatient platinum blond I saw earlier takes our order without once looking up from her pad. A few minutes later, Sam stands at the edge of our table, winking at me as he passes out our drinks.

Frankie kicks me under the table but I ignore her, reaching up to take my Va-Va-Vineapple smoothie (vanilla ice cream, fresh pineapple, and ginger ale). Sam's fingers brush against mine, sending a shock through my hand that I feel all the way up my arm.

Uncle Red thanks Sam, and seeing them breathing the same air and responding to each other's polite small talk is like seeing Frankie's fingers on my journal again — two very different and intentionally separate worlds colliding. I want to crawl down my smoothie straw and disappear in the sea of ice cream and ginger ale.

Once Sam returns to his post behind the counter, Frankie stops kicking me and we slurp down our drinks in about two minutes, anxious to get out of here before anyone recognizes us. Uncle Red and Aunt Jayne, on the other hand, act like this is the last smoothie shop they'll ever see, like smoothies are an endangered species to be appreciated and savored and drawn out as long as possible. With each passing minute, Frankie and I sink lower in our chairs, praying to the God of Annoying Coincidences that Jake doesn't show up and blow our cover.

After what feels like three hours, Red pays the bill and we're on our way back out to the anonymity of the crowded beach. I know it's risky, but I can't resist sneaking in one last goodbye. I suddenly remember that I have to use the bathroom again and wind my way back through the undulating smoothie line to get up to the counter. After confirming that I haven't been followed, I kneel on an empty counter stool and call Sam's name.

"So, midnight?" I ask.

"How about eleven?"

"Eleven-thirty," I say. "And that's final."

"Deal." He leans in and quickly kisses me on the lips, barely touching them before the frantic waitress shouts out another order for Sam.

"See you tonight." He smiles and turns back to the pastel buckets of ice cream behind the counter.

Frankie's waiting for me alone outside. "Took you long enough," she snaps. "My parents are getting postcards." She nods toward a newsstand.

"Everything okay?" Jayne asks when we catch up.

"Yeah," I say. "Just a little stuffed from the shakes. Frankie's worried that if she tries to get in the car too fast, her skirt will explode."

"Actually, Mom," Frankie says, "Anna was hanging back trying to get Smoothie Boy's cell number, but he dissed her."

"He didn't like the looks of my ugly stepsister," I say.

"That, and Anna doesn't have any boobs."

"Girls!" Jayne laughs. "What is *with* you two tonight? Is there a full moon or something?"

"I don't know, is Anna howling at it?"

"Okay, Twinkies." Uncle Red hands his postcards to Jayne and digs out his keys. "Let's head out. We still have tomorrow — I have something fun planned for our last night."

I nod. From behind Red and Jayne's trusting backs, Frankie Perino, journal-killer and two-time virgin liar — goes middle school on me and sticks out her tongue.

The time for thinking is over.

I *am* going to kill her.

Back at the house, Frankie spends over an hour in the bathroom getting ready for bed. I use the opportunity to set the vibrating alarm on my cell phone. I don't want to alert her when I'm trying to sneak out — the last thing I need is another stupid argument that could potentially wake up Red and Jayne. Alarm set, I stuff my phone under the pillow, turn out the bedside light, and pull the sheet over my head so I don't have to look at her tonight.

I don't remember hearing her come back from the bathroom, but suddenly my phone is buzzing against my cheek, shaking me from a light sleep. I use the display light on the screen to locate the flip-flops and sweatshirt I stashed under the bed earlier and notice that Frankie's bed is still made.

That means either she's asleep on the couch downstairs or she just can't stand the fact that I had sex before she did and she's out giving it up to Jake right this instant, determined to take back the center stage.

Downstairs, the empty couch and unlocked front door confirm it. I entertain the idea of locking her out and sneaking out the window over the deck, but I can imagine how that scene would play out. She'd come back and realize what happened, bang wildly on the door to wake her parents, and convince them that I threatened to sneak out to meet the Smoothie Boy and she was only trying to go after me and prevent me from doing something stupid (*sniffle*), just as a best friend ought to (*sniffle*), when she accidentally locked the door behind herself (*sniffle-sniffle-sigh*).

I follow the path we've taken so many times this summer — across the front, down the street, cut back through a neighbor's yard, down the stairs to the beach, past the pier, through the campfire labyrinth, up to the deck of the Shack, and straight into Sam's arms.

Without speaking, he kisses me hard on the mouth and I kiss him back, sobbing and crumpling into his chest like a broken puppet.

twenty-eight

"*A*nna, what's wrong? What happened?"

"Frankie. And. I. Aren't. Speaking!" It comes out in a string of hiccups.

"Did you have a fight?"

I nod, opening my mouth to tell him about it, but my brain intercepts with an urgent telegram: *Hey, dummy. Stop. Sam doesn't know about Matt. Stop. Cover blown. Stop.*

"There's so much I haven't told you, Sam. I don't even know where to start."

I pull away and lean against the deck railing to take a deep breath, watching the moon over the ocean. I wanted everything to be different here. I wanted to be someone else. Anna, cross-continental traveler, woman of passion and adventure! Not Anna, pathetic friend who breaks promises and writes letters to dead boys.

"Let's walk," he says, his hand warm and reassuring on my

shoulder. "And when you feel okay, you can tell me whatever you want to tell me."

"Okay."

We walk all the way up to Eddie's house before I've worked it out enough in my head to start talking.

"It's a long and crazy story, Sam."

"It's cool, Anna Abby. I'm here."

"Okay. So just over a year ago, there was this guy. I really liked him. I mean *really* — since I was a kid."

"Did Frankie know him?"

"The three of us were best friends. We basically grew up together."

"Complicated."

"Very. So anyway, last year on my birthday, he finally kissed me."

Sam stays quiet, focused on his feet taking off and landing against the sand. It feels strange to tell him about this for so many reasons, but the words are coming too fast for me to stop, even if I want to.

"We started hanging out all the time — even more than before. Every night. Only we didn't know how to tell Frankie, because we didn't want her to freak or feel left out or whatever."

"Makes sense," Sam says.

"He thought it would be better if he told her himself, so I promised him that I wouldn't say anything. But before he could talk to her about it, he —" I almost choke on the word, holding my hand against Sam's arm to stop our forward motion along the shore.

"What did he do?" Sam asks.

"He just — he — I'm sorry. Wait." The words of this story have passed a thousand times from my hand to the pages of my journal, but never from my lips to the ears of another living soul. I take a few deep breaths before I'm able to meet Sam's eyes and say it. "He died, Sam. He died from a heart defect that no one knew about."

I tell him about the car accident and wait for the automatic apology, the awkward bumbling, the silence, the farewell-I-can't-deal-with-this. But Sam just wipes my cheeks with his thumbs and hugs me.

"I kept my promise to him. I never told Frankie about us. But when we were at the Vista last night, she read my journal and found out."

Sam pulls away from me. "Wait, she's mad at you about *that*? But what about —"

"There's more, Sam." I shake my head. "Frankie was in the car, too. That's how she got the scar on her eyebrow. The three of us were totally inseparable. Matt is — Matt *was* — he's Frankie's brother."

Sam stares at me, eyes and mouth wide open. "Holy *sh* — I mean, *whoa*."

"He was going to tell her on their vacation here, when they'd have some time alone. He was so worried about how she'd feel — he wanted to make sure she was okay with it. They were supposed to leave, like, a month after we got together. I hated sneaking around behind her back, but I promised. A month didn't seem like that long to keep a secret.

"When he died, that was it. Anything I felt stopped mattering — Frankie lost her brother, and I was their best friend. It was simple. I would keep that secret forever." I take a deep breath, focusing on Sam's soft eyes.

"Anna, I can't believe this," he says gently. "I don't know what to say. I had no idea."

"Frankie and I didn't want to tell you guys. It was gonna be — I don't know, different here."

"What do you mean?"

"It's hard to explain. I guess people get freaked out about the whole death thing, and once they know about it, it's, like, the only thing they associate with you, and all they can do is feel sorry for you. Your whole existence is reduced to that one event."

A new wave of sadness plows into me when I think about all those nights in Frankie's room, not talking or doing anything. Sometimes after school we'd literally just sit on the floor with our backpacks still on, staring at the wall and crying.

The first few months at school were the worst — people whispering and making compassionate faces as we passed through the halls. Teachers and girls leaving flowers and notes in front of Matt's locker and looking the other way when we skipped class. Most people in our grade — including our so-called friends — avoided us as though death and sadness were contagious. Most of them didn't know about his heart, and no one could decide what was worse — losing a brother and friend, or surviving the car crash that supposedly killed him. No one knew the rules — what to say, whether it was okay to laugh or complain about things like parents and grades and new shoes when Frankie and I had "serious" problems. But by the middle of the year, Frankie was in full boy-lust mode, things got back to normal for everyone else, and the memory of Matt's death faded like the dried flowers stuck in the vents of his locker.

"God, Anna," Sam says, eyes still wide.

I nod. "We lost a lot of friends after it happened. For the past year it's basically been just me and her. And now, who knows?"

"She's probably just shocked. Maybe you should try to talk it out."

"Sam, she stole and *read* my journal. Then she chucked it into the water. And *then,* I found out she lied to me about — well, a bunch of stuff she shouldn't have lied about. I don't think we can work it out. I think we're — breaking up." My voice shakes, wavering between the dueling realms of anger and sadness.

"Come here." Sam puts his arms around me, wrapping me up in the smell of him. We stand in front of the ocean for a long time, his hand making circles on my back as I listen to his heart beat — strong and whole, like the waves.

"Thanks," I say, pulling away to wipe my eyes and let out about fourteen months of held-in breaths. "You're the only person I've actually told about Matt. Ironic, huh?"

Sam smiles. "Definitely not the 'What I Did on Summer Vacation' stuff I'm used to."

We stand silently, watching the waves for a while, holding hands. His thumb traces my palm gently, lulling me like the rocking of the water before us.

On the walk back, Sam tells me that I should give Frankie another chance.

"I'm not making excuses for her, but think about it. You're best friends, Anna."

"I don't know if I can. She lied to me about pretty major stuff. And she totally violated and destroyed my private thoughts."

"All I'm saying is that you both hurt each other. And you both lost someone you loved. Don't lose each other, too."

"Sure. I think I saw that After-School Special."

He smiles. "Just think about it, okay?"

We make plans to meet up tomorrow night for our final good-bye. Up on the street near the house, Sam kisses me and waits until I'm safely at the door before waving and turning back toward his end of the beach.

The door is still unlocked, and I assume Frankie isn't back yet, though I'm surprised we didn't run into her and Jake on our walk back. But when I get upstairs, Frankie's asleep in her bed as though she'd been there all along, her body rising and falling under the thin white sheet. The moon from the skylight throws her silhouette against the wall and reminds me of when we were kids, how we'd lie on her bed and make shadow puppets on the ceiling with our hands and a flashlight, chattering and giggling until Matt knocked on the wall from his room next door and told us to go to sleep.

twenty-nine

"Wake up, my lovelies." Red stands in our doorway, calling gently until our eyes open.

Frankie and I sit up slowly, untangling ourselves from twists of sheets and T-shirts. The first moments of being awake are neutral, as they always are, waiting for us to assign memory and meaning from the day before. In this blank zone I almost forget that I'm mad at Frankie. But it all comes back, and I stop the progression of the automatic smile across my cheeks just in time.

"Good morning, Twinkies," Red says. "Mom's making a big breakfast, so I hope you're hungry." He closes the door, silence blowing in around the space he leaves behind.

Frankie and I get out of our beds and pull on our sweatshirts. There's none of last night's unpleasantness — we simply don't speak. I want to ask her where she was last night, whether she slept with Jake, and what is going on with him. But I'm not about to break the cardinal rule of not speaking to each other just to gloat in the glory of my superior knowledge of and experience with the big *It,* which, thanks to my near nervous breakdown at the Shack last night, I completely forgot to do a second time.

Downstairs, we gorge ourselves on what is probably the best, most extravagant breakfast Aunt Jayne has ever made. The table is covered with fresh fruit, Jayne's magic vanilla French toast, eggs, potatoes, bacon, toast, muffins — everything we can't pack or leave behind. During the meal, we all laugh easily, fat and happy, talking about how much fun we've had on the trip. Everyone is tanned and relaxed, and entire *minutes* go by during which Frankie and I forget to be mad at each other. It starts with "Can you pass the butter?" and goes as far as laughing together about that first night on the beach, making sand angels with Aunt Jayne.

There are tiny fractures of time in which I want to hug her, tell her I'm sorry, tell her about my promise, put the whole thing behind me. But then I see a flash — her reading my journal in that mocking voice, her chucking it into the ocean like a flat skipping stone — and the mad and hurt come right back again. For the sake of Red, Jayne, and our last day on the beach, I'm willing to put my feelings on hold.

But I can't make them disappear.

After breakfast, we're sucked into the swirling tides of torture otherwise known as Uncle Red's Day of Fun.

First up: hard-core paddleball. Me and Red versus Frankie and Jayne.

"Come on, Dad," Frankie whines as Red passes out the flat wooden paddles. "Isn't this a little childish?"

"Sure," he says, smiling. "But last time I checked, you're still my child."

"But Da-aad!" Frankie crinkles her eyebrows and tries to work some sympathy magic on Uncle Red, but he's immune today.

"Humor your old dad, Francesca," he says, lobbing the rubber ball in her direction.

After half an hour of forced family fun, in which I score fifty points and take out at least seventy-five percent of my anger trying to blast Frankie with the ball, our game is cut short. Princess gets stung on the top of her foot by a teeny-tiny newborn baby of a jellyfish and carries on like some shark just swam away with her torso. For one brief moment I wonder if it's the ghost of my journal, reincarnated after its watery death to claim vengeance by stabbing her with its thin metal spiral. The thought makes me smile on the inside, just a little bit.

There's so much whining and limping that even *I* start to feel bad for her. I help Red get her back up to the house where she can be appropriately fed and doted upon.

My reign of paddleball terror waylaid by the tragic jellyfish incident, we spend the rest of the afternoon playing Monopoly, far away from the dangerous denizens of the deep. Frankie doesn't deal me an extra grand this time. She keeps her leg propped on pillows in a chair across from her, icing the dime-sized injury on her foot with much fanfare and taking full advantage of my temporary sympathy by asking me with a sugar-sweet smile to refill her lemonade, adjust her pillow, or find her ChapStick.

"You always take such good care of her, Anna." Aunt Jayne pats me on the knee as she brings us bowls of chocolate ice cream. "Frankie, you're lucky she puts up with you."

"Yeah, lucky," Frankie says. "Um, Anna?"

I look up from my ice-cream bowl, heart slightly thawed, considering whether to accept the overdue apology that's certain to emanate from her mouth any minute.

"Anna?"

Any minute now.

"Yeah, Frank?"

Here it comes.

"I have hotels on Broadway and Park." She holds out her hand and flutters her eyes. "You owe me twelve hundred bucks."

"How's the patient?" Uncle Red asks when we tire of Monopoly.

Frankie makes a show of readjusting her foot pillow and shaking the ice in her glass to signal a lemonade refill request.

"I'm okay, I guess," she says. "It still really stings, though."

"Do you think you can walk?" he asks.

"I don't know, Dad. I probably shouldn't risk it. I don't want it to get worse."

Must. Resist. Urge. To dump lemonade on her pretty little head.

"That's a shame," Red says with a shrug. "I guess we'll have to cancel our plans tonight."

"I guess so," Frankie says, snatching her lemonade from my hand and sighing like she's carrying the weight of the world on her tanned little shoulders.

"That's too bad," Aunt Jayne says. "What are we going to do with those fifth-row tickets, hon?"

"What tickets?" Frankie and I ask simultaneously.

"Oh, just some little show at the Fillmore in San Francisco. Airplane Pilots?" Red pulls four tickets from an envelope on the kitchen counter. "Oh, *Helicopter* Pilot, that's it. Probably a local group. I'm sure you guys haven't heard of them."

"*What?!*" Frankie and I temporarily suspend our mutual hatred long enough to exchange a pair of beaming smiles.

"HP is only, like, our number one favorite band in the universe!" Frankie says. "They're not even on tour now. How did you get tickets?"

"It's a benefit concert," he says. "Mom found out about it last month and thought you'd like to go. It's just unfortunate you're immobile. I'll have to call the box office and see if we can get a refund."

"No!" Frankie and I practically trip over each other to tackle Red before he gets to the phone.

"But, my darling daughter, you're *severely* injured." Red points to the tiny pink mound on her foot. "You certainly can't go to a concert in your condition, let alone get all dressed up for dinner at Fleur de Lys. Everyone will see your nearly amputated limb."

"Dad!" Frankie protests. "It's not amputated! And I — wait —" She walks gingerly across the living room and back, her limp fading with each step until it's totally gone. "Yes, I'm feeling much better now. It was probably the ice and everything. I'm completely convalexed."

"Convalesced," I say.

"Come on, Dad!" Frankie says, ignoring me.

"Please, Uncle Red?" Loyalty be damned — I'm fully prepared to leave Frankie home if that's what it takes to get a fancy French meal and a concert in San Francisco with my number one favorite band in the universe. Seeing lead guitarist Brandon Barry's crazy curly black hair from the fifth row takes priority over fake jellyfish injuries.

Uncle Red fans himself with the tickets and takes a deep breath. "You two better get moving. We leave in an hour and a half."

"Yeah!" I jump up and down like a little girl. Frankie follows suit, but stops herself midway, suddenly remembering her *painful* injury.

"I mean, cool! Thanks, Dad." She kisses Uncle Red on the cheek and follows me upstairs to begin the arduous beautification process a fancy dinner and favorite band concert require.

We manage to work around each other for showers, hair, and makeup, but even a mad Frankie can't leave wardrobe to chance.

"Anna, I know things aren't great right now," she says. "But we need to confer on outfits. We have to coordinate in tone and style. And also, I need to borrow your silver dangle earrings."

"Whatever you say." I'm resigned to Frankie's Fashion Hour. At least I can take comfort in the fact that she won't risk making me look bad — that could make *her* look bad, just by association.

We decide on all black with pink and silver accessories. Actually, *she* decides on all black with pink and silver accessories. I just nod and smile. Nod. Smile. Soon we'll be in the fifth row at the HP concert and none of this will matter.

Frankie puts on a slip dress with a lightly beaded neckline, a pink headband scarf, and my silver dangle earrings. Of course she looks stunning.

She dresses me in a black mini and camisole with a pink scarf tied around my hips, a silver necklace with a small heart dropping from the center, and matching heart earrings.

"You should wear your hair up," she says, eyeing me up and down. "You have really nice shoulders. You gotta show them off."

I twist my hair up with black hair sticks and pull a few tendrils down in front.

"Perfect," she says, actually smiling at me. "What about me? Is this okay?" She smoothes her hands over her stomach in the mirror, and for a single second I see a flash of old-Frankie vulnerability. It hits me like a fist, and I have to look away to keep myself from hugging her in the gushing apology that *she* owes *me*.

"You look great, Frank," I say, focusing on her shoes. "Really."

"Thanks, Anna. You do, too. Hey, we can't take the camera to the concert, but maybe we should get a few shots in here? I mean, we look *really* good."

"Sure, Frank. Here." I take the camera from her bag and get some footage of her ensemble from a few different angles. She does the same to me, narrating the plan for the rest of the evening before shutting off the camera and stowing it back in the case.

"Okay, that should do it," she says. "Ready?"

San Francisco looks totally different at night, especially when it's not raining — all lit up and magic. Uncle Red and Aunt Jayne point out sites that Frankie and I saw on our bus trip, but I smile and ask enough questions to look like a novice.

"You two look beautiful," Jayne says. "This is going to be a great night."

*   *   *

Dinner at Fleur de Lys is a jumble of creamy, decadent foods that I can't pronounce but have no trouble inhaling. I've never seen this type of food on menus back home — probably because people like our ketchup-n-mustard, festival-loving neighbors would stage a protest. *Bring back our beef! Down with escargots!*

Frankie and I manage to put all nastiness aside for the evening, solely for the sake of Red, Jayne, and the beautiful boys of HP. We aren't exactly friendly, but we aren't plotting ways to poison each other's dinner, either.

"You girls are awful quiet," Red says after the desserts arrive. "I thought you'd be more chatty on the way to see your favorite band in the universe."

"Just eating," Frankie covers, forcing a smile at me as she scoops up a spoonful of crème brulée.

The Fillmore is packed, and Uncle Red has to escort a few party-crashers from our prime fifth-row seats. We get settled in just in time to eye up the stage before the lights dim.

"Ladies and gentlemen," a voice booms from everywhere, "let's hear it for tonight's openers, Plazma!"

All around us the auditorium roars to life, pumping its collective fist at Plazma. They get the crowd rocking and primed for HP with lots of long guitar riffs and cool lighting effects. Frankie and I stay seated through most of the hour-long set, saving our energy for the main event. A few times I feel her looking at me, but when I turn to meet her eyes, she looks away.

After Plazma's final set, the houselights come up while the crew sets up for HP. I think briefly about dragging Frankie to the bathroom and finally settling this thing but change my mind when I see her chatting happily with her parents, telling them everything they need to know about our favorite band.

Matt's the one who introduced us to HP a few years ago. They weren't even popular yet, but he'd been a fan in the early years before they were a group, back when Joe did mostly solo stuff out of local bars in Buffalo. He'd call us into his room and play these random tracks he found online, blasting notes and beats from his speakers. If it was late at night, he'd pass around his headphones, bobbing his head until we caught on and followed suit. Frankie and I liked them immediately, though I no longer remember whether it was because we really *got* their music or because we just *believed* Matt, pulled into his contagious sunshine enthusiasm without question. Either way, it didn't take long for HP to become our favorite group. By the time they released their first mainstream album, we were old fans, thanks to Matt.

By the time they released their second album, Matt and I had already kissed. He surprised me with a copy of it the next day, all the lyrics printed out and stapled together. *Read them, Anna. Really read them.*

By the time they released their third album, Matt was gone.

He never got to see them in concert.

"All right, y'all," Plazma's lead singer comes back onstage, nearly hoarse after their intense set. "Put your hands together for those badass East Coast rockers we're all here to see — Joe, Brandon, Jay, and Scotty-O! Helicopter Pilot! Make some *noise*!"

Frankie and I are up from our seats with the rest of the auditorium, cheering and screaming and shouting our unrequited love. Even Red and Jayne are clapping along, bumping hips and laughing in that awkward dance that parents do when they're trying to be cool, but I'm happy to be here with them.

For three hours, Frankie and I sing and dance and laugh until our breath runs out, our hair falls, and our makeup fades. Nothing else matters — not my drowned journal or Matt or Johan or Jake or any of the secrets and lies between us. It's just us and the music, the universal language of love and hope and loss and everything else.

After two standing ovations and two encores, Helicopter Pilot finishes with their classic first single, "Heart Shadow." When Matt died, Frankie and I listened to it over and over in her room, drowning out the din of murmuring sympathies downstairs. I haven't been able to listen to it since those long, dark days, and the first words yank me right back there, right back to her room, right back to us, two broken dolls falling on the floor against the bed.

Black heart shadow,
Set my mind on fire, suffocated by the ashes.
Black heart shadow,
Spin around laughing as the space you fill collapses,
Spinning in circles as the space you left collapses.

When I think back to last year, those times in Frankie's room when we just wanted the world to end, I can't believe how much she's changed. Maybe Dad was right to say that Red and Jayne aren't dealing with her. But maybe Frankie Perino doesn't *need* her parents to deal with her.

I watch as she closes her eyes and sways in time with the most painful song in our shared history, drifting to that faraway place where I can't follow.

I watch her waving arms and the borrowed earrings that dangle in her auburn hair.

I watch her and think, maybe Frankie Perino doesn't need *me,* either.

"Meet us out front as soon as you're done," Uncle Red says as he heads to the parking lot after the show. Frankie and I line up at the souvenir booths to get HP T-shirts, standing in silence as we inch forward, still buzzing and alive from the show. There's not much anger left between us, just a great divide — like best friends in high school who go to different colleges, lose touch, and move on in parallel lives that never cross until years later, in a random bar or grocery store, and after a brief hug and five minutes of small talk, they both realize that the threads that connected them so long ago have frayed and blown away, leaving nothing to discuss.

So they nod and smile.

And bid one another farewell.

Wandering through my own thoughts, I lose Frankie when the line splits into several clusters down a long table of sweatshirts, T-shirts, CDs, and bumper stickers. I buy a black HP shirt and walk to the other end of the crowded table in search of Frankie. Beyond a group of middle-school girls trying on every single baby-doll shirt in the pile, I spot the back of Frankie's head tilted in the undeniable position of a kiss. A tattooed arm presses into her back, his other hand firmly on her butt.

I've seen this disappearing before — the night of the Spring Send-off when she ditched me for Johan for two hours. I feel like I should hide in the shadows of the punch bowl table until she's done. From the looks of it, she's getting farther with Tattoo Boy near the T-shirt table than she did with Johan on the soccer field.

I give her two more minutes before issuing a warning shot in the form of a cough. She unhooks her lips from her new friend long enough for a *"What?"*

"Our ride is here," I say.

She turns back to the guy. "The limo driver doesn't like to wait," she tells him.

He shrugs and lets her go, one hand still hovering near her ass.

"This is Rat," she tells me. "He's the Plazma bass player. You know, the *openers?* He's, like, totally close with Jay Garra in HP. He *was* going to introduce us, before you interrupted."

"Um, okay. Cool." I don't bother telling her that the Plazma bass player doesn't have tattoos — something I noticed easily from our fifth-row vantage point.

"Garra's got a way with the ladies," the Plazma wannabe announces with a wink. "So do I — it's a bass player thing. What's *your* name?"

"My name is Leaving. Leaving Now." I grab Frankie's hand and pull her toward a row of cars lined up in front of the exit as she blows a kiss to Rat.

"That makes, what, seven for me and — *how* many for you?

Just one, right?" She yanks her hand away and throws a satisfied smirk in my direction.

"That's right, Frank. One for me. Just one." I smile and head to the car with my HP shirt tucked securely under my arm, the beats from Scotty-O's intense drum solos still pounding inside my chest.

thirty

*I*t's bedtime on the eve of our departure. I change into my new shirt and a pair of jean shorts and slip between the sheets, but I've no intention of spending my last few hours in Zanzibar Bay sleeping near Frankie. Before turning off the light, I again set my phone alarm on vibrate and tuck it carefully under my pillow, T minus one hour and forty-five minutes.

I'm totally awake when it buzzes against my cheek. This time, Frankie's in bed where she belongs, mummified in the sheets and sound asleep.

Already dressed, I grab my flip-flops and sneak out of the room. I do a quick hair and breath check in the downstairs bathroom and wind my way over the familiar path to the Shack — to Sam — one last time.

Sam and I walk back out to the Vista and spread out a blanket in the sand, hoping for the same seclusion we found the other night. I

tell him about dinner and the Helicopter Pilot show, from which
I'm still radiating.

"Does this mean you and Frankie are speaking again?" He
plays with a loop of my hair, wrapping and unwrapping it around
his finger.

"Sort of," I say. "Well, no — not really. It was kind of a temporary stay of execution."

"I'm sure you'll work it out eventually."

I sigh. "Let's not talk about Frankie right now."

Sam nods and pulls me closer. We curl up together on the blanket, watching the stars and not talking. I'm lost in the night sky,
floating overhead and seeing us from above, following in the dust
of a shooting star.

"It's going to be weird when you go," Sam says, squeezing my
fingers and pulling me back to earth.

"Don't think about it yet. We still have a few hours."

He smiles and kisses me, slowly moving us into the same position as the other night. This time, I *don't* forget. This time, as he
lies on top of me, pressing his bare stomach against mine, pressing
me against the blanket and the blanket against the sand, I realize
it's no longer something I must endure; no longer a mysterious passage from point A to point B that will allow me to move forward in
an otherwise stalled life.

The air is warm, the waves blowing kisses at our feet. Out on
the horizon, the sun starts hinting as the moon still glows, their
light momentarily occupying the same space, each one making the
other more enchanting. As the stars slowly fade to make room for
the pink of morning, I know that this is probably the last time I'll
see him, and that no matter what my life brings, it will never again

be more special than it is in this moment, day and night simultaneously lighting up the black ocean just for us.

I pull Sam's sweatshirt on over my bare skin and lie next to him on the blanket, staring at the sky.

"It's strange," I say, rubbing my feet against his. "I feel like I should be sad, but I'm not. It's not that I won't miss you, but it just feels like —"

"Like everything is okay anyway," he says, finishing my thought.

I smile. "Sam, thanks for listening to me yesterday. You know, about Frankie and Matt and all that stuff that happened."

"Don't thank me," Sam says.

"You know she got stung by a jellyfish?" I laugh, thinking back on the theatrics.

"The invincible Frankie was taken down by a *jellyfish?*"

"A baby one. But when Red told us about the concert, she was magically cured. It was quite a miracle, really."

Sam laughs, locking eyes with me before pulling me on top of him for one last time.

After, the light sky tells me it's time to head back. I still have to pack, and Red and Jayne will wake up soon to start loading the car for our return trip.

I slip back into my own clothes and return Sam's sweatshirt.

"Keep it," he says. "Something to remember me by."

"I don't need a sweatshirt for that," I say, already putting it back on.

"Then keep it because it's cool."

"Deal."

Sam packs up his blanket and turns in the direction of our beach house, reaching for my hand.

"I'm gonna walk back alone this time," I say. "I want to say goodbye to the beach. Besides, they're going to be up soon."

Sam nods, slipping his hands behind my neck and pulling me into a deep kiss.

"See you around, Anna Abby from New Yawk," he whispers.

I touch my fingers to his lips, look into his eyes for the last time, and walk away along the shore. I turn back only once, watching him move down the beach until he fades into a thin beige line, a black dot where his T-shirt ought to be.

I really don't even know you, and yet, in my life, you are forever entangled; to my history, inextricably bound.

Back home, everyone is still asleep. My body is exhausted, but in this moment I feel too alive to sleep. Instead, I walk in through the front, cross the main floor, and open the sliding deck door to head back outside.

The sun isn't fully up yet and the air is still cold, infused with tiny drops of ocean mist. I walk barefoot across the wet grass like I did on our first day and situate myself on the bottom step, letting myself become hypnotized by the lull of the waves. A lone seagull paces the shoreline in front of me like he's waiting for news, but all other land, air, and sea residents are in hiding, leaving me alone with the gull to think about all the times I could have told Frankie about how I accidentally fell in love with her brother.

The night of my birthday party, before the promise, I could have pulled her back into the house under the guise of a female crisis and told her about my wish and how it came true.

All those times at the house, stealing looks at Matt over dinner. Borrowing his books. Hanging out in his room, waiting for her to interrupt. We could have sat her down and told her.

I could have told her after the funeral, as we locked ourselves in her bedroom and listened to Helicopter Pilot CDs.

Or when she told me that made-up story about Johan.

All those times, I couldn't protect her; not from the one thing that really mattered — losing Matt.

I could only protect her from the secret. I could only shield her from the knowing; from the imagining; from the inevitable suffering attached to those endless what-ifs.

What if he didn't die?

What if it didn't mean anything?

What if it meant everything?

One night, Matt kissed me. The next few weeks shot through me in a blur, a bullet speeding at the sky with no end in sight. When he pulled me close to him behind the house that first night, I saw our whole life together in the flash of his lips on mine; living next door to Frankie and her future husband so that our kids could grow up best friends and Twinkies like all of us.

But when he died, I saw — *nothing.* There was nothing left to see. It happened and it was impossible and beautiful and then it ended before it even really began, leaving nothing behind but secrets and broken hearts.

And in this moment of pale dawn in the hours before we leave California, I finally realize what has been the hardest thing for me about Matt's death. It isn't that I lost a brother, like Frankie, or a son, like Aunt Jayne and Uncle Red. The hardest thing is that I'll never know exactly *what* I lost, how much it should hurt, how long

I should keep thinking about him. He took that mystery with him when he died, and a hundred thousand one-sided letters in my journal wouldn't have brought me any closer to the truth than I was the night I pressed my fingers to the sea glass he wore around his neck and kissed him back.

For over a year, the letters were my only connection to him; the only evidence that I didn't imagine our brief time as *other*. When I first saw my journal helplessly floating on the waves, I felt a loss so immediate and overwhelming it was like being back in the hospital lobby when the doctor told us they couldn't fix him. One minute, the journal was in my hands, soft and familiar and real; the next minute, it was gone.

Just like Matt.

And just like Matt, I need to let it go.

thirty-one

*T*he sun peeks out from the morning haze behind me, turning the sky light orange. It's still cold, and I pull the sleeves of Sam's sweatshirt over my hands to warm up my fingers. When a silent shadow falls over the stairs and spills onto the sand next to me, I jump.

"Frankie? When did you get here?"

"Just now," she says, her bare arms crossed over her thin cotton T-shirt, eyes red. "I woke up last night and you were gone. When you didn't come back first thing this morning, I got scared."

I pat the step, motioning for her to sit next to me. She inhales deeply, triggering a chain reaction of sobs.

"I'm sorry, Anna. I'm so sorry. I came out here the other night to see if your journal washed up on the shore, but no luck. I never meant for it to happen like that."

It stings, and I want to walk away. To let it all go. To forget.

But Frankie and I are essentially on equal footing. I owe her just as much an explanation as she owes me.

"Why did you read it, Frankie? Why did you take it in the first place?"

She tells me that when she put her camera away at the party, she saw the journal sticking out of my backpack. She was drunk and wanted to see if I'd written anything about Sam.

"I never expected to find stuff about — well, what I found."

"Frankie, I *know* I should have told you about Matt. But he wanted to tell you himself, and I promised I wouldn't say anything. He wanted to be sure you were okay with it. He thought it would be best to wait until you had some time alone with him in California. That's the only reason I didn't tell you sooner.

"Then, the night before you left for California, everything happened so fast — I didn't want to disappoint him. I didn't want to break my promise. I didn't want you to hurt anymore. I wanted to be there and —"

"It doesn't matter, Anna," she says. "Matt was my *brother*. And I'm supposed to be your best friend. It hurts me that you kept a secret like that. You should've told me."

I look down the shore as the sun stretches over us. The runners are out now, following their familiar courses along the hard-packed sand close to the water. Two women pass us side by side, serious and intent and breathless.

I know I should've told Frankie. I *wanted* to tell her. And I — Matt — we — *would* have told her, but then . . . When I promised Matt I wouldn't say anything, I didn't know it would be for all eternity. If I thought he was going to die before confessing to his little sister, I would've added some fine print to our agreement.

"I'm sorry, Frank. I should have told you. But —"

"A whole month," Frankie continues. "And not just that, but all the time before, all the time you loved him. You never told me about your feelings for him. It's like all the times we hung out, he wasn't your friend. It was always something more for you. It was always a lie."

A lie? It hits me like a sledgehammer, releasing all the hurt and sadness and confusion I've held inside for the last fourteen months. I jump up without speaking and bolt to the shore, unable to hold it in any longer.

"How could you leave us like this?" I bawl at the sky, tears spilling into my mouth, ignoring the blurred runners who pass behind me without slowing. *Just another drunk little girl,* they must think. "Tell her!" I shout. "Tell her you made me promise! Tell her it's your fault! Tell her it was a lie for you, too! Tell her you loved me!"

Tell me *you loved me.*

I look out over the ocean, all the way to Japan, waiting for an answer.

Shhh, ahhh. Shhh, ahhh.

Nothing.

"Anna, I'm sorry, all right?" Frankie stands at the edge of the tide in tears, pulling the sleeve of Sam's sweatshirt against my wrist. Her eyes are heavy, old, the broken brow sagging and listless.

"Please, Anna. Don't," she says, wiping her eyes with her free hand. And just as quickly as it arose, the fight in me is gone.

"How can you say it was all a lie?" I ask, just above a whisper. "Matt was my best friend. I loved him that way *always*. 'We have to look out for her.' That was the last thing he said to me alone. And then he died. What was I supposed to do, Frank? Tell me?"

She crosses her arms over her chest and looks down the shore. The waves have reached our feet, icy and blue. It hurts my toes, but it's real and here and now and I need to feel it.

"You don't need to protect me, Anna. I'm *fine*." She steps back to clear her toes from the waves, shivering in her pink-and-white HP T-shirt, her knees touching to block the cold, her messy hair blowing into her eyes.

"What are you talking about?" I ask. "Your life is totally out of control, Frankie. You haven't told the truth about a single thing since Matt died."

Frankie nods slowly, refusing to look at me. She folds herself into the sand, wrapping her arms around her knees and rubbing her bracelet like she did in the hospital when Matt died.

I sit next to her and dig my feet into the sand, blowing into my hands to warm my fingers.

"Truth," Frankie says, nodding.

"Truth."

"When Johan and I got out to the field, he told me all about Maria and how heartbroken he was. At the end of it, I tried to kiss him. I thought that's what he wanted, but he just pushed me away. He said he was sorry, but he was still in love with her. I was so embarrassed that I didn't even want to go back to the dance. When we got inside, everyone was making comments and jokes and just assumed that we did it — even *you*. It was easier to go along with it than to tell the truth — that I wasn't good enough for him. I was going to tell you, but the stories just went on and on and I couldn't deal with it.

"With Jake, we messed around a lot at first, on the nights we snuck out. We almost slept together a few times, and I figured we would sooner or later anyway. So that one night when you asked me about it, it was kind of easier for me to say yes. I'm supposed to be the experienced one, right?"

I shrug, digging sand tunnels with my toes. "I guess."

"Then, he wanted to do it at the party, but I was drunk, and I didn't want to. I told him we could the next night. But when I got out there, I still didn't want to. I don't know why, I mean, we were alone on the beach and he's really hot and everything. I just — something stopped me. Maybe it's like you said — things were getting out of control, you and I were fighting, and I couldn't really think about anything else. But that was basically it. He didn't want to see me after that."

She's crying again, and my heart breaks for her. Everything is so screwed up — I don't know how to make things better anymore.

"Frankie, I'm truly sorry. I never meant to hurt you. Matt and I just —"

"No, Anna. You don't have to say anything." She shakes her head. "I read the journal. You don't have to tell me. It doesn't matter anymore. Matt's just — he's dead."

"There isn't a second that goes by that I don't know that. I'm just trying to tell you that I —"

"I can't," she whispers, squeezing my hand. "Please, Anna. Don't."

I don't want to keep hurting her, so I do what I do best.

I just swallow hard.

Nod and smile.

One foot in front of the other.

I'm fine, thanks for not asking.

We stand up and dust the damp sand off our legs, tenuously agreeing to try. To accept. To move on. To not talk about it.

"We should go in," she says. "They're going to wake up, and we haven't even started packing."

I nod, following her back to the stairs and into the house.

After packing our bags, cleaning our room, and eating a light breakfast with Uncle Red and Aunt Jayne, I take a final walk out to the ocean — my sad blue secret keeper. She's witnessed everything on this trip — albatross cast off, secrets unleashed, history destroyed, love and friendships found and broken — yet she remains the same. Reassuring. Undying.

Shhhhhhhhh.

"Goodbye," I whisper to many things at once. The water kisses my toes as the ghosts of our memories fade from the house like wet footprints, the curtains of Matt's attic room above the beach closed tight against the sun.

thirty-two

*T*he trip back home is like watching a highlights reel of our arrival in quick reverse. From the car, we turn to watch the fiery orange windows of the house vanish behind the palm trees until only the tip of the wooden iceberg roof remains. The road winds farther down and the house is all but erased, back to the photographs and fairy tales from which it sprang.

We don't stop on Moonlight Boulevard to say goodbye to Breeze or Sweet Caroline's or the postcard stand or the tourists in their lime green spandex, but Red slows down for Jayne to snap a picture of the sign posted on the far end of town.

> **YOU ARE LEAVING ZANZIBAR BAY**
> **THANKS FOR STOPPING BY!**

Along the highway, Red pulls over at the lookout where we first saw the harbor seals on our arrival, insisting that we take another official family vacation photo for comparison's sake.

The seals are right where we left them, barking and playing on the shore.

The guardrail and the informational sign and the worn picnic table are right where they've always been.

The dolomite boulders still protect the cliff from collapsing into the sea like they've done for tens of thousands of years.

My entire life has changed in the span of three weeks, but as the seals howl against the Pacific, everything around me remains exactly the same.

"You guys okay?" Uncle Red asks us when we're buckled back into the car. "I'm surprised you're not documenting this."

"Just tired," Frankie says, ignoring the camera in her backpack.

"I don't want to leave, either," Aunt Jayne says. "But I bet we'll take another trip next year."

We nod like robots and look out our separate windows from the backseat.

At the airport, we return the rental car, check in, and rush through security amid the same flux of reunions and breakups we witnessed on the way here. Same people. Same hellos and goodbyes. Same beginnings and endings. Same befores and afters.

We get to the gate with time for a Jack's Java run, but Frankie and I order separately. We don't do any mock interviews. We don't make up stories about the other waiting passengers. We drink our expensive coffee milk shakes and try to stay awake long enough to board the plane without falling down dead.

Soon we're in our seats, listening to crewmember instructions and following along with the passenger safety information card conveniently located in our seatback pockets.

Frankie lets me have the window seat again and promptly passes out against my shoulder, listening to the new HP playlist she made on her iPod after the concert. As I watch the white dots of sailboats disappear into the vast blue ocean, the Golden Gate bridge becomes a series of suspended red matchsticks, and I think about Mom and Dad, wondering whether they'll notice how much I've aged in these three short weeks. Will I look or talk or walk different? Will they *know*?

Yes, Anna was such a sweet girl, but that was before the incident. We'd rather not talk about it.

We get home after midnight East Coast time and it takes all my remaining energy to say goodbye to the Perinos, hug Mom and Dad hello, and drag myself up to my room. Save for a set of clean sheets on the bed, my room is exactly as I left it — familiar, comfortable, and expected. I know which boards in the floor will creak under my steps. I know which drawer holds my socks. I know which monsters live in the closet and which under the bed, and when I crawl between my sheets and lay my head against my old, lumpy pillow, I pull my sheets up to my chin, close my eyes, and allow myself to think that maybe I never left this safe, boring place with its old predictable ghosts.

thirty-three

*M*orning comes too soon, Mom buzzing around my room to wake me out of a deep sleep so we can have breakfast together and talk about the trip. I sit up and take in the familiar walls, remembering that I'm no longer two thousand miles across the country in a beach rental house.

The clock says eleven a.m. Ten hours isn't nearly enough to repay the sleep deficit I've built up these past few weeks, but Mom is too excited about making up for lost quality time.

Downstairs, Dad's at the table with the newspaper, surrounded by covered dishes. In honor of such a triumphant return from such a wholesome family vacation in which I did not experiment with alcohol, boys, curfew breaking, or walking outside without ample applications of sunscreen, Mom prepared a breakfast fit for kings and angel daughters alike.

I pull up my usual chair, load up a plate, and tell them all about the trip. Rather, the PG version, focusing on activities coordinated by Red and Jayne and a few strategically placed mentions of Jackie and Samantha (whose parents were of course very strict). I talk about the seafood we ate and that night when the waiter dumped the pitcher of water on Frankie's sunburn. I even tell them about the sand angels we made with Aunt Jayne. I describe the ocean and the house and Moonlight Boulevard with its eclectic mix of tourists and locals, finding it extremely challenging to reminisce without mentioning Sam and the Va-Va-Vineapple smoothie I plan to re-create in the blender later.

"It sounds beautiful, Anna," Mom says, pouring herself more coffee.

"So, anything new around here?" I ask, hoping I don't accidentally mention Sam.

"Dad has some news." Mom smiles at Dad across the table.

"Remember right before you left I won the Hoover House listing — that old mansion out on Route Five?" Dad asks. "Well, I sold it. One week flat, and we had a huge bidding war, just like I predicted."

"Dad, that's great! Congratulations."

"I'm taking us all out to celebrate tonight. The Perinos, too. Sound fun?"

I catch myself shrugging and quickly turn it into a happy nod.

"Where is Frankie, anyway?" Dad asks. "It's almost noon. I'm surprised you two can stand the separation."

I take a deep breath and gulp down some orange juice.

Well, Dad, first Frankie lied to me about losing her virginity to the foreign exchange student on the soccer field, and how your first time can't be special and all that. Then we decided to have this twenty boy contest but we only met, like, half, and she lied again about sleeping with one of them when really they just kind of fooled around naked and broke up. Meanwhile, when I was casting off my virginity with boy number five (or was he six?), Frankie read my journal and found out that I was in love with Matt for a million years and by the way, right after you took that picture of us with all the cake and frosting, he kissed me and started this whole long thing that we weren't allowed to tell her about. Frankie was so mad that she threw my journal into the bottom of the ocean, where it is banished for all eternity with a lovesick mermaid who cries out pieces of sea glass. Are you going to eat that bacon?

Dad prepares his toast, careful not to get crumbs in the butter, politely awaiting my response.

"I'll probably see her later," I say.

"Good. We already told Red and Jayne about dinner. You know, Anna, you look different." He watches me a moment longer than usual.

"What do you mean?" I hope my voice doesn't betray any guilt about the aforementioned "incident," which will completely evade his Dad-sensors, but Mom will be all over it.

"Hmm. Tan. And relaxed."

Mom nods. "We should have sent you away a long time ago."

"Ha-*ha*." Sometimes I think I'm an alien that accidentally fell off the mother ship, destined to wander among clueless earthling parents for all eternity.

After the breakfast play-by-play, it's time for the daunting task of unpacking three weeks' worth of dirty secrets. I mean *clothes*. Dirty clothes.

I start by dumping the entire contents of my suitcase — including about five gallons of sand — on my bed.

I separate out all of the nonclothes — a random assortment of beach glass, shells, and sand dollars; the striped beach stone Frankie gave me on our first day; iPod; cell phone; postcards I never mailed; a San Francisco magnet for my locker next year; the book of ocean poems from City Lights; and the takeout menu from Smoothie Shack with Sam's e-mail address scribbled in the bottom corner.

I start a new jar for my beach glass and stick the menu in the bottom of the sock drawer where Mom won't see it. Everything else finds a place in my room as if it had been here all along — even Sam's sweatshirt folds effortlessly into my drawer among the others like they are old friends reuniting after a long separation.

It still smells like him. I leave it near the top so I can wear it tonight after Mom and Dad are safely tucked away in their blissfully clueless bedroom.

I open my window and slide up the screen, hoping I can shake the sand out of some of my clothes without the breeze blowing it back into my face. I spot Frankie lying out in her backyard, perpetuating her gorgeous tan. She flips through an issue of *Celeb Style* and drops it on the stack in the adjacent lounge chair formerly known as mine.

The magazine causes an avalanche, sliding off the chair and into the grass, taking three or four others with it. She leans over to grab them but can't reach without getting out of her chair, opting instead to knock the rest of the pile into the grass and roll over on her side.

There is no expertly posed flat stomach, glistening parted lips, slightly bent legs, or heaving bosom.

There is no sparkling sand.

No roaring ocean.

No drooling, whistling boys.

Just Frankie and my empty lounge chair.

It hurts to watch, and I feel guilty for lingering in the shadows of my room like a stalker.

"Frank!" I yell down to her. "I'm coming over."

Frankie meets me in her kitchen, grabbing two Diet Cokes on our way upstairs.

It seems like years since I've been here, and the maroons and purples of her Moroccan room are a comfortable homecoming.

I sit on the bed, pulling my legs under me. Her video camera is connected to the computer on her desk, transferring the evidence of our Absolute Best Summer Ever to her hard drive.

"We can watch it later if you want," she says, nodding at the camera as she pulls a pair of boxers over her swimsuit and sits in front of the vanity. Last time I was here, I watched her get glammed up for trip planning night in front of the big mirror behind her.

I shrug. We look at each other, then away. At each other. Then away. We open our Diet Cokes and take a few sips. Neither speaks. Then both at the same time.

"Frankie, I" and "Anna, I," awkward and strained. We've never been in this place before. We don't know how to navigate.

It's her room, so I let her go first.

"I'm glad you came over, Anna. I know we already talked about this some, but it still feels weird. There's more I have to say."

"Yeah, me, too."

"Okay, so . . ." She takes a deep breath, letting it out slowly, a faint "Matt" wafting off the end of her sigh like steam.

"I understand why he didn't want to tell me right away," she says. "He was always worrying about me — even when we were kids. If I scraped my knee or fell off my bike, he was the first one to help me up and make sure Mom got a Band-Aid."

"I remember." I smile. "He was the quintessential big brother."

"He was. But that's just it — he's not here to protect me anymore, Anna. And you don't have to be, either. I know I let stuff get crazy. I didn't mean to be like that — it just kind of happened. You couldn't have changed that. I — it was something I had to go through myself."

My throat tightens. "I felt like I let him down," I say. "All that stuff with smoking and Johan and Jake — I didn't take care of you. I couldn't even keep that one simple promise."

"Anna, my brother *died*. There's no way you could protect me from that. It's up to me, now. *I* let him down. I let *me* down."

She reaches into her top desk drawer for the stale pack of cigarettes.

"I know I can do better," she says, crushing them in her hand and dropping them into the trash can. I haven't seen her so convinced about anything since she picked out our bikinis at Bling and invented the summer of twenty boys.

"Frankie —"

"There's more, Anna. When we first got to California," she says, "you asked me if I remembered your birthday party."

I nod, picking at a thread on her comforter.

"I *did* remember. Matt was acting like such a space cadet that night after we got home — like he was floating. I can't believe I didn't figure it out, but of all the things that he could have been thinking about, you were the last — I mean, my mind just didn't even go there. You were like our sister."

"But I —"

"Wait — let me get this out." She looks at me hard, her broken wing eyebrow trembling to keep the tears back. "After I brushed my teeth, I walked into his room. He was sitting on his bed, playing with that blue glass necklace he always wore, a big smile on his face. Remember the necklace?"

The necklace. "Of course."

"I asked him what was so funny. He jumped a little, not knowing I'd been watching him smile there like a goofy little kid. He said it was nothing — just that he had fun at the party. And I believed him, all the way up until the day I read your journal. That's when it all made sense. All the times he'd ask me about who you liked at school, or who wanted to take you to whatever dance."

She's quiet as I digest her story, putting the pieces together to form a complete whole from the missing half that's haunted me since that night — how did he really feel about me? Was it just one stupid moment, perpetuated a little too long, only to be forgotten as quickly as it came? As soon as he went away to school?

"I was in love with him forever — since I was, like, ten," I confess.

"Yeah," she says. "You both were in love. I know that now. We were all so close, you know? I just didn't see it coming until I read your — I'm sorry, Anna."

I close my eyes, fighting back the image of her hand on my journal. "It's okay."

"The night we got back from the hospital," she says, "when Mom and Dad were downstairs with your parents after they took you home, I went into his room. I still don't know why — it felt like he was calling me or something.

"Inside, everything was exactly as he'd left it that morning. His bed unmade. Dirty clothes on the floor. The frosting shirt from your cake fight weeks earlier — just like the one you have in your closet. It was hanging inside his closet door, blue and crusty. It's probably still in there."

I smile, picturing Matt hanging his frosted shirt behind the door that night at the same time I was stuffing mine into its plastic bag in my room next door, totally freaked out about what had just happened.

"I didn't think you recognized it," I say. "That day we went through my closet before the trip. You wanted me to throw it out."

"I didn't recognize it that day. But once I saw the picture in your journal, it started to come together.

"Anyway," she continues, "that night after the accident, his room still smelled like him, you know? It was like I could lock myself in there forever and just keep breathing and telling myself that he would come back.

"I sat on the end of his bed and looked through the stuff on his nightstand. Alarm clock. Half-empty glass of water. Loose change. Some books he was in the middle of reading. And the necklace."

"Are you serious?" I ask. "I always thought it was lost in the hospital or in the crash."

"No, he must have forgotten to put it on that morning. And the night of the accident, something told me to take it, so I did. I closed it up in my fist and cried myself to sleep in his bed. The next morning, I woke up in my own bed with the necklace wrapped around my hand. I couldn't even remember why I took it, or how I got from his room to mine.

"A few days later, Mom was wandering around the house in a trance, mumbling about the blue necklace — she wanted them to put it on him. I didn't tell her I had it. I hid it in the pocket of an old coat where I knew she wouldn't look, even on a decorating rampage. The same thing that told me to take it, told me to keep it secret. I felt terrible that Mom thought it was lost, but I knew there was some reason I wasn't supposed to bury it with my brother. I just didn't know why   until now."

"What do you mean?" I ask, still shocked that she'd had the necklace all this time; that all along, she knew so much about the secret.

She sets down her soda and pulls something from the desk drawer where she used to keep the cigarettes.

"I mean, it's *yours,* Anna. It's always been yours." She presses her fingers to my palm.

My eyes move slowly from her face to the flat, cool object in my hand. There it is, small and unassuming, two leather cords holding a triangle of blue glass. History plays itself through my head like a movie — the cake, the kitchen sink, the necklace, the kiss, the text messages, the back of the house, the second kiss, the next and the next and the next, the stars, the books, the hall closet, the ice cream, the car, the hospital. My cheeks burn. I wait for the sadness to drown me, the tears to start.

I wait.

I wait.

I wait.

But . . . nothing.

I'm — *okay.* I think about Matt and the blue triangle always on his collarbone and feel a tightness in my chest, but no tears. No crushing sense of loss. No landslide of sad rocks.

I'm okay.

I close my hand around the necklace and feel an overwhelming surge of — calm, I guess. And love. And forgiveness. And closure. A beginning, an ending, and a new beginning.

"Thank you," I whisper, stretching to put my arms around her for a long overdue hug.

"So I guess we didn't get to twenty, huh?" Frankie smiles, wiping her eyes.

"Not exactly, no."

"Oh, well. You get at least five extra points for Sam."

Sam. The sound of his name reminds me of the smell of his skin, and the hair on my neck stands up.

"You do realize I'm going to need all the details of this little rendezvous, right?" Frankie asks.

"Francesca, I'm shocked!"

"Oh, come on. You knew I'd make you spill everything eventually!"

"No — I'm shocked that you used a word like 'rendezvous' correctly! And you even pronounced —"

"And *you're* trying to change the subject." She laughs, erasing a leftover tear with her fingertip. It's different this time — her laugh. Sad and a little bit serious, but raw and hopeful and honest, too. As the red glass of her bracelet sparkles against her tan skin, I finally understand it. There was never an old Frankie or a new Frankie. Everything that ever happened is just part of who she is; of who I am; of the best friendship that I've always loved.

I press the blue glass triangle to my lips and smile for Matt, my best-friend-that's-a-boy, my last goodbye to the brokenhearted promise I carried like my journal for so long. Somewhere below the black frothy ocean, a banished mermaid reads my letters and weeps endlessly for a love she'll never know — not for a single moment.

Before the trip, Frankie and I set out to have the Absolute Best Summer Ever, the summer of twenty boys. We'll never agree on the final count — whether the boys from Caroline's should be included in the tally, whether the milk-shake man was too old to be considered a "boy," whether her tattooed rock star interlude was anything other than a rebound. But in the end, there were only two boys who really mattered.

Matt and Sam.

When I close my eyes, I see Sam lying next to me on the blanket that first night we watched the stars — the night he made me look at everything in a different way; the breeze on my skin and the music and the ocean at night. But I also see Matt; his marzipan frosting kiss. All the books he read to me. His postcard fairy tales of California, finally coming to life in Zanzibar Bay.

When I kissed Sam, I was so scared of erasing Matt. But now I know that I could never erase him. He'll always be part of me — just in a different way. Like Sam, making smoothies on the beach two thousand miles away. Like Frankie, my voodoo magic butterfly finding her way back home in the dark. Like the stars, fading with the halo of the vanishing moon. Like the ocean, falling and whispering against the shore. Nothing ever really goes away — it just changes into something else. Something beautiful.

*   *   *

Frankie smiles, arching her broken wing eyebrow expectantly. In this moment, sitting on her purple comforter with the sun shining on us through the window, I realize that we *are* lucky — lucky to be alive, just like everyone said.

I slip the necklace into my pocket and take a deep breath.

Don't move, Anna Reiley. Right now, everything is perfect.

ACKNOWLEDGMENTS

My heartfelt gratitude to all who have given me the inspiration, the encouragement, and the opportunity to write *Twenty Boy Summer* and achieve this unbelievable dream.

To my editor, Jennifer Hunt, who believed in me enough to put up a fight and whose incredible talent for storytelling brought Anna Reiley's journey to life. Thanks also to T. S. Ferguson and everyone at Little, Brown who helped make *Twenty Boy Summer* a real, live book.

To Ted Malawer, my agent, who flawlessly navigated my stalker-esque e-mails and worked long hours to give me the best birthday news ever.

To Lighthouse Writers Workshop, especially Jenny Vacchiano Itell, for your invaluable guidance; Andrea Dupree, my steadfast cheerleader; and Mike Henry, who asked, "Have you ever considered writing for young adults?" Thanks also to Bill Henderson, Jay Barry, Rachel Miller, Meredith Sale, *GIS!*, and all of my writing friends for the critiques, the encouragement, and the literary shenanigans.

To Mom and Dad, who persuaded me to write my own stuff after the *E.T.* incident of 1981; my brothers, Steve Ockler and Scott "I'm not ashamed to read girly YA books" Ockler; my family-in-law, for the Million Dollar Bims; Amy Hains, who never doubted; and all who asked, "When can I read it?" Um, *now*? Now's good!

And to my husband, Alex, who said, "Bims, you're a writer!" Thanks for reminding me when I almost forgot. Here's to those double rainbows, my love.

Finally, I am forever grateful to my dear friends John and Margaret Moyer, and to all donor families. You have inspired this story. Thank you for saying yes.

Turn the page for a sneak peek from Sarah Ockler's new novel,
Fixing Delilah Hannaford.

Things in Delilah Hannaford's life are beginning to fall apart. Her friends are drifting away. Her "boyfriend" isn't a boyfriend. And when Delilah must spend the summer helping to settle her estranged grandmother's estate, she's suddenly confronted by her family's painful past. Faced with questions that cannot be ignored and secrets that threaten to burst free, Delilah begins to doubt all that she's ever known to be true. Can even her most shattered relationships be pieced back together again?

Rich with humor and emotion, Sarah Ockler's *Fixing Delilah Hannaford* is a powerful story of family, love, and self-discovery.

Coming November 2010

Mom and I didn't sleep last night. She spent the pre-dawn hours packing and mail-forwarding and making lists with colored Sharpies while I hung out on the couch, drinking cold coffee and trying not to ask too many questions. I was in enough trouble already—and that was *before* Aunt Rachel's phone call sent her into overdrive and hijacked my summer plans.

"Here we go," Mom says now, clicking the power locks and backing us down the driveway in the dark blue Lexus sedan. Actually, it's a *black sapphire pearl* Lexus sedan, not dark blue. The bill for the custom paint job is tacked to the bulletin board over my desk—a constant reminder that I still owe her for the dent-and-scratch combo I added when she was out of town last month.

Including the backpack between my feet and a long black dress for the funeral, I brought three bags of stuff for the whole tragic summer. The rest of the *black sapphire pearl* trunk and the *cashmere* leather interior is full of Mom's matching luggage and carefully labeled boxes of file folders, gel pens, computer cables, a printer-scanner-fax machine, and—should she be required during our dysfunctional family trip to showcase her management prowess—a collection of smartly tailored pantsuits in taupe, navy, and classic black.

"Left turn in four. Hundred. Feet."

An invisible electronic woman navigates us toward the highway from the distant planet Monotone, where everyone is tranquil and directionally adept, but Mom isn't listening. As vice president of marketing for DKI Group—"the most prestigious branding firm on the East Coast"—Mom *gets* multitasking. She could eat a bagel, scan the morning headlines, *and* get to I-78 with her eyes closed. Even deprived of sleep she drives effortlessly, one hand on the wheel, the other tapping manicured fingers onto the dash-mounted touch-screen phone. It takes her eight separate calls to her assistant's voice mail to convey what I did in one text message to my non-boyfriend, Finn:

> major family shit going down. off 2 vermont
> 4 the summer. L8trs.

"Merge on right. In one. Point five. Miles."

Mom checks her rearview and eases the Lexus into the right lane. "Eyes on the road, mind on the goal, and everything will be okay," she says, patting the steering wheel. It's her corporate road-warrior mantra, and she's already said it three times this morning. Usually, Mom's mantras are pretty poster-worthy. Mom on doing homework without her help: *The more you put into it, the more you get out of it.* Mom on working weekends: *You've got to plant the seeds of hard work to reap the harvest of a satisfied client.* Mom on home cooking: *I'm stuck at the office tonight, Del. There's money in the coffee canister for pizza or Indian.*

I want to believe her today, but the view isn't looking too hot from the passenger seat.

Despite all evidence to the contrary, I'm really *not* the car-denting kind of girl. I'm also not the lipstick-stealing, school-skipping,   off-in-the-woods-with-someone-I-barely-know kind of girl, or the kind who loses all of her dignity over a scandalous cell phone picture on a trashy blog. But that *is* the evidence, exhibits A through E, all stacked up against me, and now I'm like the bad guy on one of those cop shows, handcuffed to an airplane seat. Only instead of getting the handsome, tough but emotionally wounded police escort, I'm stuck on a seven-hour road trip with Commander Mom and her arsenal of mobile communications devices.

I turn away from her and put on my sunglasses so she can't see the tears stinging my eyes, but it's too late.

"Delilah, we've been over this already. You can't stay here in Key. Period." She says it like it's some big edict passed down by the Supreme Court. It's all I can do not to play the "I wish my father was around, because he'd [insert better parenting strategy here]" card.

Mom continues, tapping my leg for emphasis. "It's not just the sneaking out or the shoplifting *(tap tap tap)*. I need your help *(tap tap)*."

"How many times do I have to tell you?" I ask. "It was an *accident!*" It *was.* I didn't even realize I still had the lipstick in my hand when I walked out of Blush Cosmetics yesterday, bored and tired from wandering the mall alone.

"An accident," Mom says. "Like the car? Like your grades?" She shakes her head. "It doesn't matter, Delilah.

There's a lot of work to do up there. Other issues aside, you'd still be going with me."

Right. I'm letting her think she's won an important strategic battle in our ongoing war, but if things were different between us, more like they used to be, I'd *want* to go—not just because I need a break from Finn and pretty much everyone I know in Pennsylvania, but because nothing would be as important as helping my family through this tragedy and tying up its many loose ends—the three remaining Hannaford women united and strong as an unsinkable ship.

But things *aren't* different. She's her and I'm me and surrounding us is an ocean of mess and misunderstanding, full of pirates and sharks just waiting to see who slips in first.

"Stay on interstate. Seventy-eight for. Fifty. Miles."

After the directive, Mom cranks the air and switches off the freakishly calm GPS woman. Back here on planet stress, it's just the two of us, all the unsaid stuff made more unbearable by the artificial cold.

"Now that I have a captive audience," she says, setting us on cruise control as the road opens up, "who did you sneak out with last night?"

Last night.

You'd think someone who's seen you half-naked would be a little more enthusiastic about picking you up on time. Not Finn "forty-five minutes late" Gallo. From the driver's seat of his old silver 4Runner, Finn crushed a spent butt into the ashtray and turned down the radio, blowing out a plume of blue smoke from between his lips. He didn't say anything like "Thanks for waiting in the dark for me," or "I'm sorry I put your life in danger with my lateness," or "Allow me to apologize with this exquisite lavender rose bouquet." He just pulled me to his mouth with one hand cool and firm on the back of my neck and somehow made up for everything bad he'd ever done in his whole entire life.

At our spot in the woods by Seven Mile Creek, Finn parked between two big pine trees and killed the engine. He asked me what was up, and I shrugged. I'd spent the whole night arguing with Mom about Blush Cosmetics and didn't feel like talking. Finn and I aren't that good at talking, anyway.

So we didn't.

Aunt Rachel says that the universe is always trying to speak to us, and that the universe doesn't waste time speaking about things that aren't within our direct power to influence or change. But if that's true, the universe needs a better signal. Because when Finn kisses me, hot and fast like each time might be the last, everything else in my life goes like the New England evergreens in a morning fog: gray, hazy, and just about gone.

Last night, I felt the familiar solidity of Finn's body against mine, midnight air cool on my cheeks, rocks and sticks and living things pinned beneath me, bits of moon falling through the branches in the tall pines bent over us.

At the end of it all, Finn sucked a crackle from another cigarette and stood, reaching down to help me to my feet. I shook out the blankets and rolled them up and he pulled the leaves from my hair. One by one they floated and swirled and fell to my feet, and when he smiled at me in his up-to-no-good way with the moonlight soft and blue on his skin, I wanted to stay there forever. To hide. To forget. To numb the dull ache of something missing. To erase my mother and her expensive car and late nights at the office. To fill the empty spaces left by my father, killed before I was even born, with something other than endless unanswerable questions.

But it was time. Finn dropped me off on the corner. He called me *Lilah* and gave me a devious smile and shook his head in that "you're nothing but trouble" sort of way that gives me chills, but he didn't say good-bye. Or wave. Or wait in the shadows until I was safely back in my house. He just drove away, and I walked on in the other direction, the distance between two points growing long and cold.

When I got back inside, Mom was there on the edge of my bed, a new eyebrow crease invented especially for the occasion of my tumbling through the open window at two in the morning with leaves in my hair.

"Get in here, Delilah," she said, tugging me the rest of the way inside. *I'm not playing games.* Only she didn't actually say the games part. She didn't have to. I climbed in and sat on the bed and chewed on my thumbnail as she recounted the last fifteen minutes in alternating bursts of finger-wagging and foot-stomping. She'd been waiting for me *(wag)* in the bedroom *(stomp)* the entire time *(wag)* with news from Aunt Rachel.

I spat out a piece of my thumbnail and met her eyes, matching the curious exasperation behind them as she passed along her sister's announcement, direct from the staff at Maple Valley Hospital up in Vermont.

Elizabeth Rose Hannaford, the grandmother whose name I hadn't been allowed to speak in over eight years, was dead.

"I told you last night," I say to Mom, inching down the window to thaw the freeze in the car. "I needed some air."

Mom's voice is about to jump an octave. I see it coming and make a silent little wish on the dash lights that somewhere among all those tailored pantsuits she's packed her Xanax. For now, I imagine how much better life would be for all of us if her lectures were delivered through the GPS device.

"Delilah I had. To. Leave work yesterday. To. Pick. You up from Blush." *In six point. Four. Miles.*

"So?"

"You were supposed to be grounded! You almost got *arrested* yesterday!" she says, as if I could forget the detective's dramatic lecture on the downfall of our nation's youth. "*One more dollar in merchandise,*" he'd warned, knuckle jabbing my shoulder, *"and we'd have to press charges."*

"Prisoners don't deserve *air?*" I ask. "Why don't you just pull off my fingernails next time."

"Unbelievable, Delilah. I really thought I could count—"

Bzzzz.

"Hang on. I have to get this." Mom touches a button on the dash and activates her public persona. "Claire Hannaford speaking."

She has a plaque on her desk at work by the phone:

☺ **SMILE before you dial! SMILING helps you sound more relaxed on the phone!**

She does it, too. Even in the car. No wonder she's so great at rebranding entire corporations for DKI. She rebrands *herself* every fifteen minutes.

I lower my window all the way down and stick out my arm. The breeze whooshes through my fingers and carries my hand over the highway, zooming past lines of orange cones and construction signs until Mom nudges my ribs. "I'm on the phone," she mouths, still smiling but eyes mad and wide as she circles her finger in the international gesture for "roll up the windows." I pretend to turn the nonexistent crank on the door, but that just makes her raise my window from the button on her side and lock the controls.

"Sorry for the background noise," she continues into the earpiece. "Yes, the final invoice was sent on Thursday with a thirty-day grace. Perfect. Thanks."

The sun is fully up now, bleaching the sky from orangey-pink to a pale, sad white. Corpse-white. It's horrendously early and the daylight hurts the stuff behind my eyes. It rained earlier this morning, though—right after I heard about our disastrous summer plans, which I thought was fitting. Now the road is all patent-leathery and sets our wheels to a whisper, raspy and hypnotic like the ocean. The sound reminds me of this Memorial Day road trip Mom and I took to the Connecticut coast when I was six—just the two of us. New London—only time I've ever seen the ocean. We couldn't swim the first day because it rained, so we just walked along the shore with bright yellow raincoats buttoned up over our bathing suits, looking for shells and sea glass and dizzy little hermit crabs. The rain kept coming the next day so we stayed inside the motel eating Doritos from the vending machine and watching movies on cable—a luxury for us back in Mom's pre-DKI days. Even when I accidentally pulled the pin out of the motel fire extinguisher and shot a blast of white haze across the floor, she laughed, chasing after my little white footprints as I ran into the bathroom to hide. On the last day, the sun came out and we swam in the ocean.

On the way back to Pennsylvania, late at night on the road, she smoothed her hand on my cheek and sang classic rock songs with the radio on low, and I pretended to be asleep so she wouldn't stop.

After her call ends, Mom clicks on the radio and I turn away, my breath fogging the glass of the passenger window. As the all-news-all-the-time station drones on about the latest economic trends, I trace a bead of leftover rain along the bottom edge of the window and watch it pass over my shoulder. Sometimes I think about telling Mom how much I hate coming home alone every afternoon, turning on the television just to pretend there's company. All those takeout dinners at the big dining room table, chairs empty, invisible guests eating invisible soup and drinking made-up wine in my head. I want to shake her and scream and tell her that for all her hard work to pay our bills, the snake plants in the foyer know more about my life than she does, that I'd strike a single match and raze the whole damn place to the ground if it meant we could start over with nothing but the ocean, potato chip vending machines, and free cable.

Then again, I don't need an arson charge on my record.

"At this rate, we'll never get there," Mom says, turning toward me to check the right lane as she merges back in. In the stifling beige-ness of the car interior, she looks weak and defeated and ten years older than she did yesterday, before she knew her mother was dead. She wears it like makeup: a paper-thin layer of unwavering resolve flaking away to reveal all the broken parts underneath.

"Mom, I'm . . . I'm really sorry about—"

Bzzzz.

"Hold on, Delilah." Mom keeps one hand on the wheel, the other searching for the right button, fingers poking around the dash like a bird for worms as the unsaid end of my sympathy stumbles and slips back down my throat. On the phone, Claire Hannaford Speaking betrays none of our troubles, but as she engages her award-winning, smile-as-you-dial communication skills for the caller, a thing that's been sitting like a rock at the bottom of my stomach grows an ounce heavier.

Dread.

Cold and unmoving, it drips with the murky memories of that place we're going to. That place where she and Aunt Rachel shared their childhoods and, though my recollections are hazy, part of mine. That place I was ordered to forget right after my grandfather's funeral more than eight years ago. That place yanked suddenly from the dark of the cellar, all those black-tarred Hannaford secrets still stuck to it like giant, undustable cobwebs.

The tension is crawling across my skin and making me itch.

I dig a Snickers bar from my backpack and offer Mom the first bite, but she refuses, waving her hand in front of me as if shooing a fly. After her call, she lets out a long sigh, tugging the phone device from her ear and flipping the GPS back on.

"Recalculating route for. Red Falls. Vermont."

"Mom?"

"Not now, Delilah. I'm driving."

"Location triangulated," Lady GPS announces. "In two hundred. Four. Miles. You will reach your destination."

Stories about love, loss, and, just, being a girl.

Sweethearts

Story of a Girl

Once Was Lost

From National Book Award Finalist
Sara Zarr